COMFORT & JOY

COMFORT & JOY

a novel

by JIM GRIMSLEY

Algonquin Books of Chapel Hill   1999

Published by
ALGONQUIN BOOKS OF CHAPEL HILL
Post Office Box 2225
Chapel Hill, North Carolina 27515-2225

a division of
Workman Publishing
708 Broadway
New York, New York 10003

This is a work of fiction. While, as in all fiction,
the literary perceptions and insights are based
on experience, all names, characters, places,
and incidents are either products of the author's
imagination or are used fictitiously. No reference
to any real person is intended or should be inferred.

Library of Congress Cataloging-in-Publication Data
Grimsley, Jim, 1955–
    Comfort and joy : a novel / by Jim Grimsley.
        p.   cm.
    ISBN 1-56512-250-X
    I. Title.
    PS3557.R4949C6   1999
    813' .54—dc21   99-32033
                                                    CIP

10 9 8 7 6 5 4 3 2 1

First Edition

For Carlos Daniel Schröder

COMFORT & JOY

To find a hiding place. Close the front door and lock it, *click*. At the end of the driveway, Dan's luggage sat amid foliage that was still green in December. He had locked the blue door; the house beyond lay empty and silent. Now the journey was beginning, and he needed to find a hiding place. Shelter. But instead he headed to the street where a taxi was waiting. The driver, in dreadlocks and yarn hat, stepped out of the car and loaded Dan's bags into the trunk. He dipped his head politely, high hat and dreadlocks shivering. Dan slid into the back seat.

"And where do you go?" the driver asked, settling behind the steering wheel. Dan answered and the driver shifted the taxi into gear. The house vanished, obscured first by interlaced limbs of cedar, later magnolia, a deep green veil.

To the airport. Dan counted the bounces of the driver's

hat, ballooning against the roof of the car. Dan to the airport. With suitcases. The driver had understood everything, what more to do but sing? So he sang softly, in a baritone, some snatch of tune Dan sometimes heard plainly and that at other times was lost in other sounds. Dan watched the dark column of the taxi driver's neck, hearing the low song like a purr, and answering even more softly with singing of his own, as the shadows of bridges and sweeping curves wheeled over his face and arms. They rode through Atlanta in a cocoon of glass and light, orderly traffic surrounding them on all sides, the stately proceeding of many lanes of highway south through the city. Moving away from the towers and canyons of downtown.

"You are home for the holy days," the taxi driver said.

"Oh, yes," Dan answered.

The man grinned and nodded his head. "Every body is going to the airport. All day. I drive back and back."

The car swept down the road, encountering less traffic than Dan had feared. Once the vehicle raced a commuter train moving unimpeded along its track, the train vanishing as the curve hurled it out of sight. Dan had a feeling, matching the gradient of asphalt to the graceful neck of the taxi driver, that the whole world was in motion all at the same time; that it was good to travel along slashing inclines; that it must be good, sometimes, to travel at all.

Sometimes. But this was Christmas, and Dan was going home.

At the airport Ford had already arrived and was waiting in the zone where automobiles let off passengers and luggage. Ford stood on the walkway, somehow calm, wrapped in his black overcoat, tall and bareheaded. Black hair shining. Already standing at the curb, already waiting, when Dan had guessed he would be late.

Dan lay his hand on the door latch. The driver opened his door and got out. Dan opened his door and got out. The cold air chilled his face as he waited for the driver to open the trunk. The driver lifted the first of the bags and Ford reached for it; the driver looked at Dan, who said, "It's all right."

So Ford grinned and took the luggage to the curbside baggage check, and Dan paid the taxi driver but watched Ford, moving so easily in the crowd. Ford had already tipped a porter to help him with the bags and this transaction was completed with such dispatch that he had the claim check stapled to his ticket before Dan had pocketed his taxi change. Ford folded the tickets and slipped them in his coat. He stood serenely waiting. "You didn't think I would be here, did you?"

"No. I was sure you'd be late."

They plunged into the airport, through the hiss of electric doors into the echo of North Terminal, where a gallery of unfortunates, who did not have Ford to arrange their travel, had still to stand in line, check their bags, and fiddle with their tickets. Ford steered Dan by the elbow through a crosscurrent of off-duty Marines who were wandering through the ticketing arena, bewildered in tight jeans. The flight was an hour away, no hurry. Ford removed his gloves. Wandering, Ford calmly surveyed the crowd, the midway of the Hartsfield aerodrome. Dan kept beside him and studied them as well.

Ford said, as they were walking, "I liked his hair."

"The taxi man? So did I."

Ahead, lines were forming at the security checkpoint. Ford directed him toward one of the lines, then stopped. Dan placed his bag, flat, on the belt. He pictured his underwear, files, pens, lozenges, comb and gum wrappers under radiologic illumination. Beyond the gate Ford lifted the bag and touched Dan's elbow again. With the drone of voices and near collision of bodies on all sides, Ford guided Dan forward. Dan said, "Ford."

"Yes?"

Dan watched Ford's hand. Now, descending on the escalator, the fine hand gripping the black rubber railing. "Nothing," Dan said. "I said your name."

"Did you forget who I was?"

"No."

The voice closer, uncurling in his ear. "Say it again."

"Ford."

In a plush scarlet bar they found a table overlooking the whole panorama. The bar itself was pleasantly crowded but not full. Dan slipped neatly into a silver-armed chair. Ford spoke to a waitress, then joined Dan at the table.

Watching Dan, he stripped off his overcoat, laying it across the table's third, empty, chair. Ford wore no jacket, only the white shirt and tie. The waitress brought drinks and Ford sprawled in the chair. "Just as well you stayed home from the hospital. The place was dead today."

Dan fingered his glass. "Always is, at Christmas."

The two men touched glasses and sipped. Ford yawned, letting his head hang back. He closed his eyes. "I do feel like I'm getting here," he said. "Am I?"

"You are."

The young man smiled. The boy inside him did the same. Eyes still closed, throat still longing to be touched, there, on that pulse. Dan asked, "Did you get any sleep last night?"

"No. But I got a shower."

"I thought you said the place was slow."

Ford yawned again. "Was. But I had this sick kid."

"Bad?"

"Yeah." Sipping. The tone said, *Don't ask.* "Little guy. Nine years old." Ford met his gaze, briefly. "I'm okay, just tired. The kid's going to pull through."

The bar itself was filling up with servicemen heading home for the holidays, young couples, husbands taking a break from families to gulp a beer. Two accountants were discussing the end-of-fiscal-year procedures at their places of employment. On the television over the bar flickered the comforting images of intensive Christmas marketing.

"You run around on me last night?" Ford was still slumped in the chair.

"Well, no, I stayed home packing just like I said I would. Why do you always check on me?"

"I don't always check on you." Ford lifted his empty glass. "I'm still thirsty. You think I have time?"

"I doubt it."

Ford rolled the empty glass on the tabletop and leaned over the table. They stood to go. Ford left money and so did Dan; Ford saying, "You could let me buy you a drink." Dan pretended not to hear, laying bills in place. They crossed the concourse as the gate attendant announced that the flight to Raleigh-Durham was ready to begin pre-boarding.

Ford, being a McKinney, had bought first-class seats. Dan had a suspicion that the McKinneys of Savannah, Georgia, had bought first-class and only first-class tickets on every form of conveyance since the Ark, and that no McKinney had ever so much as walked through coach. In Ford's case, since he was not merely a McKinney but a McKinney the Third, and a doctor, the question had simply never come up.

Whereas the Crells of North Carolina had only recently taken to air passage at all, and were in fact unfamiliar with most forms, and even the idea, of travel.

Ford settled Dan by the window, himself on the aisle. The spacious first-class seat always surprised Dan at first, and he settled back with a sigh into its soft embrace. He was feeling the warm flush of liquor, a slow creeping of comfort through his arms and legs. From close by came Ford's mellow voice. "Here's your boarding pass. I'm going to call the hospital. Don't let these folks take off without me."

Dan closed his eyes and waited. Ford was gone until the last moment, the plane full, final boarding already called, Ford slipping through the cabin door and sliding into his seat, smelling of the cold wind in the jetway. "I got through," Ford said, as the flight attendant blinked. Ford rubbed his hands together. "It's getting cold outside."

He was happy. Meaning the phone call had gone well, and the child was probably okay. Dan had learned only to ask when invited to do so. But this time, Ford leaned close again. "The kid's doing great. Just great."

The doctor settled his head back against the seat and closed his eyes, grateful for any moment of rest. The jet lurched backward, and the flight attendants began their demonstration of seat belt function, oxygen mask protocol, and the paths to exits.

Lights were dimmed for evening takeoff. The fasten-seat-belt sign glowed overhead. In the forward cabin, one reading lamp poured down its tinted cone of light. Beyond the windows, below on the murky tarmac, glowing lines of blue and orange paraded past the taxiing aircraft. The jet rolled forward more or less smoothly. Nearby, on the interstate highway, rivers of red and white lights traced sweeping arcs beneath the soupy clouds into which the jet would soon hurl itself. Beyond the runway, parking lots unfurled in bluish haze. The jet lumbered toward its point of departure, engines flaring and subsiding.

The pilot turned the nose into near-darkness at the end of the runway. With some pilots there was a pause here, a moment of stillness before the jets rose to takeoff pitch. With other pilots—like the one tonight—there was no such pause; there was only the jet turning, creaking weight quickening forward, faster, down the slight incline of the early runway and then lifting. Into the sky stepped the machine, the groan of metal subsiding, wheel carriages lifting into their beds. The aircraft tested the air, found that its ungainly shape made sense at this speed, and climbed. Over the roofs of East Point into heaven.

The jet broke into a peaceful sky above the clouds, attaining its cruising altitude of twenty-two thousand feet, a flight time of forty-odd minutes, and in Raleigh-Durham the weather was clear and cold.

"Did you call your mom?" Ford asked.

"She called me. Early this morning."

"Does she believe I'm really coming?"

"I don't even know if I believe it." Their faces, in the dim cabin light, were close. Ford's clean jaw and dark beard line, his perfect mouth with the full lower lip and strong, straight nose. He said, "You're not worried are you, old man?"

"Don't call me old man."

"Your mom likes me. We've talked lots of times. You don't have to worry about a thing."

"I'm only four years older than you are." Pause. "Your mother called, too."

"Did she?" The slight shift of Ford's expression signified his wariness. "Did she talk to you, or did she act like she didn't know who you were?"

"She was actually rather pleasant. She asked how I was doing, that kind of thing. She's never done that."

"But she didn't say anything about Christmas."

Dan leaned close this time, into the circle of Ford's seat. The balding gentleman on the opposite aisle quickly averted his eyes. "She did the best she could, I think. She said she guessed I had heard you wouldn't be coming home for Christmas." Ford's stillness became frozen. Dan went on. "I said I didn't think it was quite as simple as that."

Ford idly touched his cocktail glass to his lower lip. Dan went on. "Then she asked if I knew where you would be, and I said you were coming home with me."

Ford set down the glass and then the weight of his hand settled onto Dan's arm. "What did she say?"

"She didn't say anything. She pretended not to hear. She said she hoped you would at least call on Christmas. Then she wished me a Merry Christmas and said the maid was calling her, and that was it."

The man across the aisle was watching out of the corner of his eye. Ford said, "Serves her right to know. I wonder if she'll tell my dad."

The question did not require answer. His fingertip

worried the cotton sleeve of Dan's sweater. Touching. Rarely did Ford touch him so freely in public. The boy within the man must be afraid. The boy who had always gone home to Savannah at Christmas must wonder who would take care of him now.

But where to find the boy? Where to lay one's hands? Within so large a frame.

Ford reclined further, listening to the monotone keening of the jet turbines. Soon the captain announced their descent to the Raleigh-Durham airport. Ford glanced at his watch and said, "We don't have to drive far tonight, do we? We can just get the car and find a hotel."

"Whatever you want."

"That's what I want." Ford turned on his side toward Dan. Dan thought, *This is my hiding place.* This wall of McKinney. But something about the thought made him uncomfortable. So he looked out the window, as the jetliner descended, and Ford said, "What was that?"

"What?"

"That last thought you had. I didn't like it."

"Nothing," Dan said. "General anxiety."

"Save it for tomorrow."

Treetops, roofs rising toward the window.

"Hey." Ford's voice close to his ear. Hungry. "I said, save it for tomorrow. Can't you? You don't have to be anxious tonight. Right?"

"Okay."

Breath on his cheek. In public. "How many of you are there? Right now?"

"One," Dan said, and looked Ford in the eye, as the flight attendant reached round Ford's sidewise bulk to collect their glasses. She was clearly startled by their intimacy. "Just one," Dan said. And thought, *Shelter. Not hiding place*. This wall of Ford was, would be, shelter. That was where the thought was wrong.

———∞∞———

Leaning over from the passenger seat of the rental sedan, smelling new vinyl, Dan unlocked the driver-side door. Ford slid behind the steering wheel and smoothed his hair. For the moment he was all discipline, averting his exhaustion. He reached into his shirt pocket and handed Dan folded paper. "Read this. We have a room there, wherever it is. Our friend the travel agent says it's on I-40 east between here and Raleigh."

The drive was long enough for a sleepy speechlessness to settle over both men, which lasted till Ford parked the car in the hotel lot. Ford registered with the front desk while Dan carried the luggage down a lane of young magnolias into the lobby, a large, airy cage of glass and steel, hung with wreaths, red bows, and small white lights. The whole effect was adequate, even somewhat warm with its restrained Christmas finery. To reach the registration desk, one crossed an expanse of sectioned carpet, passing a fir trimmed in more white lights and golden balls. But Ford was already turning away from the desk, and coming toward him. "This place looks like Christmas in hell," he said, hefting his share of the luggage.

Their room was large, peach-colored, with the usual assortment of chests, chairs, functional lamps, and a bed with what seemed like an acre of mattress. Only one bed, Dan noted, and caught Ford watching him. Ford said, "I asked for what we needed. One king-size bed."

"I see."

"Are you proud of me?" Smiling just slightly.

"Yes." Moving forward, setting down his suitcases. The door closed safely behind them. Dan slipped out of his overcoat and threw it across a chair. Ford touched the buttons of his own, still holding the room key, and watched while Dan hung the garment bag in the closet and opened all its straps, zippers, and snaps, unpacking what they would need for the night. Ford studied him straightening the jackets and shirts on hangers.

"Give me your coat," Dan called from the closet. But then he walked over to Ford and unbuttoned the coat and eased it off Ford's shoulders. Ford all but held his breath. Dan's slim hands brushed his shoulders, the sides of his arms, the heavy coat slipped across his back. Ford said, "There's a restaurant downstairs, and a bar that serves sandwiches. I saw a Waffle House further up the exit ramp, if that suits you better."

"I can find something in the restaurant, if you can."

"That's what I thought."

Dan slid the tie through the white collar. Ford unbuttoned the top button of his shirt.

"Do you need to call the hospital?"

"Not this minute," Ford said. He reached his arms to the top of the door jamb.

Dan ran his hands along the contours of Ford's chest, knowing now that the boy was in there. To be found. Ford moved closer. "Who's this?" he asked.

"Danny Crell."

"Nice guy," Ford said. Then said nothing. Lowered his arms around Dan's waist. Dan had wondered whether Ford would kiss tonight—there had been nights when he seemed reluctant, even after two years—but tonight he was willing. Dan could feel the ache in Ford then, all the way to the bottom of him, pouring out of him but unrelieved. He touched Ford's face, fingertips to cheeks, along his neck.

"I laid some clothes on the bed. So you can stop looking like a doctor."

Ford refused, for a moment, to release Dan. He held their faces close. Then, walking to the bed, he stood over the folded sweatshirt. Turning, hands rising to the buttons of his shirt, he watched the floor, as if he had gotten lost in the turn from the bed. He unbuttoned the shirt slowly. His body was powerful, the product of much labor, the muscles of shoulder, chest, and abdomen moving beneath the white cotton T-shirt. He stretched his arms and stood there. Laughing softly, his mouth just open. His heart beating. Across the room, the sight of his body quickened Dan's pulse.

Once, Dan had found this terrain to be terrifying, this

iteration of the McKinney genetics, out of its clothing. Even now he was transfixed, touching the bare chest. Watching the movement within movement of Ford's strong arms. He felt a rush of ease; the flesh welcomed him.

Their closeness had been a struggle from the start. Now as they stood, chest to chest, they found peace in all their territories, unexpected. To stand so near, to allow touch, to love with the fingertips, were victories. "No T-shirt," Ford whispered, "in this weather," taking off Dan's shirt. Dan's laughter blew against the soft of Ford's neck. Dan felt Ford's hands low on his back, sliding inside his pants, caressing. The two were one weight standing, one balance, and in due order, like blossoming, one face opened to the other.

Easing off after the first long phrase, they opened their eyes. Everything said, *Go slow, you are in another kind of time*. "Oh," Dan said softly, breath stirring the black hair of Ford's chest, "you've been practicing that with somebody."

"Yeah," Ford said, "and it's a good thing too, don't you think?" He ran a hand through his hair, taking a deep breath. "Do we have condoms?"

"You know we do."

Laughing softly, Ford stepped past a suitcase. Gray eyes on Dan. They were facing each other, Dan touching fingertips to Ford's shoulders, tracing the full curves of his chest, the flatness of his abdomen, down to the cool buckle of his belt.

Ford cradled himself against Dan's chest, and for a long time lay there drowsing. He started awake. Stretching, he leaned over Dan. "If I don't turn on this light, I'll fall asleep."

"I bet that restaurant is closed by now."

"It's not that late," Ford said, "it just feels that way."

Reluctant to untangle their limbs, they lay quietly until Ford said, "I need to call the hospital." Dan could feel his search for words. Pulling Dan close, Ford continued, "We did the right thing this year. About Christmas."

"I think so, too."

The shower was good. As he toweled himself dry, he could hear Ford discussing medication with his friend Russell Cohen. A crisp conversation about incisions and drainage. Tomorrow the child would have a second session of computed tomography to determine the size of the swelling somewhere in the head. Ford hung up the receiver. "I'm glad Cohen's the on-call. The kid's doing okay. Not great, at the moment. But okay." Then, moving away from the phone, "I'm sorry, I shouldn't be talking about it."

"Why not? I don't mind."

"That's all my dad ever did with Mom. Review cases." Ford found the black jeans and put them on, but simply held the sweatshirt in his hand. "Did you bring my silk sweater?"

This had been a gift from Dan. Ford slipped the pale blue sweater over his bare skin. "What did you do with the cats?"

"Took them to board at the vet."

Ford sat down to tie his sneakers. "I don't see why you couldn't just leave some food out."

Had it not been for these same cats, Dan might have moved into Ford's house six months sooner, or so Ford always claimed. "They'll be safer at the vet."

"How much does that cost?" Ford asked, finding his wallet.

"Not much." A slight edge to his tone. "I can afford it."

Silence. Ford, coming up behind, put his arms around Dan and said, in his ear, "I can afford it too. That's not what I meant."

The warmth of the body surrounding Dan reminded him that he was, by agreement, safe. "Ten bucks a night," Dan said. "They stay in the same cage."

The lone waitress scanned the empty rows of tables, inviting them to choose their own vantage. Ford selected a table by the window, where wind pressed against the broad glass pane, whipping real and reflected treetops. Below, in the gulf of highway, traffic moved in slow ribbons. "We must be close to Raleigh," Dan said.

"Right outside." Ford sat back, rubbing his stomach. "How long does it take to get to your mom's from here?"

"Two hours. Something like that." Dan opened his menu.

"We can sleep late."

Dan hardly heard this. The thought of what lay two hours away struck him cold. *Tomorrow we will drive to my mother's house.* Tomorrow. Dan reached for distractions and found his water glass.

Ford said, "One of the guys on the ward was talking about you today."

"Was he?" Dan asked.

"The nurses took him to hear you sing. In the Christmas concert. He liked it a lot."

Dan said, "I thought I sounded pretty bad," but was pleased nevertheless.

"The nurses said you sounded good. They went on and on about it. Made me feel terrible, for not getting there."

"You couldn't help it."

"That's where I first saw you. Way back when I was a senior medical student. You were singing, 'God Rest Ye, Merry Gentlemen.' I had never heard anything like you. It was one of the saddest sounds I ever heard. You got under my skin." This with a look of deep brooding. Something beneath attempting to surface. "I think I knew something about you that day."

"What?"

"Something about where you came from. What you could do. So I remembered you."

Something about where you came from. The phrase echoed as the waitress, Marlene, presented supper.

During the ride in the elevator, Ford leaned against Dan and closed his eyes. Dan led him through the empty corridor by the hand, fishing the key from Ford's pocket.

Ford stumbled dramatically to the bed and sprawled

across it. Ford's need for sleep had long been a joke between them. He got little rest at the hospital, even when he was called upon to remain there for thirty-six- or forty-eight-hour shifts; consequently, he had no time for anything else when he was at home. Dan sat quietly beside Ford, watching, hearing the change in Ford's breathing that indicated he would soon be asleep. Dan unlaced Ford's shoes, and Ford stirred, murmuring. Dan undressed him with practiced gestures. Dan read for a while, sitting in one of the chairs. When Ford's breath fell and rose in waves, Dan lay down beside him.

In the small hours of morning, waking out of sound sleep, Dan heard Ford talking in low tones on the telephone. Ford was speaking to Russell again. His voice, cool and crisp, belied his fatigue. The child had lost a good deal of blood. Dan couldn't hear all that was being said, but for some reason he had a feeling this boy had hemophilia, too, and that this was a cause of Ford's worry.

"Is everything all right?"

"The kid's having a bad night." Ford's weight settled against Dan's back. "But Russell says he'll make it."

Closing his eyes, Dan returned to shadowland and let Ford's warmth and nearness lull him into sleep again. Through dawn and after, they lay drowsy, basking in the unaccustomed peace, having no alarm to answer. Mornings to lie abed had been scarce. Drifting in and out of dreaming, Dan was sometimes certain he wandered in Ford's house, where the sick boy cried nearby, in a room Dan had never seen and could not find, even though he heard the child clearly; in the dream Dan himself was bleeding and needed to take his medicine, but Ford had already departed for the hospital. . . .

At other moments he was aware of Ford's heavy leg flung across his own, beneath sheets of harsh texture. The comfortable thigh and fleshly warmth drew Dan nearer consciousness, but he lay quiet within the soft blankets, studying the pattern of acoustical tile in the ceiling. Ford's heavy sleep weighed like a stone in the bed beside him, the young man sprawled across pillows, hair tangled over his brow, bare dark nipple peering above the sheet's edge.

Soon Dan returned to the territory of the dream.

This time, because Dan himself was closer to waking, the dream image was more vivid. In Ford's house, Dan waited in the kitchen just after dawn and the boy was cry-ing. His clear voice sounded a note of hollow cold and loneliness, a thread of vibration, now and then broken by soft sobs. On the kitchen counter lay the apparatus of the hemophiliac, the vials of dissolving medication, syringes, alcohol prep pads, butterfly needles, a tourniquet—was the medication for the boy, or for Dan?

As the sobbing continued, Dan searched the house, trying to find the boy by the sound of his voice. For a while he suspected it was his brother Grove; then he was certain it was Ford; then he became convinced it was he himself, he was crying somewhere, a smaller, younger, lesser Danny, and Dan the Elder had to find him. But the boy was always crying from some farther room. So Dan wandered.

He woke finally to the tightening of large arms around his waist, to the press of a familiar heat at his back, Ford's breathing torso moving against him and the sleepy voice murmuring in his ear. Saying no words, only the soft, slow pressure of Ford's thighs against Dan's back, till Dan turned.

When they were dressed, they bought breakfast at the same table in the same restaurant as the night before. "Did you pack your medicine?" Ford asked. "I looked for it in the suitcase but I couldn't find it."

"I have it in a separate case, in the closet. Why?"

"Just making sure," Ford said.

He had already found time to call the hospital again, a conversation he had shielded from Dan, though Dan knew it had taken place. The sick boy had lived through the night.

———— ∽∾∽ ————

Traveling east of Raleigh in the rented car, through flat farm country studded with paint-peeling farmhouses and winter-gaunt pine forests, Ford had the feeling it was Savannah, Georgia, that lay at the end of this journey and not the Wickham, North Carolina, of Dan's family. There was, in the flatness of the land and the poverty of the countryside, much to remind him of the territories of his own boyhood. Overhead blazed a sky white and bare as any winter sky Ford had seen, the morning sun a searing single eye into which the automobile plunged headlong. Along the roadside, beyond the bland fast-food-tainted suburbs of the Raleigh beltway, stood evidence of the lost commerce of other generations—the small wood-frame crossroads stores advertising Pepsicola; the ubiquitous, rusted Quaker State motor oil signs nearly lost behind brown weeds; wooden tobacco-curing barns, rotten and leaning over the trim, metallic bulk-curers that had replaced them. A small farm town hugged every curve of the road, streetlights bedecked in tattered Christmas decorations, streets for the most part empty of traffic. The quiet country spoke more to Ford of bleakness than of peace, so that, as he steered the car deeper into the eastern forest, he kept watch on Dan.

He and Dan had enjoyed relatively few such mornings with only one another for company, without the pressure of Ford's being on call at the hospital or Dan's being late coming home. Dan's face, a curious amalgam of homeliness and handsomeness, had a clarity in this white-washed light that reminded Ford of their first morning, Dan asleep in Ford's east-facing bedroom, Ford studying him, trying to fathom this strange attractor.

It was the sound of his voice that had stopped Ford in the first-floor lobby of Grady Memorial Hospital, the eerie minor-key vibrato, pure and clean, a cappella, tingling the skin at the back of his neck. Ford, then a fourth-year medical student, was only dimly aware that the hospital sponsored a Christmas concert, but here it was, spilling over from the lobby to surround the information desk and congest the elevator court. Curt Robbins, the resident who was in charge of Ford for that month, cursed the traffic and the delay for the elevator, but Ford moved away from him into the fringes of the crowd, feeling the silence around him as the song hovered in the room. The voice rang on the tile walls and terrazzo floor. The man who was singing stood on a raised dais, nearly blocked from sight by a structural column. He was an odd, tall man, angular, with a childlike face, a high, clear brow, dark hair, and a full, soft mouth. His face was cleanly planed, his jaw all sere lines. At first Ford thought him homely, but after listening for a while he could no longer be sure.

The song kept him there. In the midst of the decorated lobby, trimmed in potted poinsettias, the familiar carol belied the joyous season and mocked, gently, the attempt at gaiety through evergreen and velvet decorations. This man's song was about the sadness of Christmas, and the singer, as far as Ford could tell, was aware of it, was in fact filling the spacious room and all its occupants with the certainty of it. Tidings of comfort and joy. Ford was mesmerized.

The song ended, and the singer received his applause. It seemed to Ford that those who had listened to the true nature of the altered melody applauded, as he did, with vigor surpassing the usual polite appreciation. He watched the man, the slim figure and odd face, descend and vanish quietly into a knot of friends. For a few more moments he watched, before shaking his head clear of the echo of the voice and song. Then he and Curt

Robbins, who had listened as rapt as Ford, returned to their duties. But as the elevator opened, Ford spied a stray concert program on the floor. He lifted the bright green-and-red Xerox, reading the names of the singers, the bell ringers from Coral Baptist Church, and Amanda Zed, the operatically trained business office representative who sang "O Holy Night" every year.

The name of the other singer was Dan Crell, and he worked in administration. Ford folded the paper and tucked it into his pocket with his patient care notes. In the elevator he said to Curt, "Christmas sucks, anyway."

Later that same evening, in the apartment he shared with his dog, Hammond, and a friend named Allen Greenfield, he found the program mixed in among the scribbled SMA-18 results for one of his admits. The card on which he had scribbled the lab values belonged to a child who was in the terminal phase of leukemia, and Ford was expected to present this patient during tomorrow's morning conference. The concert program, lost in this chaos, seemed out of place. Laying the notes aside, he unfolded the paper and read the name again.

He hummed a few notes of the carol idly and thinly, with noise from the refrigerator as his only accompaniment. He tossed the program into the trash along with the rest of the paper to be purged from his pockets. The song would not leave his mind, was by now almost maddening, for it had stuck in his head and replayed itself all day.

Months later, Ford moved into a house on Clifton Heights, a pretty brick bungalow with a deep yard stretching back to a patch of woods and a mostly dry creek bed. Here he lived, alone, with his dog. He had bought the house using income from a trust established for him by his grandfather. His ownership of the house, combined with his departure from roommates in general and Allen Greenfield in particular, had made Ford aware that he was at an important juncture in his life. He had reached his late twenties, and his parents reminded him regularly that he ought to be thinking about marriage. His parents were certain to continue their lectures on the subject, assuming their harangues to be for his own good. But Ford imagined himself in marriage only with difficulty.

Ford had lately begun to worry at the number of Allen Greenfields in his life. He had lived with Allen for only a few months. During the beginning of their rooming together, they had made love twice, in Ford's bedroom, on the Sunday afternoons of succeeding weeks, without speaking of the event before, during, or after. These sessions took on a kind of frenzy and violence, the memory of which haunted Ford far beyond the moments of climax. Ford had returned to the apartment from his Sunday morning workout, his body flush from exercise, and Allen followed him into his bedroom, where they talked. Allen had appeared fascinated with the details of Ford's workout. He admired Ford's brawny body, and Ford had offered particular brawn for further admiration. Silence had settled over them both. Ford sensed the tentativeness of Allen's seduction and responded, at the crucial moment. Stripping in front of Allen. Standing close. Finally telling Allen what to do, how to do it, by gripping the smaller man's head with his hand, easing him to his knees. Their two bodies had tossed violently on Ford's big bed, and when they were finished, Ford stepped immediately into the shower.

But on the third Sunday, Ford returned home from his workout to find Allen's door closed, Allen asleep or feigning sleep.

When Ford's father's attorneys arranged the down payment on the Clifton Heights house, the thought of moving away from Allen relieved Ford. The two men never discussed the sex, though sometimes Ford would find Allen's eyes on him, momentarily devouring, as he passed from bedroom to shower. In those moments, Ford knew, he might have forced the issue. Feeling Allen's guilty admiration. But he refused.

The last month found Ford busy with the closing of the house and the details of the trust, with his parents and their attorneys visiting Atlanta from Savannah to obtain signatures on the necessary deeds, loan papers, and documents. With the rigors of his first year in the residency program closing in on him, Ford barely spoke to Allen at all.

Because admiration had always flowed to him from others, he never before felt himself responsible for any of its by-products. One day, as he wrestled with an older boy, Scott Elliott, in the shower stall at Savannah's Country

Day School, Scott's sudden arousal led to a kind of mutual fumbling during which Scott came, rapturously, on Ford's thigh. Ford himself felt curiously detached. What he remembered afterward was the taste of power he had over the older boy. This seemed only natural, since Ford was the larger of the two, and yet the fact that Scott was older made the whole incident more significant. When the scene with Scott recurred intermittently, Ford began to take this homage as his due.

The fact that he was physically freer with Scott than with any of the girls he dated never occurred to him. That thought only came later, when he actually made love to Susan Wariner in his dormitory room at the University of North Carolina at Chapel Hill. He had met her through a student Methodist organization, and she submitted herself to him some months later, after reading to him from the Bible and asking him to pray with her. Following the sweetest, gentlest of prayers, they made out on Ford's plaid bedspread, and she sighed and gave up the ghost, his hand sliding in and out of her clothes. Susan's religion had not stunted her physical development, nor had it dampened her sense of experimentation. But her expectation was that her mere yielding was enough. Ford had grown accustomed to the fervor with which his boys admired him, and Susan's praise of his broad shoulders and the size of his biceps did not strike quite the same chord.

Soon afterward, in the gymnasium, when a slim, handsome blond named Tucker lingered in the shower to watch Ford following a workout, Ford took the boy to that same dorm room, and they acted out a scene which was more to Ford's liking. Tucker adored that body which had awed him in the gymnasium, and Ford basked in the radiance of Tucker's lust, answering it with his own, leaning back on the bed and letting Tucker drink, the two boys rolling around on that same plaid bedspread, reducing the room to chaos corner by corner. Following Tucker's departure the normally tidy room was a shambles, while after Ford and Susan had restored their clothing they might have served tea on the premises immediately.

But Tucker he saw no more than twice, while he dated Susan on and off for more than a year. Their lovemaking did improve, but with Susan he never entered into that territory of adrenaline and fever. Because he understood, instinctively, that this failure was not Susan's but had to do with him, he never spoke about the subject. As far as he was concerned, he was perfectly comfortable seeing Susan now and then, and might have gone on dating her far beyond the time during which they courted. But near the end of a year, Ford realized Susan might expect something more from him in the future. After that he became conscious that he was distancing himself from her, and soon they agreed to stop seeing each other altogether.

His parents expressed relief at this breakup of what had appeared to be a vigorous college romance. Susan Wariner was far from the sort of girl they wished for their son—she was neither from Savannah nor of particularly good family. As for Ford, he accepted the approval of his parents as tacit evidence that he had acted properly in freeing himself of this entanglement. But as he continued to pick up boys in the gym, and as his delight in the subsequent acts of conquest continued unabated, he became aware that his own maturity was taking a different road than the one prescribed for him.

As a college senior, with his parents beginning to wonder why he showed so little interest in the kind of women suitable for a proper match, he himself discovered mutuality of desire. With McKenzie Donnelly.

McKenzie lived next door to Ford in a bungalow on Wyrick Street that had been rented to so many prior college students it had taken on the aura of a dormitory. McKenzie owned a dog named Hammond, a hulking brown mongrel with paws the size of grapefruit and a tongue so long it trailed the ground as he ambled through the neighborhood, terrorizing garbage cans in his search for gourmet tidbits.

Ford had noted the presence of the homely dog in his neighborhood, but only met McKenzie one autumn morning while righting his own overturned garbage can. This was early, about the time garbage pickup was due, and Ford hurried out of his kitchen when he saw the mess at the street.

McKenzie found him at the task. Hair disheveled as if he had only just stumbled out of bed, he bounded to the end of Ford's driveway and said, "Let me help you with that. Since it was my dog that did the damage."

The two men introduced themselves, and Ford learned that McKenzie lived in the red-shingled bungalow with a graduate student whom Ford had only seen and never met. "I think Kenneth is getting a little tired of my dog," McKenzie said, taking Hammond's ungainly head by the ears and shaking it gently back and forth. "Of me too," he added, giggling, scratching the nest of his hair. "We got our marching orders last night, when I got in."

"Your roommate kicked you out?"

"Oh, yeah," McKenzie said, laugh still sparkling. "Put my ass right on the street, as of today. I don't blame him either. I'm such a son-of-a-bitch."

As the conversation progressed, Ford found himself more and more intrigued. He invited McKenzie inside, and they sat at the kitchen table. The fellow was raucously good-looking, with a rakish, slant-grinned face that reminded Ford of the fair-haired villains in cowboy movies.

He claimed to be the scion of an old southern house, the great-great-grandson of one of North Carolina's Confederate generals, and a troublemaker since the day he was born. When he laid claim to this heritage, his blue eyes glazed, and he spoke of his family with brittle callousness. Because of his endless misbehaviors his father refused any contact with him, and he existed on student loans and the occasional dividend from rarefied family stocks. He also attended the university, asserting himself to be a philosophy major and naming the requisite professors, whom he claimed to have bested in one classroom debate after another. Ford hardly knew whether to believe him or not; McKenzie spoke so glibly, it was easy to believe he could best even the experts in their chosen fields. The conversation amused them both to the point that Ford cut his morning class and drove McKenzie to the local package store, where they obtained gin and bloody Mary mix—gin being vastly preferable to vodka, even in a bloody Mary, according to McKenzie, because of the effects of juniper on the human dream state. "When I drink gin, I wake up with an erection the size of a telephone pole," McKenzie claimed. "If I could figure out how to write down my dreams before I forget them, I could have a pornographic bestseller."

That they ended up in bed together before noon surprised neither of them. But what astonished Ford was his own reaction to the man. In the face of McKenzie's liveliness, Ford abandoned his own preferred game of self-absorption. McKenzie led him step by step, ravenous and lovely, his touch sparking heat in every line of Ford—in the living room of the Wyrick Street house, under the moving shadows of tree leaves on the carpet that had belonged to Ford's Grandmother Strachn. McKenzie's lithe shape drew Ford's hands irrevocably along its every plane, Ford fumbling with the buttons of McKenzie's shirt, almost tearing the T-shirt over McKenzie's head in his eagerness to get at the firm torso, the hairy chest, the pink, soft nipples. When the two men lay naked on the historic carpet and Ford brushed his lips down the length of McKenzie's cock, the fact of this initiation escaped Ford. He had lost himself somewhere within McKenzie.

Late in the evening, after they moved to the bed and

continued their long ritual of acquaintance, McKenzie moved his few belongings into Ford's house. The next-door graduate student, Kenneth, watched the whole moving process coldly from his porch, lit by a single bare bulb. Finally Kenneth glared at Ford and said, "You'll live to regret this, let me assure you," before returning inside and slamming the door. Hammond, confused, dashed back and forth between the houses, his club-like tail wagging wildly. At last, with the move complete, Ford welcomed the ungainly mutt into his kitchen.

The honeymoon with McKenzie lasted for weeks. To Ford, who had never before felt compelled toward anyone, the interval wore all the trappings of eternity. That he could lose himself completely in the presence of McKenzie came as a continual surprise; that he could desire McKenzie to the exclusion of nearly everything else shocked him even more deeply. He had never before had to wonder about his future, but with McKenzie in his house he began to do so.

Already he had aimed at Emory medical school, from which his father and grandfather had graduated to their cool, ordered lives among the Savannah elite. Ford's choice of Emory aimed in part at family tradition and in part at a desire to appease his father, who had strongly disapproved Ford's decision to attend the Chapel Hill university rather than its perfectly good counterpart in Athens, Georgia. Ford had never doubted he would achieve admission to Emory, and, indeed, had never before doubted that he would go on from medical school to the requisite residency at Grady and the eventual ascent to the throne of his father: the house off Calhoun Square and the carefully established medical practice whose patrons included the best and oldest families.

But in the wake of McKenzie, in the flood-tide of feeling the man stirred in him, he understood that he might never have a wife. Further, he understood that without the wife, the whole studied and perfect life that his family —that he—had envisioned became suddenly at risk.

At the same time, the honeymoon with McKenzie ended, and the young man's self-destructiveness resurfaced.

McKenzie drank. At first this seemed reasonable enough, and Ford took up the sport, too. He had nothing to lose, after all, being in the last weeks of his senior year in college, his grades earned, his admission to medical school assured. He allowed McKenzie to lead him, and drinking became part of his general infatuation. But Ford soon tired of it. Waking into a cotton-headed stupor each morning wearied him to the point that he began to quarrel with the need for the stuff, at first intermittently and then all the time.

McKenzie reacted by descending more deeply into haze.

When the quarrels between them began in earnest, McKenzie retreated, as he had always done. He went to bars and stayed out all night, stumbling home toward dawn or after, drunken and wrecked, falling over furniture and cursing Hammond's attempts at affection. Some mornings he had himself delivered to the door by whatever pickup had sheltered him for the few hours between bar-closing and morning light. At the first such incident, Ford withdrew from him in cool shock. After some weeks of this, Ford moved McKenzie into the second bedroom of the house. The quarrels ceased. The physical heat that had dictated their life together turned to frost.

This cooling had not disturbed McKenzie while he was with other men; with Ford, he became terrified, flaunting his night encounters more openly. Taunting Ford, ridiculing him, doing anything to provoke response. But no response came. The arctic chill of the house reached even to Hammond, who wandered from one man to the other, utterly confused.

When McKenzie brought one of his pickups home from the gay bar in Durham, a final, savage argument began. Ford, alone in the room he had reserved for himself, heard voices in his living room, one he recognized and one he did not. Instant anger flooded him, and he rushed out of bed wearing only loose pajama bottoms.

In the living room he found McKenzie and a boy wrapped round each other on the same carpet where McKenzie and Ford had begun their tryst, what now seemed a lifetime ago. At the sight of Ford, the stranger leapt to his feet, backing toward the kitchen as he rearranged his clothing—later, Ford would wonder just how palpable his anger had been that the boy should feel it before Ford said a word. Ford gazed down at McKenzie, trembling, and said, "Not here."

McKenzie, drunk, gestured beatifically toward the rug. "Come on, come join us."

"Fuck you," Ford said. "Get him out of here."

"But I can't," McKenzie said, still smiling the drunken smile. "He doesn't have anywhere to go. Do you?" Turning from the frightened figure huddling in the kitchen doorway to Ford. "His parents won't let us go to his house."

"I said, get him out of here, I don't care where you take him."

McKenzie laughed. "Come on, Fordie, it's all right. We'll be quiet. Don't spoil my fun."

Ford turned to the stranger, a scared kid. "Wait for me outside. I'll take you home."

"Now you wait just a minute," McKenzie said, struggling to rise.

"Shut up!" He trembled, looming over McKenzie. Who froze in the midst of clumsy attempts to right himself and buckle his belt. "I said I'm taking him home, and I mean it."

"Just because you won't fuck me anymore doesn't mean I can't have any fun."

"You can have all the fun you want," Ford said, "but not in my house."

"Oh, yes," McKenzie said, "your house. That your parents buy for you. But they wouldn't, would they? If they knew what you do in it."

"You're drunk," Ford said.

"Oh, yes."

"So shut your mouth."

"Oh, no," McKenzie said, "I'm planning to use my mouth. As soon as you get out of my way."

"You're too drunk to do much," Ford said. "You probably can't manage sex anyway. Why don't you put yourself to bed, if you think you can manage that. And get plenty of rest. Because tomorrow you're getting out of here once and for all."

"Fordie doesn't like us faggots, does he?" McKenzie turned to the frightened boy, who fumbled with the doorknob trying to open it. "Fordie doesn't like being a faggot. Fordie doesn't like being a fucking cocksucker like the rest of us, oh, no. But Fordie is a cocksucker, and when Mommie and Daddie find out —"

The sound of the harsh slap echoed. McKenzie fell flat again, the side of his face reddening. Eyes glazed, he lay silent. Ford's palm stung. He looked at the hand, at McKenzie's face. Stunned at himself, he felt the shock of the moment reverberating, and for a moment he longed to say something tender.

But then he heard the door closing, the shadow of the terrified boy falling against the glass from outside. Anger returned; Ford whirled to the bedroom, found his car keys and a robe and stormed outside. Through this, McKenzie lay motionless on the rug.

Ford drove the boy home. Few words passed between them, but Ford did learn that the boy's name was Johnny

—no last name—and that he claimed to be eighteen. Beyond that, Ford felt no need to know anything, leaving Johnny to contemplate this sudden end to what must have seemed a wonderful adventure. His home lay beyond Durham, a twenty-minute drive. From the small size of the house and the old truck parked in the front yard, Ford wondered if this were a standard evening for the kid, out all night and no one to care. Ford parked the car momentarily, and Johnny studied the house, suddenly lost and frightened. He turned to Ford and appeared to want to say something. Eyeing Ford up and down. Ford became acutely aware that he was in pajamas, in a strange town in the middle of the night. Johnny opened the door and bolted from the car, and Ford watched him fumble for keys. The slim body slid into the house, and Ford drove away.

Till dawn he drove around Chapel Hill, parking for a while near Kenan Stadium, watching the silhouettes of the sentinel pines against the moonless sky. He cruised residential streets, drove around University Mall, even headed the car toward Sanford and opened the windows, letting the cool night air flood the interior. The lump of anger refused to dissolve.

When he finally returned to Wyrick Street, he found the house open, lights on throughout, and McKenzie's car gone from the yard.

Inside, except for the lights, all was in perfect order. McKenzie had cleaned out the bedroom; nothing of his person or his possessions was to be found. Not even a note.

Ford expected never to see the man again, but late the next afternoon the battered Chevrolet returned to the driveway and McKenzie, haggard and unshaven, stepped one foot out of the car, standing in the open door with the motor running, to ask if Ford had seen Hammond.

Ford came to the door and waited there. He could see the bruised side of McKenzie's face, the nearly blackened eye, and wondered if the single slap could really have left such a mark. The question of Hammond surprised him, since he assumed the dog had moved out with McKenzie. Ford answered no, calmly. McKenzie nodded. "He ran off last night," McKenzie said, "I can't find him."

"Tell me where you're staying, and I'll call you when he comes back."

"Never mind," McKenzie said, "I'll just check again," sliding behind the steering wheel and hurriedly backing away.

For a moment Ford felt the fleeting return of that first feeling, that ache for McKenzie; but this soon fled, and in its wake came hollowness and sorrow. He closed the door and returned to his house.

If McKenzie ever returned to check for the dog, Ford never saw him. As for Hammond, Ford presumed him lost as well, until a week or so later the dog showed up at the kitchen door, clumsy tail wagging heavily, tongue trailing the window glass as he begged for entrance. Ford let him in, fed him, scratched his ears.

Since he knew of no way to find McKenzie other than to patrol the bars, he simply waited, assuming that the man would someday return to claim the animal. But Ford's senior year of college soon ended, the commencement ceremony came and went, his parents flying to town for the occasion and taking the opportunity to comment on the astounding ugliness of the hound. When Ford moved from the Wyrick Street house to Atlanta, Hammond moved with him. After that, Ford stopped thinking of the mutt as McKenzie's dog and simply referred to Hammond as his own.

———————

Four years later, on a night in late July, Ford unlocked his front door and found a curious stillness. At first Ford thought the problem was that he had entered by the front door, when Hammond was accustomed to welcoming him in the kitchen. But Hammond always found him, wherever he was. In the absence of the dog, Ford's spine tingled, and he called quietly, "Hammond. Hammond, fellow."

He searched the house. Finding Hammond stretched out on the floor of the bathroom, flat and motionless, fur stiff, nostrils spilling a little pool of blood onto the white-and-blue checked tile. Behind him, along the bottom edge of the porcelain bathtub, lay most of Hammond's disgorged breakfast.

Ford sat stupidly and watched the dog for a long time. He had no idea what to do or who to call. He had been awake for nearly two days and wanted rest, but now he could hardly think of anything except Hammond, the fact of Hammond, cooling and stiffening before him. Finally he called the veterinarian who had last given the mutt his shots. Wrapping the hound's corpse in a blanket, Ford drove the necessary blocks in the twilight of Druid Hills.

Hammond had suffered a cerebral hemorrhage, the veterinarian concluded, days later. What had caused the hemorrhage? The veterinarian offered only that the skull appeared perfectly intact, that the cause was internal, that there was really no way to tell exactly what had happened. The veterinarian charged him a small fee for disposing of the body and a large fee for the autopsy that Ford had required.

The silence of the house first offended and later frightened him. Each night, when he entered the house, he heard the emptiness anew. After a while, not only the silence but the largeness of the house brought Ford disquiet, and he wandered from room to room, restless, through the few hours of off-duty time his schedule afforded him. He understood his reaction to the dog's death to be disproportionate, out of kilter, but he only watched himself as if totally detached, as if happy to note that he was capable of a reaction that frightened people.

Frightened, at least, his parents, his mentors on the medical school faculty, to the point that someone suggested psychotherapy, and his parents agreed. Ford had begun to lose weight, his eyes had gone dark-circled, and, though he remained mentally precise in his hospital training, he showed signs that his fatigue might soon affect his thinking. He confirmed everyone's suspicions of his instability by breaking up with his girlfriend even more abruptly than he had broken up with his past girl-friends. Ford could feel himself slipping into a fog.

But he already understood his fear quite well. For this reason he could be helpful when the psychotherapist, a friendly woman with wire-screwy hair that wafted in a cloud around her face, offered her hand at their first session, introduced herself as Shaun Gould, and asked, "Why are you here?"

"My dog died and now I'm so lonely it's driving me crazy."

His directness brought her forward in the chair, and she said, "I'm very sorry you lost your dog. That must have hurt you."

"Yes."

"Did you know you were lonely before the dog died?"

"No. But I know now."

"What do you know about it?" Shaun asked, and the question bore just exactly the right ring of interest, nothing feigned or enacted.

As she listened to his answer, he studied her comforting body, its thick waist and generous curves lounging in the black leather chair. He told her about breaking up with his current girlfriend, and he told about breaking up with the previous girlfriends. Each time he described one of the girlfriends, he got a sick feeling in the pit of his stomach, and finally he said, "But that's not what I want to talk about."

"I didn't think it was," Shaun said.

"I want to tell you about Allen," Ford said. "And then I want to tell you about McKenzie."

He expected to tell the story with detachment, but failed. He stopped talking and waited, shivering. Shaun had listened with occasional changes of expression, small nods, and careful encouragements for him to continue. He told about Hammond and McKenzie, and those months in Chapel Hill when he had been with them both. He trembled, but Shaun sat calmly, hands folded in her lap. When he said, "But he never came back to get the dog, and so I kept him," and then fell silent, Shaun sat motionless. Finally nodding once.

"Why did you tell me that?" she asked.

"To tell you something about me."

"What are you telling me?"

"That I must have cared about him a lot."

"That you must have?"

He thought carefully. "That I did. I cared about him. More than I cared about anybody else that I can think of."

Ford visited Shaun once a week for a period of several months. While he declined to discuss these sessions with his parents, they were relieved to note he had regained his weight and color. He slept well, after the first few weeks. Returning to the empty house no longer paralyzed him. Abandoning the image of himself floating above himself, he caressed the physical objects around him, the exquisite antiques that had belonged to his Great-grandmother Bondurant, the Waterford vase full of silk daisies, the stainless frame of the Matisse print over the Victorian sofa.

At the hospital, he proved himself to be a better prospect as a pediatrician than many would have guessed, moving with authority from nursing unit to clinic exam room, charismatic, with a knack for getting along with nurses and ancillary staff. Even after thirty-six- and forty-eight-hour shifts, Ford remained even-tempered and clear-headed, proving his value repeatedly.

"Why do you want to be a doctor?" Shaun asked, in late September.

"I don't know," Ford answered, "I never really thought about it."

"You're working very hard to become something, and you don't know why you want to be that something?"

Ford enjoyed the game of framing his answers in words that Shaun would allow. "I want to be a doctor because my father was a doctor and my grandfather was a doctor. I never really thought about my own reasons. It was enough to think about my father and my grandfather."

"Don't you think you should do a little thinking about what you want?"

"I guess I already have. Because I'm going into pediatrics. My father wasn't too happy about that because pediatricians don't have the same prestige that surgeons do. Don't make as much money. So he wasn't very happy with that, on top of the whole business with Hammond."

"Do you think there's any connection between the two things?"

"You mean, the fact that I'm going to keep disappointing my father for a good while to come?"

Shaun fingered the plain gold band that she wore on her right hand. "That's one way to look at it. But I think it might be healthier just to think of it as one more step toward honesty with your parents. With both of them. Your mother is involved in all this, too."

Honesty. With the white house, the cool rooms, the yard filled with oleander, the Vietnamese gardener moving among the blossoms. Honesty with the cool china, the polished silver, the framed pictures of parents, grandparents, great-grandparents, collateral couples, the great paired beings of his past. "I know what you're trying to say, Shaun. But it doesn't matter what I call it, honesty or anything else. My dad's going to hate it. So will my mom. In my family, in Savannah, you get married. You just do it. No matter what. I'm already late."

By early fall, his parents' concern over his matrimonial future became acute. At dinner with his father one evening, the two of them supping in the elegant affiliated men's business club (which remained a men's club even though women occasionally won membership), Dr. McKinney Sr. brought up Ford's old girlfriend, Haviland Barrows, who had recently married Red Fisher, one of Ford's high school acquaintances. "Settled right down in the historic district in a little stoop cottage. Renovated beautifully, right out of a textbook. I don't think that's such a bad way to start out." Father dabbed his lips with the napkin, preparing to engage his almond torte. "Of course, he'll get the Jones Street house when his grandfather dies. Your uncle Hubert drew up that will. God knows what she gets. Some of the Barrows don't have a cent, from what I hear."

"I hope she's happy," Ford said, signaling the waiter to bring more coffee. "She deserves it."

"I never did understand how you let her get away, son," Father said.

"It was easy," Ford answered. "In fact, I wonder if I'm likely to get married at all."

"What are you talking about? Of course you'll marry. Your mother and I wonder why it's taken you this long."

"If it's taken this long," Ford said, "that has to be because I've wanted it that way."

"Nonsense. First you had to get through medical school. That's what we've always expected." Dr. McKinney adjusted his collar. Ford spooned his own torte. "But now you're out of medical school, and it's time to think about your future. You're going to be a busy man, and you need someone to take care of you at home."

"You got married when you were in medical school."

"That was different. When your mother and I were coming up, people got married when they were younger. These days it's better to wait, the way you have. But you do have to stop waiting sometime." His father laughed, self-consciously, underlining the jovial atmosphere he attempted to create for serious discussions.

"I don't think I'm waiting." Ford spoke with all the finality he could muster. "I've had plenty of chances. I don't think I want to get married."

"You can't possibly be serious."

"I can." Folding his napkin and laying it on the corner of the table.

His father paused, then changed the subject to the politics of Emory University Medical School, the appointment of yet another dean. "This one may be worse than the last one," Father said. "We don't know if this one can even function with a—" falling suddenly silent.

"You don't know if he can what?" Ford asked.

"Well, anyway, he can't be worse the last one."

"But what about Dean Rouse?" Ford asked. "What are your buddies at the club saying about him?"

"Just idle talk," Father said uncomfortably.

"Did you know he's a bachelor?" Ford asked, after a moment.

"Why, yes. I did hear that." But his face was set as stone, and Ford watched him carefully. Frost settled over the table, covering their dinnerware and the remains of the dessert. Ford sipped his coffee.

Later they discussed his trust funds and other financial matters. Ford asked after his mother. Father answered that she was well. The conversation cooled even further, and the two men parted company in the porte cochere as the liveried driver handed Father the keys to his vintage Mercedes. At the last moment, the elder doctor said to the younger, "Don't forget we talked, Ford. You need to think about what you're doing. You've come through a bad time, and I think all that trouble started because you need somebody to take care of you. You need a wife."

"I'm thinking about all that, Father."

The two shook hands, and in his father's eyes glimmered ghost lights of real affection, sodden and held back.

———— ◦◦◦ ————

At about the same time, while awaiting an appointment with his chief of service, Dr. Milliken, Ford chanced to read a memorandum posted in the Department of Pediatrics office suite. The memorandum, like others layered on top of it on the bulletin board, might have merited little of Ford's attention, being unremarkable—but it was signed by someone in administration named Dan Crell. The signature itched at Ford for a few moments before he remembered the Christmas concert, the eerie voice, and the name on the concert program.

At the end of September, Ford rotated out of Grady for two months of training at Egleston, another of the teaching hospitals that Emory staffed. By the time he returned to Grady, in December, with the hospital adorned in poinsettias and decorated doors, he had allowed the name to lapse from active memory once again. But one morning early in the month, he became aware of someone watching him from the back of a nearly empty elevator.

Since he was ultimately headed for the operating room, Ford wore the green surgical scrubs that are ubiquitous in hospitals; the particular suit Ford had scrounged fit him snugly, the shoulders somewhat narrower than his own. The short sleeves rode high on his shoulders, and apparently the young man at the back of the elevator found the sight of Ford's shoulders irresistible. Nothing new. Ford turned a little and allowed himself to return the man's gaze coolly.

But the face shocked him. Recognition came at once. Ford looked for the man's identification badge and saw it hanging from the pocket of his shirt. Mr. Crell noted the motion, and this discomfited Ford somewhat. He felt suddenly naked in the green scrubs. But he met the man's gaze again.

This time Mr. Crell averted his eyes, as if shy. The moment gave Ford an interval in which to study the face again.

Dark curls framed features that seemed sharp and soft at once. The face broadcast innocence, as if a child were entombed in it. The face as a whole shimmered from awkwardness to moments of grace. Or seemed to, until the young man met Ford's gaze again.

"This is our floor," said Crell's companion, a nurse whom Ford had failed to notice.

"I guess I'm falling asleep," Crell said, "it's all those late nights," easing away from the elevator door. Even in those few words Ford could hear the singer in Dan's voice, the rich soothing undertone that, for a moment, filled the elevator car. That was it, or so Ford thought. But as the elevator doors began to close, the man looked back at Ford. They simply watched each other, and the door closed, and that was that.

———∞∞———

December of that year brought more sick people to Grady than any previous December of record, with patients in every available bed and new admissions sometimes waiting for hours in the emergency clinics. Every morning, the faculty and staff of the various medical disciplines met to determine which patients, while not fully recovered, might be well enough to go home anyway, in order to make another bed available for someone even sicker. During the height of this crisis, a school bus turned over while rounding a curve on Johnson Ferry Road, and suddenly the Pediatric Emergency Clinic filled with injured children.

The hospital implemented its disaster plan, called in extra staff, and coordinated the distribution of the injured to other area hospitals. Ford saw the first of the injuries following the interruption of morning rounds, when word of the bus accident rippled through the nursing units. Dr. Milliken chose Ford for part of the team that was to assist the trauma surgeons. He helped the emergency medical technicians unload the first child and rushed the broken body into the makeshift trauma room. Skull crushed on one side, delicate, throbbing brain tissue naked to the air, a little girl already intubated and strung with intravenous lines. Ford heard himself asking crisp questions about what had already been done for the girl, his voice nearly disembodied, almost as if he floated above himself once again, detached as he had been when Hammond died.

That moment of disembodiment—seeing the child with her head opened like a blossoming flower—was the last he allowed himself for hours. He assisted with six of the twelve children, all pitifully bruised, cut, blood oozing onto starched sheets and dripping off the side-rails of stretchers. His mind felt white and clean in the midst of all this motion, his orders crisp. Once he corrected a third-year resident on the proper dosage of painkiller for a nine-year-old with a body weight of eighty-seven pounds; once he started an intravenous line on a child when even the nurses could not find a vein. He felt himself elevated by all that motion into a state of grace, and while in it he moved through medicine as a dancer through music.

Inevitable problems occurred. The emergency clinics ran out of stretchers, and hospital administrators ordered a search of every floor of the massive building, sending unit managers to herd stretchers to the ambulance ramp. The telephone computer glitched, half the clinic phones went dead, and for the ten or fifteen minutes needed to restore service in the area, chaos reigned. At about this point, when a little girl with massive bruises had waited two hours for a bed, Dr. Milliken sent Ford to find a phone and get some word about beds.

He found the few working telephones in the clinic area already occupied by administrators calling to complain about the tardiness of telephone repair. However, a few days before, Ford had learned that the Admitting Office lay just around the corner from the emergency clinics, and since he wanted to get away from the clinic scene for a moment, he said to Dr. Milliken, "I can't find a phone working. I'm going around to the Admitting Office."

He passed through a crowded waiting room and stopped at the first desk he saw, at which a young woman was busily filling in a form as she conducted a telephone interview with a patient's next-of-kin. Ford hovered in her doorway for some moments, but she ignored him. Ford searched other offices and found nearly everyone occupied in similar work. But one of the desks, tucked into a small room at the back of the office suite, belonged to someone called an admitting officer, and because this title sounded promising, Ford waited in the doorway till the woman finished her phone call.

"Hi, what can I do for you?" she asked after hanging up the phone, patting her hair.

"I need a pediatric bed for Connors. You have the paperwork. The phones are out across the hall, and I walked over to see what was happening."

"No beds," waving her hands, "I got beds empty, but the nurses tell me they're not clean and the housekeepers tell me they have crews coming up to clean them. But when I talk to the nurses they tell me the crews never get there and the beds are still dirty."

Ford paused briefly to rearrange the information in his head, answering, "We've got a lot of kids needing those beds. Don't you think somebody can do something about getting them clean?"

"Doc, I've already called three times."

"Well, call again."

The woman sighed, patted her hair again, reached for the phone and dialed. "This is Rollins, get me James. Yeah, I got another problem." On hold, the woman tapped on a pad of Post-it notes from a pharmaceutical company. "James. Hey, honey. Yeah, you knew I'd be calling you again, didn't you? Listen. Did you get those Peds beds cleaned yet? 9A and 9C, right. Honey, we don't care about adolescent beds right now, we're putting everybody up there we can fit." Pause. "Well, the nurses tell me nobody's cleaning." Pause. "Honey, I know you need more people, so do I, but we got to get beds clean from someplace and you're the only one I know." Pause. "The doctor's standing right here. Little girl been waiting two hours to get a bed. That's right, from the bus accident." Pause. "Well, James, girl, you better get after somebody. The nurses tell me nobody's cleaning anything on the ninth floor, and we have to do something about that. You call me. All right? You call somebody, and then you call me and let me know what's going on." Cradling the receiver, she looked at Ford and shrugged. "I'm working on it, doc. What else can I tell you? Call administration, maybe they can do something."

She gave him a phone number to call, Mr. Franken's assistant, she said, because Mr. Franken was in charge of admissions. Ford went into another office, asked to use the phone and dialed.

A voice said, "Administration, Mr. Crell." Soothing, even through the telephone cord.

"This is Dr. McKinney in Pediatrics," Ford said. "I have a problem, and I think you can help me with it."

A moment's silence. Dan said, "I'll be happy to do whatever I can."

"I'm in your Admitting Office and I can't find out why we're having to wait hours in an emergency situation to get beds cleaned for the kids we're holding in the emergency room."

"How long have you been waiting?"

"I've got a little girl who's needed a bed for two hours."

"What did the Admitting Office tell you?"

"That there are empty beds on the ninth floor but they can't find the housekeeping crew to clean them."

"Well, it sounds like somebody ought to go to the ninth floor and find out whether anybody is cleaning beds," Dan said, "so why don't I do that? Then where can I call you?"

"You can't," Ford said, "the phones aren't working down here. I had to come to Admitting and grab a phone to call you."

"Well then, I'll come down there."

Returning to the Surgical Emergency Clinic, Ford passed Dr. Milliken and said, "I couldn't get an answer from the admitting officer, so I called Mr. Franken's office and spoke to Dan Crell. He says he'll find out what's going on with the beds and let us know as soon as he can."

Dr. Milliken's brows rose slightly. "Good work," he

said, mildly surprised. "I was planning to speak to Franken myself."

Word that ninth-floor beds had been cleaned and assigned came to them from Mr. Franken himself, however, with Ms. Rollins, the admitting officer, in train, and no Dan Crell in sight. In the press of events Ford felt no disappointment. He shook hands with the associate administrator at Dr. Milliken's behest, then busied himself with the transport teams who would escort the injured children to the nursing units.

Only later, in the first moment of stillness, a vague disappointment overlay the other fragments whirling in his brain. The guy might have found a reason to come in person, if he wanted. Not that it mattered to Ford. But he went on sitting at the tiny desk shoved against the corridor wall, unable to complete the order he had begun to write. He let himself drift, listening to the myriad voices, aware of motion but detached from it. Remembering the day in the elevator, the way the man had admired him. Remembering the easy voice on the telephone today, *Well, then, I'll come down there.* He had thought Dan Crell might be attracted to him. That hardly seemed such an odd thought, since so many people were.

In the midst of this reverie, a voice behind his shoulder said, "Dr. McKinney."

He could have sworn breath touched his neck. But when he turned, Dan Crell stood much too far away for the breath of that voice to have caused the tingling along Ford's skin. The single moment telescoped: Ford saw himself sitting there with the useless pencil, saw Dan hold a sheaf of disorganized papers like a shield between their bodies, noted the delicacy of the skin along the tops of Dan's hands. Each detail clear.

Dan said, "I came down to tell you about the mess with the beds a couple of times, but you were so busy I thought I ought not to disturb you. But my boss talked to Dr. Milliken."

"I know," Ford said.

"Is everything taken care of, then?"

"Yes, I think so."

Dan watched him intently, then averted his gaze. "I guess that takes care of the problem." Smiling, but not raising his eyes.

He was afraid, and Ford knew it. He was hungry too, and Ford felt the hunger. Ford said, "Thanks for your help." To draw those eyes up again.

"The cleaning crews were actually already there cleaning the beds. Everything was happening the way it was supposed to happen, it's just that nobody knew about it. So I told the nurses the beds were actually being cleaned and then I called Ms. Rollins."

"Thanks."

The moment ended when an arriving nurse asked for orders on one of Ford's patients. Dan withdrew. Later Ford wondered why he had found no opportunity to shake the young man's hand at least. At home, later, he savored the look in Dan's eyes and the open admiration with which Dan approached him, the warmth of Dan's remembered voice, and the gentleness of his presence.

A few days later, after twelve hours of a twenty-four-hour shift, he went to the hospital cafeteria for breakfast. Seated with Curt Robbins, Russell Cohen, Allison Roe, and a couple of other residents, he rubbed his night's growth of beard and listened to the discussion of a juvenile who had just been admitted to the ninth floor with acute diabetic ketoacidosis. Robbins described the fruity smell that accompanies the onset of this state, and Ford settled back for another ritual meal of diagnosis and discussion.

But across the cafeteria, framed by louvered windows and yellow blinds, Dan Crell carried a breakfast tray to a seat by the window wall.

Something in his demeanor alerted Ford to the likelihood that Dan had already seen him. Dan set his tray lightly onto the table and arranged himself behind it, unlidding hot coffee and releasing steam from the Styrofoam cup. When Dan finally looked up, he saw Ford watching him and immediately returned his attention to his tray.

Ford found himself staring at Allison Roe's emerald and diamond ring. He lost all contact with Curt's explanation of disease process and felt his breath come short. He told himself this was not the time, meals at Grady being as much a part of teaching as grand rounds, but when he glanced at Dan again, he felt a tightening in his chest. He pictured himself sitting here through the whole meal, watching that odd face across the room, then turning his back on Dan and leaving. Consciously he believed this could not make any difference, while to walk across the room to speak to the young man now would be to declare himself publicly, in front of his peers.

In that light he tried to focus on Curt—or was it Russell now?—discussing critical lab values and the immediate need to replenish body fluids, electrolytes. But the thought of Dan across the room made it impossible for him to concentrate. Russell tapped him on the shoulder and grinned. "You look like you've seen a ghost."

"I'm tired, that's all." Ford shoved his chair back from the table.

When he stood, Dan watched him. Ford took a deep breath. "I'll be back in a few minutes," he said to Curt.

He studied all the changes in Dan's face as he crossed the room—frozen unbelief, recognition, the whiteness of terror. At the table he loomed over Dan's tray watching Dan's cereal spoon suspended in midair. "Good morning," he said. "Can I join you for a minute?"

"Please."

Ford sat, folding his hands in front of him, careful to place his back to the table of doctors he had abandoned. He spoke at once, in order to forestall paralysis. "I wanted to thank you again for what you did the other day. During the accident."

Dan still watched his cereal. "I really didn't do very much."

A line of red crept up Dan's neck into his face. At

once, understanding Dan's fear, Ford lost sight of his own. He said, "I think you did enough." He wanted to make Dan look at him, and continued, "But that isn't why I sat down here."

Dan nodded. "I figured that." His voice almost vanished. "I've been staring at you ever since I sat down. I'm sorry."

The statement stunned Ford. An ache welled up in him, and he said, "I came over here to ask you to go to dinner with me. Sometime soon." Speaking now to keep his own breath even. "I was looking at you, too, you know."

Ford could detect each change in the man's lowered face, initial disbelief giving way to comprehension. Dan's grip on the cereal spoon tightened till his knuckles were white. He took a long breath and looked at Ford.

They watched each other in silence. Not since Mc-Kenzie had Ford read so much in another face. He felt himself opening and relaxing, drawn to the body across the table as if they were falling toward each other. Ford laughed. "Well. Answer my question."

"Yes, I want to have dinner with you." Shock still registered in Dan's expression. "Have you been planning this for a while?"

"Since last week. Whenever the accident was."

Dan shook his head in wonder. "I've been watching you for a long time. Since you were a medical student. I can't believe it."

Ford blushed himself, as if no one had ever admired him before. He glanced back at the table of physicians still engrossed in their medical discussion. Turning to Dan again, he said, "I need to get back to my ongoing learning experience before my senior resident comes after me. When can we do this?"

They negotiated the date, shy of watching each other but drawing out the process in spite of Ford's need to return to his duties across the cafeteria. Ford was on call for several nights running, and Dan was busy with rehearsals for a musical at a local community theater. They settled on a Friday evening in a week, and Ford noted the engagement in his pocket calendar. This business finished, they sat.

"I don't particularly want to go right now," Ford said.

"I don't either," Dan replied. "I haven't eaten very much of my breakfast. But if I don't get back to my office, I'll never dig myself out from under the morning mail."

They rose from the table together. Standing, Ford could feel the intense charge between his body and Dan's, acute now that the gates had opened. He could find no words delicate enough for the moment, but Dan said, "Thank you for doing this. May I call you Ford?"

"Yes. Please."

"Thank you for doing this, Ford. I've wanted to talk to you for a long time, but I've never had the guts to do anything about it."

"I never would have either," Ford said, "before now. So listen, I'll call you next week about arrangements, right? You'll be here?"

Allison Roe greeted Ford coolly as he adjusted his

chair. "Getting acquainted with hospital administrators, Dr. McKinney?"

"I was just thanking him for his help with the beds last week when we had the bus accident." Ford made a business of getting his napkin in place.

This exchange seemed small enough at the time but took on more significance as days passed. The short walk across the cafeteria divided his life by apprehension, beginning with Allison Roe's silken remarks. What would she say if she knew Ford had asked the administrator to dinner? Worse, if she knew the reason for the asking? If his other friends found out?

In his pleasant kitchen on a morning when he was free of hospital duties, he understood his courage to be failing. He poured a second cup of coffee and drank it in the early quiet on his side porch, wrapped in a thick sweater against the slight December chill. Holly in the yard gleamed deeply green. Loneliness poured into him with the stirring of winter breezes, but even in the cold he sat on the porch for a long time in his pajamas and sweater, bare ankles in bedroom slippers, numbed fingers on the warm coffee mug.

He tried to remember the feeling that had led him to cross space, to sit down at the table of a stranger and ask the stranger to take a meal with him. He pictured the stranger's face but the image formed only as a blur in his consciousness. What expectations did Dan harbor? *I've been watching you for a long time. Since you were a medical student.*

By the time he left the porch, he had resolved to break the date; but even that act would be public, would require courage. He must either telephone Dan or else, worse, walk into his office. Briefly Ford considered calling Dan at home but found the idea too personal, worse than any public scene. Would he tell the truth, or would it be better to pretend that his on-call schedule had changed? Dan might not get the message right away, but soon enough, when Ford refused any attempt at rescheduling, the picture would become clear. Dan was, after all, far from the kind of person Ford wanted in his life; surely even he understood that.

This left only the question of timing. On this issue, Ford's thinking failed him. He meant to call at once. Each silent telephone reminded him. But Ford lacked the certainty that he could carry off the conversation with good grace.

Finally he wrote a note to the young man, mailing it to his hospital address. Ford simply wrote that the dinner they had planned was proving impossible for him to schedule. He signed himself "F. McKinney" and attempted to make the scrawl as little like his usual signature as possible, in case Dan Crell attempted to make some sinister use of the note.

He placed a call to Shaun Gould, canceling his weekly session and wishing her the merriest of holidays.

On the Friday of the impossible dinner, with Christmas looming the next week, Ford headed through first-floor corridors toward the Pediatric Appointment Clinic

where he was scheduled to see patients under Dr. Milliken's supervision. Though the clinic occupied a large area
on the second floor of the hospital, Ford went to the trouble of descending one floor and crossing to the clinic on
that level. Out of fear. Dan Crell's office lay on the second
floor in a suite of offices between the two clinics.

But Ford found Dr. Milliken at the juncture of corridors near the first-floor lobby, standing in a large crowd,
and as Ford approached Dr. Milliken signaled him. Ford
smiled the crisp smile of the proper young medical resident, heading toward his chief of service. "I want you to
hear this," Dr. Milliken said, and a piano struck soft notes
as across the crowded lobby Dan Crell mounted a dais
and prepared to sing.

"Let's see if we can't get closer," Dr. Milliken whispered. "He has a wonderful voice."

Ford muffled his panic and followed, entrapped. Dan
began a lullaby to the Christ child, a song Ford had heard
in his childhood but not since. At the first full notes, a
ripple of response passed through the gathering as the
song was recognized; then rapt silence fell as the voice
swelled to fill the lobby, to permeate every corner. "Lo, lay
thou little tiny child," the young man sang, and the
mournful tones sent a chill through Ford. He lost himself
in listening. His eyes followed every movement, tracing
the slim figure of the singer as the song poured from him,
the radiance of the sound matched by the luminescence
of his face, his wholeness. While Dan sang, he remained
oblivious to everything around him, motionless but for

the throbbing of his tender, touchable throat. Again his singing told those who listened that the joy of the saved is the sorrow of the savior, that the tiny child might wish another fate. Again in minor keys and throbbing tones he undercut the merry decorations of the lobby, and from within Ford responded with the same deep sadness.

The song ended, the last pulse vanishing, and the room exploded into applause, far greater than Ford's memory of the year before. Dan received this quietly, with a look of deliberate containment. The stillness of his features burned an image into Ford. Before descending from the dais, with an air of perfect peace, he surveyed the crowd as the applause continued.

He could hardly help but find Ford, who stood inches above every other occupant of the room. Their eyes locked, and suddenly Dan's moment of perfect beauty fled. He froze on the dais, broke off the eye contact by act of will, took a breath and gathered himself together, each phase of the change visible to Ford. His flesh went ashen, his eyes dimmed. When he could move again, he let the crowd take him.

"He's wasting his time at Grady," Dr. Milliken said, "anybody who can sing like that."

Ford said, all hollow, "I heard him in the concert last year."

Only the sickness of his patients kept Ford intact through the remainder of his shift. He moved through the clinic corridors with perfect whiteness of mind, obliterating every thought but that of his next action, the counting of a heartbeat, the proper curve of sinus rhythm on an EKG strip, the correct test to order for the white blood cell count of a child one week past strep throat. Once, in his empty exam room, before summoning his next patient, he dialed Dan Crell's hospital extension; closing his eyes, holding his breath, he told himself he would think of something to say. A crisp-voiced secretary informed him that Mr. Crell had left for the day and would not return to the hospital till after Christmas; would there be any message?

His shift ended, and he drove to Clifton Heights. The iron control with which he had braved the long day refused to release him now, and he could hardly feel his own heartbeat. Pouring himself a large glass of gin, disdaining all lights, all television, all music, he wandered from room to room, his brain a burned-out blank. When he recalled the events of the day, he could hardly believe any moment of it after Dr. Milliken's voice in the lobby, *I want you to hear this.*

He had heard. He had also remembered, past his fear.

When the telephone rang he rushed to answer. But this voice was without resonance, was his mother asking about his plans for arrival in Savannah, would he drive or would he fly? Her mellow, cool questions returned him to the kitchen, facing wooden shelves, studying his grandmother's colanders and the telephone directory. He reached for the directory, saying to his mother, "I only have about thirty-six hours, if I drive I'll do nothing at home except sleep."

"I agree that flying is sensible, Ford, but if you haven't booked a flight by now you'll never get a seat."

"That's not what I told you, Mother, I said I hadn't decided which flight to take because I wasn't sure of my schedule. I have seats on two different flights and I'll know tomorrow which one I'll be on. My travel agent has everything under control."

"I don't mean to be a bore about it, dear, but you know what Christmas means to all of us." She laughed electronically across the scores of miles. "We want to make sure you get here in time for your grandmother's party."

"I get there Christmas Eve night," Ford said, "and I'll probably make it to the party, but I won't make dinner. Then I fly out early the morning of the twenty-sixth, just about dawn. That's the most likely schedule at the moment."

"Do you have any shopping I can do for you, or have you managed it all?"

Ford rubbed his brows, biting back impatience. Reaching for the telephone book, he said, "Why don't I call you about that sometime Sunday. I need some help, but I don't have myself organized about it right this minute."

"That's fine, son, but please don't push this off to Christmas Eve. You know how much I have to do this time of year."

Shortly afterward they said good-bye and hung up, and Ford looked up Dan Crell in the telephone book. There was only one listing under that name, on Blue Ridge

Avenue near North Highland. Standing in the dark, taking deep breaths, Ford lifted the phone receiver again.

After a dozen rings he gave up. Dan had indeed gone home early, or he had decided to do something else for the evening, or he refused to answer the phone. Leaning against the countertop, watching moon-cast tree shadows moving against the windows, Ford gave up for the night.

Christmas in Savannah followed the course of every Christmas he remembered, as far as the family was concerned. But the change in him was evident to his family at once. His sister, Courtenay, picked him up at the airport, full of news about Smith College and warnings about Dad and Mom. "Sounds to me like they want to start matchmaking for you as soon as you get in the door. They've invited the oldest Stillwell girl to Grandmother Strachn's for eggnog."

"Christ," Ford said, "that's all I need."

"Chin up, Fordie. She's so shy she won't say a word. And she's only tall enough to come up to your ribcage, you can always pretend you don't see her."

"Why can't they mind their own business?"

Courtenay, nearly six feet tall herself, reached across the car to pat his forearm tenderly. "As far as they're concerned, Ford, your marriage is their business. Family business. Just like mine will be, whenever I get around to it."

"Are you seeing anybody?"

"Oh, yes. The same guy I told you about, the carpenter. Mom will love it when I finally tell her about that one."

Ford laughed. Courtenay turned down Abercorn Street and finally onto East Gordon, where Grandmother Strachn's well-kept mansion occupied the corner off Calhoun Square. Ford convinced Courtenay to park on the other side of the square, and they walked slowly through the moss-hung trees, arms around each other's waists.

"Cheer up, big brother," Courtenay said, sensing trouble in his silence. "You've always got me. Frankly, it suits me if you wait a long time to get married. As long as the prince of the house is single, the pressure is off the princess."

"I doubt I ever will."

"Will what?"

"Find a wife. Raise a family."

She let the statements stand for a moment. "You sound as if you've got a good reason for saying that. Do you want to share it with your sister?"

He shrugged, affecting nonchalance, but feeling the flutter of tension in his stomach. "I'm not seeing anybody at all right now. I haven't dated since Haviland."

"Is something wrong, Ford? Is there something you need to talk about?"

They looked each other in the eye. Ford smiled wryly. "Are you asking for direct communication, in the McKinney family?" They remained beneath the draping of Spanish moss. Ford reached for another joke but stopped himself. Without a plan for this moment, he had managed to engineer it anyway. "There is somebody I want to start seeing. A man at the hospital."

Courtenay accepted this in silence, gently drawing him against her side. From Grandmother Strachn's parlor drifted the sound of recorded Christmas carols. "Have you talked to Mom or Dad about any of this?"

"Sort of. To Dad. He deflected the whole thing, and I wasn't very direct."

"How long have you known?"

"About this guy? Not long. About me? I don't know. I'm just now getting around to facing facts." Remembering the Christmas concert, the empty Friday evening, now a week past but fresh and aching nonetheless. "I haven't been very good at it, so far."

He told her the story of the last few months, including his therapy sessions with Shaun, and his pattern of more-or-less anonymous sex. Her lack of surprise gave him to understand that the news neither surprised nor shocked her particularly, and she listened as if there were all the time in the world. Finally she said, "I guess I knew something was going on. You're too good-looking to be having trouble finding a woman."

"How do I deal with Mom and Dad?"

She blew out misty breath, turning to the imposing house that overshadowed them both. "I don't know. Let's think about it." She ran a hand through his hair and pulled him against her side. "But I wouldn't rush into anything."

"If they're planning to parade half of Savannah's finest in front of me, I don't know if I can stand it."

"You're not here that long; hold your breath and drink

a lot of eggnog." She kissed his forehead and they wandered toward the parlor lights. "Wait till you get yourself straightened out with this man. Or till you get somebody else you care about. You need a little support before you take on the whole twenty-nine generations of McKinneys and Strachns."

Christmas Eve at Grandmother Strachn's followed a script written before either Ford or Courtenay was born, beginning with the formal dinner Ford had missed, ending with gift exchanges and half-hearted caroling around the antique Steinway in the middle parlor. As at most Savannah social occasions, everyone drank throughout the evening, and when Ford entered, still arm-in-arm with his sister, the room glowed with flushed faces and bulbous noses etched with broken capillaries. Ford greeted Grandmother Strachn at once, seated in her high-backed chair at the center of her family. He kissed the delicate old skin of her cheeks. Aunt Rose had just seated herself at the piano and, after Ford had kissed his mother and the other aunts and had shaken hands with his father and the men, Aunt Rose struck up the first chords of "Hark, the Herald Angels Sing." Glass in hand, Ford joined the circle of voices. His mother contrived to have Lisa Stillwell stand next to him. They had rounded their way through "Joy to the World" and into "While Shepherds Watched Their Flocks by Night." Flushed with his success (and with what he considered to be his rather good baritone), Ford managed to speak politely to Lisa as Aunt Rose flipped the pages of her yellowed music book. He caught his mother watching with a look of private satisfaction as he complimented Lisa's singing. Aunt Rose reached her destination and struck up the opening chords of "God Rest Ye, Merry Gentlemen."

The song catapulted him back to Atlanta. He tried to control himself, but after the conversation with Courtenay, his heart refused control and he knew he could not stand here. Not with this sinking in his gut. He excused himself quickly. He shut himself in the downstairs bathroom and locked the door, leaning against the wall out of sight of the mirror.

He could still hear the song, but not as sung by his family's ragged choir. The voice in his head, rich and full, filled him with loneliness. But he played the memory through, beginning to end, the sadness and beauty of the voice, and at its end he looked himself in the eye in the mirror. Taking a deep breath, he let go of the ache and willed it to subside. "I will take care of this," he said, "I promise," though he himself did not know for whom the promise was made.

After that, even the most superficial conversation with Lisa pained him, and he avoided her presence. Once his mother whispered, "You've hardly spoken to poor Lisa, and she was so happy when she found out you were going to be here tonight. Why don't you ask her about her internship? She's working for Senator Nunn this summer, you know."

"She's so much shorter than I am, I have to shout at her to get her to hear me, Mother. It's just no use."

She laughed, her strand of pearls trembling against her bosom. "Ford, how awful. She's really not so bad."

"Don't start, Mother. I'll pick my own conversation partners, even at Grandmother's Christmas party." To forestall any heightening of the argument, he kissed his mother's powdered brow and sat on the floor beside Grandmother Strachn's chair.

"There's my Ford," Grandmother said in her dry voice, pressing her feathery hand against his cheek. "Merry Christmas. Do you know what you gave me this year?"

The question reflected a standing joke between them, begun in his first year of medical school when Ford's mother bought a diamond brooch for Ford's gift to Grandmother Strachn, and Ford failed to recognize the gem when she wore it for Christmas morning service. He laughed. "No, I don't. But I hope you liked it, whatever it is."

She joined his laughter. "You gave me a lovely silk shawl. Just what an old lady needs for drafty nights in her parlor."

"Is it a good color?"

"Oh, yes, a lovely cream color with robin's-egg-blue embroidery. Your mother has good taste." She leaned closer, whispering. "She invited the Stillwell girl for you, did you guess?"

"I didn't have to guess," Ford said, "Mother made it **very** clear that I was neglecting Lisa. How old is she, anyway?"

"She's in graduate school, poor thing." In her own

day, Grandmother Strachn had disdained any notion of college as training for a career; college had been viewed as a social obligation for well-brought-up women. Marrying Charles Strachn had proven to be career enough, one that she had not always relished, as she liked to let people know, now that Charles was dead. "How old are you now? I should know, of course, but at my age everything is beginning to blur."

"Twenty-seven. Not yet going on twenty-eight."

"High time you were married, then. That's what I'm supposed to tell you."

"Have you all been rehearsing this?"

"Of course we have." Grandmother sipped her trembling cup of eggnog. Her voice was firm. "Your mother is the tactician, but I understand it's your father who's really frantic about the whole thing. He can't help it, I suppose. You were already born by the time he was your age." Delighted at her own wit, she gave out her heartiest laugh, her thin bosom shaking beneath the staid white collar of her dress. A sudden, brilliant smile lit her features. She kissed his cheek. "Don't take it to heart. You'll find a wife in good time."

"Or something like that," he said. She smiled, pretending to understand him, and kissed his cheek again.

When he looked up from the kiss, he caught his father watching the whole exchange. The two men had hardly spoken all evening but acknowledged each other silently now. His father raised his glass to him, face clouded by a slight scowl that knit his heavy brows together.

The party ended, as always, with Aunt Rose leading Grandmother to the stairway, where the departing guests lined up to bid her good night. Grandmother's two maids brought coats and hats to the gathered family, and soon everyone bundled up. Ford helped Lisa into her white wool jacket with the sprig of mistletoe at the lapel, and as he did, Mother called out, "Oh, and Ford. Borrow Courtenay's car and drive Lisa home, will you? Courtenay can ride home with your Father and me."

Lisa looked at him hopefully, and Ford tried to smile. Courtenay gathered herself into her own coat. "Mother, for heaven's sake, I'll drive Lisa home, and Ford can ride along with me if he wants. But I'm not about to turn him loose in my car when he's falling over asleep."

Ford adjusted the white collar of Lisa's coat from behind. "I'd probably drive across the square, tired as I am."

"Whatever you do, don't be out all night," said Father, pulling on his driving gloves.

To appease his mother, Ford carefully held the door for Lisa and walked with her down the stone steps. "It was lovely of Mrs. McKinney to invite me," Lisa said. "My parents are abroad this year, and I had no idea what to do with myself on Christmas Eve."

"Mother's so crazy about the holidays, she can't stand the thought of anyone being alone." Ford casually looked over his shoulder to find Courtenay.

She appeared, heels click-clacking on the tabby sidewalk behind them. She deftly allowed momentum to insert her between Ford and Lisa, taking both their arms.

"Don't you just love holidays," she said brightly, turning from one to the other. "I used to think December was cold here, too, before I went to Smith."

She and Lisa chatted about Smith as they crossed the square. Ford let himself be pulled along in their wake, playing the familiar, acceptable part of the silent male in female company. Courtenay handed the car keys to Ford, assuring him that she wouldn't let him drift at the wheel, and he and Lisa arranged themselves in the front seat for the short drive to the house on East Gaston. Courtenay maintained a wall of chatter during the drive. At the large, well-lit house, Ford parked in the porte cochere and rounded the car, walking her to the steps and shaking her hand. From the car, Courtenay called, "Call us sometime, Lisa, it was truly wonderful to talk with you."

Into the house she vanished, casting one lingering glance in Ford's direction.

Courtenay took over the front seat, and Ford drove home. "Mother's very pissed that I didn't let you do this little duty yourself."

"Whereas I've never been so grateful to anybody in my life," Ford said.

At home, Father and Mother awaited them in the family room. Father knelt in front of the fireplace, stoking the new flames of the fire he had lit. Ford took the small brandy his mother offered, settling himself into the easy chair that faced the Christmas tree. Mother always insisted on two Christmas trees, the large one at the front of the house, for the neighbors, as she said, and the small one in the family room. As Ford sat down, his father said, "Well, I think Grandmother Strachn and Millie outdid themselves this year. Did you have any of the caviar, Ford?"

"Yes, wonderful," Ford yawned.

"I'm sure Mother had it flown in," his mother said. "She takes care of this whole occasion herself, you know. Rose likes to take credit for it, but Mother's the one who makes the arrangements. I liked those cheese straws too. Millie makes those so well."

"I'd like to hire Millie away from her," Father said.

Mother laughed, patting her hair with studied irony. "When Mother dies, God forbid, the biggest fight we'll have will be over who gets Millie."

"Rose will keep her," Father said. "Don't you think Millie will want to stay with the house?"

"Rose isn't getting that house," Mother said. "What would she do with it? A maiden lady with a house that size? It's ridiculous."

"Please, dears, let's not start this." Courtenay rounded the sofa, barefoot, to nest on the floor beside Ford. "It's Christmas, and Grandma isn't anywhere near dead yet."

"She certainly isn't," said Father. "She's as sharp as she ever was. Don't you agree, Ford?" Father unknotted his tie and unbuttoned the top button of his shirt. Gray chest hair curled over the fabric. Soft firelight rendered him younger, though every bit as stately as usual. "What's wrong, son? You're awfully quiet tonight."

"I'm tired from the flight, I guess. I got a good night's sleep, the hospital is pretty slow this time of year."

"I hear good things about you from Carter Thompson. He says your faculty is pretty impressed."

"That's good to know. I don't see much of Dr. Thompson. He spends most of his time at Emory."

"Well, that's easy to understand. He gets at least ten thousand dollars every time he walks into the operating room over there."

"I figured he was doing pretty well."

"I think it's disgusting how much money a person can make for dipping his fingers in blood," Courtenay said.

Mother leaned forward and said, firmly, "Stop that. You and your father are not going to start that fight on Christmas Eve. Your father works very hard for what he makes."

"Don't worry, Jeanine," Father said. "The little strumpet can't get me going tonight. I'm too much in the Christmas spirit."

"As long as you don't get paged," Courtenay said.

"You don't let up, do you? Well, Missy, there won't be any interruptions this Christmas. We've got a new junior man to take night calls."

"What's his name?" Ford asked.

"Elman. He's a Harvard man. Mike Neighbors brought him in. I think Mike was getting tired of my pushing Emory people down his throat."

"Mike's not from Harvard, is he?" Ford asked.

"No. He's just very impressed with anybody who is." Heat from the fire pressed Ford's face, close as a mask, and the varieties of alcohol he had ingested began to sing in his brain. Mother hummed softly, scattered bars of "O Little Town of Bethlehem." Father said, "It's good to have our children home for Christmas."

"How long are you home for, Courtenay?" Ford asked.

"New Year's Eve. Classes don't start for another week, but I'm moving to a new apartment."

"I don't particularly like the idea of your living alone," Mother said.

"Please, Mother, let's talk about this after Christmas, all right? Ford's home, and I don't want to argue."

"As long as you remember that we do have to talk about it." Mother's polite voice concealed a well-known blade.

Father eyed him from above the glass. "I thought Lisa Stillwell looked just lovely tonight."

"She has the sweetest little figure," Mother agreed.

"She certainly thinks the world of you, Ford," Father added, weighting each word. "She was quite excited when she found out you would be at the party."

Suddenly Ford remembered the careful telephone interrogations conducted by his mother, each pointedly reminding him of the vital need to arrive on time. A small knot of anger rose in his throat.

Courtenay said, "Lisa certainly does have big front teeth."

"Courtenay!"

"I didn't notice anything about her teeth," Father said.

"You didn't? They're as big as a beaver's."

"Courtenay, that certainly isn't a very kind way to talk about the poor girl. Do you remember how terrible you used to feel when the boys made fun of you for being tall?"

"Yes, mother, I certainly do. But now I'm six feet tall and drop-dead gorgeous, and Lisa Stillwell's teeth are still too big."

Father laughed in spite of himself, setting down the glass on the sideboard. Mother said, "Keith, don't encourage her."

"I'll be perfectly happy to be quiet, Mother," Courtenay said, drumming fingertips on Ford's knee, "if we can just stop talking about that dwarf."

Ford said, "She's a perfectly nice girl. I just don't want to marry her."

The fire hissed. The top of the brandy decanter chimed. Otherwise the whole house fell silent. Father sipped, swirled the glass, looked at it. "What brought that on?"

"I was trying to be funny."

Mother said, mildly, "I don't see the humor."

Father crossed his arms and faced Ford with his legs spread slightly. "Tell me, son, who do you want to marry?"

"Nobody," Ford said. "Right at this moment."

"Well," Mother said brightly, "I'd like a Christmas cookie. Would anyone else care for one?" She glided from the room before anyone could answer, calling, "Courtenay, come help me, please."

When Courtenay refused to move, Father said sternly, "Courtenay, go and help your Mother with the cookies."

"Mother doesn't need any help with a plate of cookies, Dad, and I'm not going to leave here just so you and Ford can go at it."

"Ford and I are not going at it." Father spat the phrase, which he considered to be inelegant. "Ford and I are simply talking and that's all. Now be a good houseguest, young lady, which you certainly are by now, and help your mother."

"Go ahead," Ford said, patting her head. "I'm fine."

In the uncertain world of gesture, one never knew what would anger Father most. Tonight, that touch on Courtenay's head was it. "That's right, Courtenay," he snapped. "You have your brother's permission to leave."

She stalked out silently. Father faced the curling flames, took a deep breath and waited till his flush had faded. "Now, Ford, your mother and I had the best intentions in the world when we invited Lisa to the party. I don't want to hear any more unkindness about that. But let me say this. If she won't do, look for somebody who will. You're too old to be single. When I was your age, I had two children, I had settled down, I was living my life. Even in the middle of a residency, I was living my life. That's all I want for you. That's all your mother and I are trying to achieve."

"Maybe what I need to do is stop coming home." Ford set down the snifter beside the chair.

"Don't make childish threats."

When he stood, he towered over his father, and the

realization came to him that Father had more to fear, right now, than he did. He spoke as calmly as he could. "This is no threat, Dad, and I'm not a child. I don't need this. No, listen for a minute." Ford took a deep breath. "Now, you and mother need to face facts. I might not ever get married. I might marry somebody you don't like. One way or the other, it's going to be me who picks and me who decides." He lifted his overcoat from the couch. "I'm going to bed. I'll see you in the morning. Tell Mother I said good night."

Retrieving his overnight bag from Courtenay's car, he lingered in the small garden behind the house, standing beneath the broad mimosa. At this hour of Christmas Eve, the city lay in silence, occasionally interrupted by a whisper of traffic. He walked to the wooden fence that separated the yard from the service lane. Wishing for his own bed, his own house, he studied the few stars bright enough to pierce the haze of streetlight. Wind had begun to shift, and he smelled the first dingy scent of the paper plant blowing into the city.

He could find no place for himself here and now, in the backyard of this house in which he had spent most of his childhood, or in the lives of his parents.

He passed a nearly sleepless night in the room of his boyhood, long since transformed by his mother into another showplace for antiques. His speech to his father replayed itself in his head through most of the night. Toward morning he dreamed he had brought McKenzie home with him for Christmas, a long, formless dream that he failed to remember on waking. But the renewed image of the young man left him aching and full of dread.

Christmas Day passed peacefully, despite the tension that remained from the night before. Before breakfast, Mother approached him in the sun room and told him that both she and his father had agreed to let the subject drop for this trip, for the sake of the holidays. "But Ford," she said, "it's really time we had a long talk about this whole subject. This is twice you've told your father you don't want to get married. And while you may be an adult now and this may be your decision, it's certainly something that involves your family. We all know how busy you are and how difficult it is for you to travel, so your father and I would like to come to Atlanta to talk to you about this."

"I think that's a better idea than trying to deal with it on Christmas." Ford felt suddenly exhausted.

"Good. Now you think about when you want us to come and let us know. But I'm perfectly serious about this."

"I'm taking you seriously, Mother."

"I thought this was what you and that therapist were supposed to be working on," with a slight lift of her upper lip.

Ford contained a flash of anger. "I thought we were going to save the whole subject for another time. All right?"

The social guise, which he had seen her assume in many other situations, kicked in automatically. "You're right. Now, I've got to get Christmas breakfast. You know, I actually do feel like cooking this morning."

Father awaited them in the kitchen, leafing through the thin Christmas morning edition of the *News-Press*. Already showered and shaved, he had dressed in the battered green cardigan with red buttons that Mother called his Yuletide sweater. He folded the paper and lay his reading glasses atop it. Mother said, "Ford agrees we have a wonderful plan for settling this whole issue, Keith. I think everything's going to work out just fine."

"That's good to hear." Father wore the placid expression reserved for cocktail parties and difficult legal negotiations. "I'm glad no one wants to spoil Christmas with the kind of talk we had last night."

Ford put out his hand and Father shook it firmly. "No one wants to spoil anything. I'm just happy to be home for the holidays."

"You can't expect this kind of easy schedule every year. I remember a couple of Christmases I had to miss, when you and your sister were young."

Christmas breakfast proceeded, managed with aplomb by Mother in spite of the fact that she rarely used the kitchen. Courtenay stumbled into the kitchen for coffee and found Ford and her father sharing stories about Grady. Ford told the story of the bus accident and the ensuing headaches. "The place is stuffed to the gills now," Ford said. "The administrators talk about renovating, but nobody believes they'll ever get it done."

"I was there the first day we rolled a patient into the

new building, out of the old White Hospital. I was a student, I believe. I'll never forget it."

Following breakfast, the family proceeded with the opening of gifts. Ford helped set up new woodworking tools in Father's shop, an immaculate room in the basement. At the center of the room stood Father's current project, a large chest with an elaborately carved lid, partially completed. Cedar smell permeated the room. Father indicated the chest. "For your sister. Your mother wants to call it a hope chest, but I told her I don't think modern girls have hope chests anymore."

"It's lovely. You're spending a lot of time on it."

Father chuckled. "Time I don't have, you mean. You're beginning to see what it's like, aren't you? Trying to take care of sick people and have a life too."

Ford ran his palms lightly over the surface, from the smoothed, finished middle to the rough edges. Dad continued, "It all gets easier after a while. Don't worry. Just listen to your mother and me. We got through it."

Upstairs, Mother and Courtenay were putting together a modest Christmas dinner intended to feed the immediate family plus Father's uncle Paul, one of the elders of the McKinney clan. Later in the day, the whole clan would assemble on the Isle of Hope in the home of the ranking elder himself, Father's uncle Reuben. The visit to Uncle Reuben had been customary since as far back as Ford could remember.

Once the holiday settled into its usual shape, a spirit of peace did finally overtake each of them. The children remembered what it had been like to depend on these adults, to be protected by them, to be within their power. They remembered how it had felt to be small in this house, to wake up on other Christmas mornings, when the promise of gifts had meant sleeplessness and anticipation. The parents remembered their own benevolence, which had seemed so automatic when the children needed everything, which was sometimes absent now that the children had grown.

Ford drew his usual assignment, fetching Uncle Paul. The drive to the large house on East Oglethorpe gave him a moment of solitude in which to breathe. Uncle Paul waited in the front parlor, clutching his ivory-handled cane and his favorite lap rug. Since he rode everywhere in a wheelchair, the cane served a purely ornamental function, but he refused to part with it.

As Ford started the car, easing the vehicle onto East Oglethorpe, Uncle Paul asked, "Is this a new car?"

"No, it's not." Ford shook his head no. Uncle Paul looked at him skeptically. He turned to face out the front window, hunched forward. According to Father, Uncle Paul once stood nearly six feet tall himself—short, for a McKinney—but due to curvature of the spine and general decay he could barely see above the dashboard now.

Uncle Paul was allowed the head of the table, where he confined himself to peering between water glasses and drinking a good deal of wine. When he decided to speak, he reared back in his chair, bringing his head above the level of the glassware, and sighed deeply. Conversations with Uncle Paul were generally brief, as today, when the maid poured his second glass of wine and Uncle Paul lifted it from the table, fixing Father with a stare. "You got a new car."

"No." Father found it unseemly to raise his voice in order to be heard, so he sat next to Uncle Paul and spoke close to Uncle Paul's ear. "You know I would never sell that car. Too many good miles on it."

Uncle Paul had sold Father the vintage Mercedes a decade ago, but lately had become convinced that Father had traded it in on a new model. No one knew why, exactly. Uncle Paul announced, "It's not the same color." Setting the wineglass on the table, he lowered himself below the rims of the glasses once again, indicating the conversation had ended.

Father asked Ford, "Did you remember we called you Ford Jr. when your grandfather was still alive?"

"That's right," Uncle Paul said, surprising everyone, since Father had been speaking in a normal conversational tone. "Our mama was a Ford, so my papa named his oldest son Keith Ford, after the both of them, and that's where your name came from."

"I didn't know that," Courtenay winked at her brother.

Explained Father, "Your great-grandmother didn't come from the right kind of family, quite, so the Mc-Kinneys never really accepted her. That was what my father used to say. But he adored her. Her father came south during Reconstruction, and that was the kiss of death here. Savannah in those days was a closed circle."

"Do you think it's better now?" Ford asked.

"Depends on what you mean by better, I guess," Father said.

The talk about family history echoed through Ford, underscored by the parlor's infamous arrangements of family pictures, some dating back as far as the birth of the photograph. Courtenay referred to the room as Mom and Dad's museum, and today Ford wandered from display to display, studying the evidence of his forebears, mulling the poses of the couples, the taut arms of the husbands embracing the stiff waists of the wives. Faces presented the bland, impersonal expression with which well-bred people greet portrait photography. Every picture possessed its own history. Ford remembered only scattered names among the older photographs but recognized dozens of his modern relatives. Sipping brandy, he brooded over each expression. Mother joined him, circling his waist with her arm. "Are you having a good Christmas? Are you glad you came home?"

He returned the embrace, "It's nice to do nothing but eat and drink for a change."

Lifting one of the heavy silver frames, she tested the glass for dust and said, "Esther hates all this. Nothing but dustcatchers, she says. But this is my favorite part of the house. I do just what you're doing, I wander around and look at all the faces. Do you have any of the family pictures at your house? I can't remember."

"No," Ford said, "just you and Dad and Courtenay. And Grandma."

"Well, we ought to give you some of ours, I guess. It's time I started dividing these up between you and Courtenay."

"It's a little too soon for that. Whenever I need to re-visit history, I know where to come."

"For once, I wish we could stay here for Christmas night. I wish we could all be together, the way we are right now."

"Is this my mother, trying to get out of visiting Uncle Reuben?"

She laughed softly. "Doesn't sound like me, does it? To tell you the truth, though, I hated going out there the first few years, when you children were young. I wanted my children and my husband and that was all the Christmas I needed. But when I got older things changed. I got used to it all, I guess. And now I can't do without it. Without this," indicating the pictures, the room filled with polished antiques. "Not everybody comes from a family with so much of its history preserved. I think we have a duty to that."

"A duty to do what?"

"To continue." She sipped her dark sherry and rested her head briefly against his shoulder.

"I thought we weren't going to talk about all that right now."

"I'm talking in general. Christmas makes me senti-mental these days, with you children grown. So when you're here, I start to remember how things were when you were little, how happy I was to be a mother." She straightened, looked him in the eye. "There's so much happiness in raising a family, Ford. In continuing the family that you're part of. That's all I'm trying to tell you."

"Thank you, Mother," he said, "I really am listening." But walked away from her, nevertheless.

At Uncle Reuben's party, within the gathering of the McKinney clan, he deliberately behaved like a stranger. Paying due courtesy to Uncle Reuben, he withdrew afterward to the side porch, choosing to study twilight over the intercoastal waterway. Courtenay searched him out. Ford said, "I really don't need this much family this year. Do you?"

"I don't want to think about it," Courtenay said. "I still have a week left. And I have a feeling Mother and I are headed for a fight before I go back to school. The truth is, I'm going to live with my carpenter." Courtenay watched his face for reaction. "We've been talking about it for a long time. If Mom and Dad ever figure that out, I don't know what they'll do."

"What can they do?"

"Behave the way they always do. Get very cold and pretend Mike isn't alive whenever we're together. Talk about Savannah boys I ought to be dating. Make sure to tell me every time one of my friends gets married to the right kind of boy. It will be just like what happened when I told Mother I wouldn't make my debut. World War Three."

"Except you don't live here anymore," Ford said.

"You can bet Dad will cut off my money."

"Don't worry about that. I have money. So do you,

you just can't get to it yet. I'll loan you whatever you need till you're twenty-five and you can pay me back. And there's not a thing Mom and Dad can do about that."

She leaned her head against his shoulder. "Thanks for the offer. I hope I don't have to take you up on it, but believe me, I will if I need to." Moving to face him, she took his face in her hands. "What about you? What are you going to do?"

He watched the last light on the water and the deepening shadows of the yard. "I'm going to visit my singer as soon as I get back to the hospital. And then I'm going to see what happens."

The two of them returned to the family gathering together, arm in arm, and through the rest of the evening stood guard over each other. Through Uncle Reuben's continual goading of Uncle Paul, through the stories about boat purchases and extravagant vacation plans traded among the uncles, through the cool comparison of clothing among all parties and of jewelry among the aunts, Ford and Courtenay watched, back to back, then moved along parallel lines into the formal parlor, where Uncle Reuben and Uncle Paul argued about the exact date of Uncle Ellis McKinney's wedding. "I said during the war!" Uncle Reuben shouted, inches from Uncle Paul's ear. "During the war! He already had children after the war!"

By the end of the evening, as happened every year, Uncle Paul and Uncle Reuben refused to speak to each other. This had become the signal for Father to collect his own branch of the clan and return to Savannah, since Uncle Paul preferred to retire from the battlefield once a satisfactory round of hostilities had been completed. Father's theory held that Uncle Paul and Uncle Reuben had lived as long as they had mostly out of spite and anger toward each other. Father asked Uncle Paul if he was ready to leave, and Uncle Paul said, "Leave? By god-damn right I'm ready to leave! Who can sit here and talk to a fool like Reuben all night?"

"Fool hell!" Reuben said. "You're the fool! Can't tell 1942 from 1948 anymore. You're getting too old, Paul, you ought to go on and die."

Uncle Paul waved his hand in dismissal at Uncle Reuben. Holding his mother's coat as she slipped grace-fully into it, Ford smelled the sweet pungency of her good cologne. She said, evenly, "Well, that's over, anyway," and smiled at her son. "Now we can go home."

At his parents' house, Ford counted the minutes till he could excuse himself and retire. Having prepared him-self to discourage any attempt at conversation, he was re-lieved when none took place. He rose, finally. "Tomorrow morning I'm taking a taxi, so you folks can sleep it off." He rubbed the back of his head idly. "In fact, if I'm going to be awake when I get to the hospital tomorrow, I'd bet-ter go to bed now."

Saying good night to all, kissing Mother, shaking Father's hand, he thanked them for a fine Christmas and headed to the bedroom in which he slept as a guest of the house. Knowing now, and vowing to remember, that home lay in front of him, in the crass big city nestled at the foot of the Georgia mountains.

———— ⚬⚬⚬ ————

But his mother rose to see him off that morning, greeting him in the predawn kitchen with a kiss on the cheek. Fresh from sleep, she was suffused with gentleness, and he remembered the mother of his childhood. In the long morning robe with the net cap over her hair, she seemed younger, softer, than on the previous evening in her formidable makeup and fashionable evening clothes. She set the coffee in front of him and stroked his hair to the proper line across his brow. Naked of its disguises, her face seemed innocent and whole.

"I couldn't let you get up and leave us without anybody around." Even her voice lacked its subtle edge of judgment. "No matter how old you get, you're still my son."

For the first time since he had arrived, he felt at ease with her. She asked what time was the flight and he told her. "I need to call the taxi and make sure it's coming," he said.

"I'll call," she said. "Sit and drink your coffee till it gets here."

The car arrived before the coffee cooled, and Ford lifted his overnight bag as Mother stood close by. He embraced her thin shoulders and wondered at her slightness. Sudden sadness gripped them both. "Please take care of yourself," she said. "We worry about you."

"I'm all right," he said in mild surprise, hearing the taxi horn sound on the dark street.

He slipped into the taxi, turning once to wave. Framed by the substantial porch, wrapping the quilted robe against her sides, she had become almost a girl again. Her face filled with sorrow as the taxi pulled away. He felt the sorrow echo in himself, along with fear. Could he really mean to do what he planned?

The glorious crimson clouds blazed for the whole of the short jet flight, and Ford sat suspended in the bleeding light. He tried to remember Dan's face and recalled only a vague blur. Any feeling concealed itself.

The house on Clifton Heights awaited him with calming silence, the soft rush of air through the vents and return, the flush of morning light along the kitchen walls. He wandered through the emptiness, touching the familiars that grounded him: the dumbbells in the den, the black bag that had belonged to Ford McKinney Sr.

Hours remained before he needed to report to the hospital. He stood in the bedroom, near the place where he had found Hammond. A cold ache filled him, and another memory followed that one: of himself, wandering through the dark house, the evening of the Christmas concert, the Friday of the aborted dinner. The sound of the telephone ringing in his ear but no one answering.

Memory of Dan's face returned to him, vivid in detail, and Ford remembered the eerie voice, singing not the lullaby of this year's concert but the well-known carol of the year before, *To save us all from Satan's power, when we were gone astray.*

Gathering his gym bag, Ford headed to the hospital.

At the top of the C-wing of the huge edifice, the medical school had installed a gymnasium for the use of residents, who were often trapped in the building for long shifts and unable to reach their usual exercise clubs. Ford headed there, parked in the sparsely populated deck, and strode through the quiet corridors. Hardly anyone had returned from the holidays. He found the gym empty but for one third-year student, a woman named Dorothy Ballard whom he had met here before. "I stayed in town this Christmas," she said. "I learned a long time ago that going home is useless. My lover made Christmas dinner, and we had the best holiday I can remember in years."

"I wish I'd had the good sense to stay here," Ford said, pretending for the moment that this were actually an option.

"Do yourself a favor and get listed for Christmas duty next year."

"I think I'll do that." He headed for the bench press.

My lover made Christmas dinner. He remembered what Dorothy had said while he showered in the on-call suite one floor below, stashing his gym bag in the locker and dressing in scrubs. Taking a deep breath, running a hand through his hair to get the look of it just right, he spoke to the face in the mirror. "Whatever happens, I'm fine," he said. "Whatever happens."

The wait for the elevator seemed endless, but when he entered the car a wave of dread engulfed him. At the outer door to the office suite in which he would either find or not find Dan, he took a deep breath. Let him be here, he thought, let this be over. The other voice attempted to intercede as well, to say, no, not yet, you haven't planned what you're going to say, wait a while, but Ford placed his hand flat on the door and pushed.

The secretarial office lay empty, desk clean of paper, and one of the inner offices, darkened, bore witness to the quiet of the day. But the second of the inner doors opened onto a well-lit room, and Ford could see window blinds and the fragments of a light court beyond. On a table, at right angles to a desk, sat a personal computer, screen facing the desk's occupant. Ford watched the doorway, the corner of the desk, his fear rising. He should announce himself, but he could find no voice.

Dan called from the office, "Hello, I'm in here."

The fullness of sound touched Ford from many angles at once. He found he had been holding the door open all this time and released it to close behind him. He cleared his throat and said, "It's Ford McKinney. I'm here to see you, if you have a minute."

Silence. Followed by the sound of a chair releasing weight.

Dan's shadow crossed the doorway, paused there. Dan himself emerged a moment later.

He stood in the doorway. Taller than Ford remembered, though not as tall as Ford. Watching Ford with an expression neither cold nor warm, a simple blank. "This is a surprise. I didn't expect to hear from you, after your note."

Ford fought off breathlessness and leveled his gaze to

meet Dan's. "I'm sure you didn't. Can I talk to you for a minute? Are you busy?"

A telephone buzzed. Dan turned to face it, then turned to Ford and watched him as the buzzing continued. "Yes, I can talk to you." He turned again into his office. "Please come in."

The phone continued to ring, then stopped. Dan folded his hands and looked at Ford. "I got your note. Is there something you need to add to it?"

Ford flushed, feeling his heart beat harder. "I'm sorry. It was a stupid thing to write."

Dan shrugged. "I don't know about that. If you were going to cancel, a letter was as good a way as any. A lot better than doing it in person."

The blunt, unforgiving words collided with the image of innocence, leaving Ford speechless. The rising of steam through convector pipes covered the silence. Finally Ford said, softly, "No, that's not what I meant," drawing a long breath, forcing himself to look Dan in the eye, to show some of what he felt. "What I mean is, I got scared. I wanted to take you to dinner, but I got scared. I was sorry later. But it was too late to do anything about it."

"You could have called me. I would have been glad to let you change your mind."

"I did. But your secretary said you had already gone home for Christmas. I called you the Friday we were supposed to go to dinner." A flush still heated his face, and he was beginning to feel like a fool. "I called you at home, too. The phone rang for a long time. I guess you don't have an answering machine."

"No," Dan said, "I don't," and for the first time his expression softened. He studied the desktop. With sudden understanding, Ford said, "You were there, weren't you."

Dan's face shimmered from its cool control to another expression, and Ford saw in that other face the man whom he wanted to reach.

"I wish you had answered."

Dan shrugged. "I wish you hadn't written the letter."

Beneath the cool voice lurked another, and Ford answered. "I'm sorry I did. I already said that."

"Well, you might have to say it again."

Outside, in the light court, dying breezes tossed potato chip bags idly on the roof below. Ford said, "I'll say it as often as I have to."

"Why? What do you want?"

He would never have guessed from the brittleness of Dan's tone that this same voice could soothe. Ford concentrated on the face he had glimpsed, the softness he had reached for a moment. "I want to convince you I'm not a jerk so maybe you'll agree to go to dinner with me tomorrow."

Dan absorbed this. "What will that prove? That you're really okay, that you're not a jerk, like you said? And that's it?"

"What do you mean, that's it?"

"We go out to dinner, and that proves you're an okay

guy. But what about me? Am I okay?" His voice had begun to tremble, but he quickly brought it under control. "I already know you're not a jerk, I don't care about that. One stupid note doesn't make you a jerk. But I don't want to go out with you because you feel sorry for me, or because you feel sorry for something you've done."

Ford stepped closer, sat on the desktop, nearer than before, and when Dan turned each could feel the heat of the other. They watched each other for a while. Ford wet his lips. "So you'll let me take you to dinner," he said quietly. "Tomorrow."

When Ford went on duty in the Pediatric Emergency Clinic, he focused his concentration. The work absorbed him completely through the day. Near evening, realizing the time, he hurried upstairs for a shower and change of clothes. Dorothy Ballard joined his downward elevator ride, entering on the thirteenth floor and greeted Ford with the carefully casual tone used by medical students when addressing their hierarchical elders.

"You don't look like you're just getting off thirty hours," she said, "you must have plans for tonight."

"I do," Ford said. "I'm going to dinner with a friend. I've been looking forward to it all day. You headed home?"

"Yes," Dorothy flexed her shoulders, "I'm going to spend the evening with my lover for a change."

The elevator stopped, bounced a little, and the doors

opened. The two looked around the cab as if it had suddenly become precarious, then laughed.

He found Mr. Franken still in his office, the partly open door revealing several other men in dark suits as well. Dan looked up from a large, bound report and set down his yellow highlighter after carefully capping it. He tried to move casually and to mask his delight, but Ford could see the changes in his face. Ford asked, as a greeting, "Did your secretary tell you I stopped by this morning?"

"She spelled your name McKenzie but I figured out who you were. She said you just came to say hello, but I was a little afraid something had come up."

"McKenzie," Ford said, laughing softly. "That's pretty good."

"Ms. Vaughn's eyes aren't that good," Dan said.

"She sure scared me to death this morning." Gesturing toward Franken's office, Ford asked, "Can you go?"

In the dim, quiet parking garage, Ford felt Dan's physical presence acutely. Dan seemed calmly aware of this, but his face betrayed little. "Nice car. I like the smell."

"The smell?"

"Leather seats."

"It's a good car. My dad drives one."

"Is your dad in Atlanta?"

"No. My folks are from Savannah. So am I, I guess. Though after this Christmas I don't know. You?"

"North Carolina. From the backwater, way down east, where they grow tobacco."

"You must have lived in Atlanta for a while. You've been around Grady since I've been there."

"Sometimes it feels like I've been at Grady forever," Dan said, with a slight scowl. "But it's just five years. That's about how long I've lived in Atlanta. I like it here, I guess."

Ford had maneuvered to the down ramp and drove through the open gate. "So do I. Better than Savannah, I think. But that's not supposed to happen."

"Savannah boys grow up to be Savannah men, don't they? Something to do with evolution of a higher order of being."

"Do you know much about Savannah?" Ford asked.

"I was there for a while, once. A couple of months. I was in New Orleans longer. It's the same way there."

"I was in New Orleans once, when I was a kid. Before I was old enough to remember much about it. We went on a steamboat ride. And we ate seafood I didn't like. And I didn't like the French Quarter because there weren't any rides. That should give you some idea how old I was."

He navigated toward the expressway. Dan nested in his winter coat, surrounded by the dim of winter evening, by Ford's low-slung coupe and by the highway monuments of downtown Atlanta. Enormous bridges, loops and rivers of prestressed concrete, dressed steel beams, and arcs and torrents of masonry dropped shadows across the windshield. Dan's awareness moved from shadow to shadow; he leaned forward to look up at the sky, his face catching the low light. Ford found himself watching, at odd moments.

"You drive well. Do you like this car a lot?"

"What do you mean, a lot?"

"Do you drive it a lot, do you take it out in the country? Does it mean as much to you as a horse to a cowboy?"

"No," Ford chuckled. "I like to drive it but I hardly ever get to. Why are you making fun of my car? Do you think it's ostentatious?"

"It's certainly conspicuously consumptive." Dan crossed his arms and inspected the interior once again. "But I don't think it's offensive. Maybe it's just the smell of the leather, maybe that's what reminds me of cowboys."

"I don't think I ever reminded anybody of cowboys before," Ford said.

"I bet you have, it's just that nobody ever told you about it."

Ford steered through traffic, and Dan smiled faintly. Ford said, "It's a flattering image, anyway. Are you at all curious as to where we're going?"

Easy silence followed as the automobile cruised past buildings too new to have either name or reputation. Into a side street the car turned, and Ford parked.

The restaurant, a converted bungalow, nested behind twin cedars, each tall and full based. A brick path led them to the dwarfed house. In summer the patio in front, shaded by an old pecan tree, housed outdoor tables, but these were cleared since the winter cold rendered them useless. Leaves beat across the red tile, tumbled by sharp wind. Ford found himself remembering his last date here with Haviland Barrows, which had taken place at a table in a bay window in what had once served as the parlor of the bungalow. His restlessness that night had been evident to Haviland, and when she asked him about it, the whole long conversation leading to their breakup began. Tonight, standing in the small foyer waiting for the owner, a polite Frenchman, to seat them, Ford wondered if this gesture, this dinner, were truly the end of that cycle.

As they were about to be seated, Ford stood, blankly eyeing the neat arrangement of china and silver, then turned to the owner. "Could we have the window table in the parlor? I'd prefer that one, now that I think about it."

The owner assured him the table was available and led them through low-ceilinged rooms to the front of the house. Dan walked ahead of Ford to the table, Ford watching him. The man moved with a precision that approached grace; but also with undeniable softness, a trace of effeminacy.

Ford savored newness. He sipped a drink and studied the menu while Dan cradled a tall wine glass in one hand. They ordered from a small, neat, mustachioed man. Dan accepted Ford's recommendations on most items, folding the menu. He considered the wine. "I can't drink more than this. Unfortunately. If I'm going to rehearse tonight. I'm having trouble remembering the words to my songs. I do three songs in this show."

"You sing other places too? Other theaters?"

"Sometimes. I also act sometimes, but I'm not very good at it. It's something to do besides push paper at Grady.

I grew up singing in the choir. At least I joined the choir once my family started going to church. One of the times when my parents were trying to save themselves."

The tinge of sarcasm in the tone and the sudden hardness of Dan's expression surprised Ford. He asked what Dan meant by saving themselves, and Dan answered, coolly and with that same distance, that his mother and father had spent eighteen years fighting, with time out to regroup every couple of years. During time-out they attended church passionately, prayed on their knees in their bedroom every night before going to bed, taught Sunday school classes and Baptist Training Union sections, and generally pursued a path toward whatever salvation they could thus earn. Dan told the story easily, not as information that was difficult to give, but articulated quickly, in an offhand way. As if he had been merely an observer all those years.

Throughout, Ford was struck by the ease with which Dan spoke, no matter what the subject, and by the liveliness of his mind. Surrounded by the flux of Dan's charm, Ford found himself free to talk as well, and he told, without any forethought, the story of Christmas and the coming Atlanta summit during which he and his parents would hash out the subject of his marriage. He talked about his mother's coolness at the altar of family photographs and the sudden return of her kinder self at the moment of his departure. "The whole visit was like an essay on why I should marry well," Ford said, "and there I was, very quietly trying to tell them that I'm not the marrying kind."

The words dropped into space before he heard them in his head. But he knew as soon as he spoke that he must have had a plan. He watched Dan carefully for response.

Dan met his eye and said, "My mother and I got through that stage. I finally told her I was gay a few years back, and she stopped asking about my girlfriends."

"I hate that word," Ford said.

Dan shrugged. "There isn't another one."

Ford conceded the point, though with an inner resistance that puzzled him. "How did your mother react?"

Dan's face filled with gentleness. "She had been worried about me, because she knew I was keeping a secret from her. So I finally got up the guts to tell her I was gay, and she shrugged. She still doesn't like to talk about it. She hates the word 'gay' too, but I make her say it every now and then, to get her used to the idea."

"What about your father?"

"He's dead," Dan said.

Something in Dan's tone warned Ford to ask no questions. Ford waited till the chill passed from Dan's features, a visible change. "I don't think my parents will react very well," Ford said. "My sister was fine. But Courtenay's just like that. We've always had to take care of each other."

"My sister was fine about it too, when I told her," Dan said, "but she always hates it when I have a boyfriend."

Ford laughed. Framing his next question with careful casualness. "Even the current ones?"

Dan met his eye again. "There aren't any right now."

Silence. After which Ford asked, "Are you sure about that?"

Dan flushed slightly, abandoning the dinner, turning to the window. Deep emotion stirred in his face, and he spoke as if to the cedars beyond the glass. "I hope you mean that. Because I really like you. And I don't want this to be the last time I see you."

"I feel the same way," Ford said, suddenly breathless.

Having accomplished this much, they sat in silence, each flushed. They were jointly aware of the need to shelter this intimacy from the other couples in the restaurant. With his composure once again secure, Dan turned from the window to sip wine. "I'm going to be a wreck at rehearsal, I can tell."

"You've only had one glass."

Dan looked at him evenly. But the face had changed again, illuminated from within by what must be joy. All hardness had fled from him, and the mask was no longer a mask. Ford said, "I could pick you up after rehearsal."

"You'll be asleep."

"I could wake up. For that." Swallowing.

The moment receded, Dan touching his fork again, and Ford realized clearly that Dan controlled the distance between them, that he had closed a gate which had stood open a moment before. "Not yet." Dan seemed momentarily afraid. "I'd be a fool to say yes. Until we've had more chance to talk."

"I can wait," Ford said, heart sinking at little. "I don't mind. But I promise I won't hurt you."

"It isn't you." The mask returned, secure and implacable. "It's me."

"What about you?"

"Let's leave it at that for right now." Voice uncertain. Brows knit together.

"I don't want to leave it at that. I want you to tell me what's wrong."

Dan froze with the fork nearly to his lips. A slight shudder passed through him, and he set the fork at rest at the side of his plate.

As suddenly as the space of that small gesture the gentle man vanished and a mocker inhabited his face. "All right. I may as well say it. This has probably gone on long enough, anyway." Dan was no longer able to look Ford in the eye, and trembled. "I have hemophilia. You know what that is."

"Of course I do." Ford was numbed. "I've treated hemophiliacs before. Type A?" Trying to keep his voice even and calm, trying to betray none of the fear that gripped him in the pit of the stomach.

Dan's smile was heartless. "Yes. Less than one percent activity." Taking a long breath. "You know why I'm telling you that, don't you? You know what that means?"

"No," Ford said, looking out the window, hardly able to see the cedars in the dark. "No, I don't."

"All right. I'll spell it out for you. I'm HIV positive. I have been for years." Voice trembling. "It's really funny. I guess 'funny' is the right word. I've had two lovers in my life. Two. But I've had blood from thousands of men. In my veins." Silence. Senseless noise from wherever they were, whatever place this was. Dan's voice, softer. "I'm sorry, Ford."

The next moments passed in a jumble, and Ford was never sure exactly how they got out of the restaurant and into his car. He drove through the clean, well-kept Buckhead neighborhoods with Dan rigid beside him. Ford had never seen anyone under such terrible self-control, as if at the least move Dan would shatter into shards. Hardly a word passed between them.

Ford parked near the theater and turned, but Dan had already swung open the door. "I'll call you," Ford said, and Dan paused to let him know he had been heard. Dan faced him for an instant. Something desolate in his expression. He started to speak and then shook his head. In a moment he had vanished altogether.

Ford started the car and pulled away. For a long time he drove without thinking much about where he went; streets and houses streamed past in a blur. The world beyond the window paled, compared to the world he was still seeing inside his head: he might as well have been in the restaurant still, with Dan in front of him, his face washing white as ice, his knuckles brittle as the stem of the wineglass.

When he stopped driving and shook himself back to awareness, he had parked in front of the entrance to Stone Mountain. The park had already closed, but in the moonlight the shadow of the mountain loomed overhead, a dome of rock like a turtle's back, or like a gigantic river-smoothed pebble. He opened the windows and sat in the darkness by the gate. After a long time, thinking nothing articulate, he drove home again.

Near sundown the next day, he headed down North Highland Avenue, looking for the street sign labeled Blue Ridge, his stomach in knots. Parking the car in front of the apartment building, he stared straight ahead, unable to release the steering wheel until he remembered the moment at the table in the restaurant, the hoarse voice, *I'm sorry, Ford.*

He locked the car and found the number on a door at the back of the building. Taking a deep breath, he knocked.

Silence beyond the doorway made him expect Dan had already headed for his rehearsal, or that he refused to answer the door just as he refused to answer the telephone. But Ford knocked again, firmly, and whispered, "Come on. You're here. I know you're here."

Footfalls approached, the door lock rattled. Dan faced him. Ford said, "I've tried to call you all day. Can I come in?"

A cat sidled along the wall behind Dan and tried to lunge past his feet. He scooped the cat from the floor, draping it over his shoulder, saying, "I have to get to rehearsal soon."

In the neat apartment Ford waited for Dan to close the door. He turned from trim bookshelves to tall windows, walls adorned with oil paintings, simple furniture, a stereo and television of basic proportion, other rooms opening off either end. Steam heat rattling pipes. "Sit anywhere." Dan deposited the cat on a chair, where it stretched and watched him adjust the stereo. "I've been trying to get these songs right," Dan said. "One of them is giving me the devil of a time." Then he sat with his arms folded across his chest and looked at Ford.

The moment grew long. Now Ford must explain why he had come. He spoke simply, as if he dropped by Dan's apartment every afternoon about this time. "I called your office today. They sound a little crazy without you." Leaning back, as the cat perched beside him on the adjacent cushion, "I don't usually just drop in on people. But tomorrow I go on duty for a couple of days and I was afraid if I waited to talk to you it would be too late."

Dan nodded, expression blank.

"I've been thinking a lot about last night. Obviously."

"You were very kind."

Something about the tone or the words made Ford angry, and he said, "I wasn't being kind." He ran a hand through his hair. "I'm a doctor. I know I can't die from being near you. I can't catch this virus from lying in bed next to you, or touching you, and I probably won't even catch it if I do more than just touch you." A phone began to ring but they both sat still. The phone soon stopped. "I don't know what's happening here. I really don't. But I don't want to give up yet."

Dan had frozen in the chair, gazing blankly at a pattern in the hardwood floor. The cat lay peacefully in his folded hands. "I'd be so much better off if I could be mean enough to make you go away," he said. "And you would too. But I don't know if I can do that."

"I don't think I'd be better off. And I don't think you would either."

"When will you know if you want to give up?"

In answer, Ford knelt in front of Dan, laying his arms across Dan's lap and leaning his head into the center of Dan's chest. The contact shocked them both. "I could ask you the same thing. When will you know?"

———— ∞∞∞ ————

Ford rushed into his house on the afternoon of New Year's Eve. He had officially gotten off duty at 6:00 A.M. but had been held over at the hospital for clinic, a favor to Dr. Milliken, who found himself shorthanded. He had talked to Dan twice since then, once in person in a hallway outside the public cafeteria and once more on the telephone. Running from one clinic to the auditorium, trying to reach a lecture on head injuries in children under five, he happened on Dan in the corridor near the entrance to the Pediatric Appointment Clinic. They talked in the middle of the hall, lingering in the midst of moving bodies; then Dan stirred to depart. At that moment Ed Harknight appeared down the hall, raising a hand in greeting to Ford. Dan rearranged the papers he was carrying and looked on disinterestedly as Ed said, "Ford, fellow, it's nice to see I'm not the only one who's late to the lecture." Grinning, he looked from Ford to Dan.

His expression flickered uncertainly, as if he sensed their intimacy. He turned to Ford almost for explanation, and at the same time Dan said, "Well I'd better get back to pushing papers, Dr. McKinney."

"I'll talk to you later, Mr. Crell," Ford said, and Harknight nodded pleasantly to Dan, who nodded pleasantly in return.

As Dan vanished into the corridor's maze of moving bodies, Harknight turned to Ford with obvious curiosity. Ford flushed slightly. Knowing that Harknight would have thought nothing of Ford's talking to a pretty dietitian or to one of the female nurses. Ford prepared simply to ignore the moment and to proceed to the lecture, but Harknight said, "You better watch out for him, big guy. I hear he's gay."

"Oh, yeah?" Ford asked, calmly. "From who?"

"From what I hear, he's pretty public about it. He's an administrator, right? He works in the Nursing Office?"

"I don't think it's Nursing," Ford said.

Harknight shrugged. "Wherever. Come on, let's see what old Federson has to say about kiddies with a bump on the noggin."

He slapped Ford on the back with presumed familiarity. Ford let himself be led to the auditorium, staring resentfully at the back of Harknight's head.

As if to prove to himself that this public warning had no effect, he called Dan from the cafeteria the next morning, to ask whether Dan could join him for breakfast. Dan thanked him for asking but said it was not a good morning; even so, Ford felt pleased with himself after he hung up the phone.

———✷———

He was dressed and ready with time to spare. He made a sandwich and ate it. Thinking how odd it was, on this night of all nights, to be alone until an hour before the New Year began. For a moment, in the dark, he had a feeling this was his mother's house, that through one of these doorways, if he opened the door properly, he would find the Savannah rooms waiting for him. He peered gingerly into some of the doorways, then laughed at himself. He could almost hear his mother's voice. He slipped on a jacket, found his car keys, and drove.

A winter evening in the Druid Hills neighborhood, the lights of Christmas trees shimmering through Palladian windows. Tasteful wreaths on tasteful doors. On Blue Ridge Avenue he parked behind the old public library and locked his car. He had come early, and waited on the ledge beside the steps to the apartment building, legs dangling. Impatient. One moment wishing he had defied Dan's wishes and attended the show opening, and the next glad of the peace.

The wait ended more quickly than he had expected. A slim figure appeared among nets of leaves and branches, halting at the brick retaining wall. "You look good, sitting there. You look natural. I like it."

Ford laughed. "How did it go? The show, I mean."

"Fine. We had a big crowd. We got a lot of laughs. There was a critic there and he enjoyed himself. At least he said so."

"I started to come anyway," Ford said. "I couldn't sleep."

"Thank God you didn't. We'd have been there all night. There's a party. There's always a party. And everybody stands around and talks about their next project."

In the light from the apartment door, Dan's face revealed its flush. Uncomfortably, fingertips brushing eyebrows, allowing Ford to see. "I haven't taken off all my makeup yet," Dan said.

Ford simply smiled. His fear dissolved into another feeling at the sight of the face, transformed by rouge and shadow, lips daubed with red, lashes showing traces of mascara. As if Ford had caught Dan in the act of transformation. Suddenly he knew what his fear had been, earlier: that, at this moment, he would find himself without desire. Now at the presence of this face, he found himself consumed, and his hands rose to that neck, palm over Dan's pulse. Desire ate him. "Do you need to go inside?"

"I want to wash my face." The hand along Dan's neck held him pinioned, and a charge passed through him; Ford could feel the power shifting between them. As surely as he had understood Dan's power before, he felt his own increasing. In the apartment, Dan's pale body shimmered as he slipped the clean shirt over his torso, nipples lovely and roseate, tender-tipped. A different kind of man from

Ford, his lean hardness, different from the men with whom Ford had kept company in the past.

When Dan was ready, they exited, descended stairs, and hurried to Ford's car, where Dan sat erect and carefully controlled, staring straight ahead. Without warning, Dan lay a hand along Ford's, atop the gearshift. Ford felt as if the hand were reaching much deeper inside him; their two skins, colliding, shimmered. So many doors were opening, and until now he had seen only the obvious ones. Dan said, "Happy New Year."

Through quiet residential neighborhoods Ford drove, avoiding thoroughfares, avenues, selecting tree-lined streets overlooking murky ravines, where the large houses peered down at them from the crests of hills, the occasional yard lined with cars, describing the New Year's parties within.

"I'm glad I'm not in any of these places," Dan said. "They look so smug." Soon enough, they turned onto the dark twists of the street where Ford lived, Clifton Heights, and Ford braked the car to a halt at the beginning of the driveway, near the large brick mailbox stenciled with the clear, silvered "McKinney." The headlights washed the broad porch at the front of the house. "Does this look smug?" Ford asked.

Dan studied the façade and answered, so quickly Ford was taken aback, "No. Just satisfied. But I like that." He gazed straight up at the sky, obscured by interlaced pecan and oak; he took Ford's elbow, the lightest touch, and guided him away from the house into the yard.

In silence they rambled through the cold winter night, first beneath the broad limbs of the pecan that dominated the nearer part of the yard, then under the more distant oak. They stopped at a swing in which Ford himself had never sat, except briefly when the real estate agent showed him the house. Dan sat and beckoned. Ford joined him and, so naturally it seemed as if he had done so a hundred times, opened an arm around this stranger who had become suddenly so familiar.

Close to midnight, they went inside. Dan hung their coats in the closet while Ford listened to the muted chime of coat hangers, the rustle of fabric and leather, Dan's soft humming. Ford felt something unnameable was changing in the house. Not simply when Dan entered tonight, but when the thought of him had begun. The emptiness had receded. Ford no longer heard clocks ticking, water dripping, silence. A man moved, and his motion made sounds.

"It's five minutes to midnight. Do you want to turn on a TV or anything?"

"I'm fine," Dan said. "This is good. I like your house. Your furniture has stories, doesn't it?"

"What makes you think that?"

"Either you've been collecting this stuff for years or you've had some help."

"My mother picked out most of it. Part of it is from my grandmother, and part from an aunt's house, and some of it Mother bought."

"It's lovely." Dan spoke with a hint of coldness.

They wandered to the room his mother called the library. He knelt in front of the fireplace and set to work. But they had lingered too long in the yard; his watch finally gave off its alarm before he had the fire lit. "I'm too slow," he said, lifting his glass. "It's midnight. Happy New Year."

Dan knelt close to him and kissed his eyelids gently. "For luck," Dan whispered, and kissed his lips.

After a moment, trembling, Ford kissed him back for the first time.

The sensation spread fear through his whole body, the touch of that male mouth, full and ripe, against his own, Dan tasting of champagne. They remained side by side near the hearth, Ford finding reasons to brush his arms against Dan's shoulders, and Dan leaning into the touch. The small room filled with firelight, dancing on the inner surfaces of windows. Embers cracked and spit, flames coursing round the wood. Dan's head eased against Ford's shoulder. Ford leaned against dark curls. He had pictured the gesture as simple, but as the weight and texture of Dan became real, his body responded. Dan lay a hesitant hand on Ford's chest, and the touch penetrated deep into the bone. Ford moved toward Dan, reaching to draw the face of the man nearer, closing his eyes.

From outside, distant, the sound of fireworks penetrated the walls. Dan leaned up, and heat played over Ford's back as he lay the tip of his tongue on the pink of Dan's chest, the eye of the nipple. Fear washed away. They pressed and pulled and laughed softly into each other's mouths.

On the floor in front of the fire, flickering shadow dancing against their different flesh, Dan slid Ford's socks off his feet, the jeans down his thighs, shyly caressing the fine hair. Ford drank the sight of Dan's fresh nakedness as deeply as he drank Dan's admiration for his own, tracing the line of neck and shoulder with his mouth. The two overcame the awkward flatness of their bodies, the clumsy joining of erections, the tedious friction; forging passion and joy.

Finally Dan rose over Ford, drawing Ford to a hardness, painful and sweet, that seemed to last forever. Till Ford came.

Dan spent himself against Ford nearly at the same moment, helplessly pressing as if trying to find some point of entrance into his flesh. At the last moment, he tried to pull away from Ford, but Ford sensed the withdrawal and held him close. Wet lips in Dan's wet hair. Naked, moist, collapsed, they lay quiet in the library amid the wreckage of their clothing.

"I should have worn a condom," Dan said.

"Hush," Ford said. "Let me worry about that. Okay?"

"I can't help it."

"Yes, you can. We haven't done anything to worry about yet." Pulling the man close, he laughed softly. "We'll get to that part in the bedroom. Where there's some cushion."

Dan laughed too, relaxing. Ford closed his eyes and allowed elation to fill him. In such safety he could even admit the little fear kenneled in his brain, the minute dread of the sticky wetness on his thigh. Dan's gift of danger. *I can beat you*, he thought. *You can't stop this. You can't.*

—⟨∞⟩—

Dan rose and headed to the bathroom. Ford leaned up on one curled arm and watched, amazed, the naked body walking in his house. Dan came back with towels. He cleaned Ford's thigh and his own and sipped lukewarm champagne.

"I don't have to take you home tonight, do I?"

"I think I'm all right where I am."

In the morning, soon after dawn, Ford woke with his limbs twined round Dan, the thick taste of champagne in his mouth. They had stumbled here toward morning, drunk and exhausted, leaving clothes and ash in the library.

Now Ford studied Dan's feline sleep. Not only had he made love to Dan Crell but now they rested together in Ford's bed. When Ford stood to find the bathroom, he was careful to be quiet. He returned to the bedside and stood there, watching Dan, curled like a geisha in the folds of sheets and blankets, a flower in Ford's bed. Someone with a heartbeat, waiting for Ford.

—⟨∞⟩—

Familiar pines alerted Dan to the fact that Ford and he were approaching Forrester County. Gaunt, stunted branches swayed atop shaggy trunks, ragged against a pale sky. Silent, he fought apprehension, as across the front seat Ford waited and watched.

Whenever Dan returned to this country, he carried with him the conviction that the land would swallow him. Through the early part of the ride, from the Raleigh-Durham airport to the wastelands surrounding Smithfield, Princeton, and Goldsboro, his dread manifested itself as a tautness across his chest. He watched the procession of devastated landscape, ruined farms, and collapsing shanties, wrecks of unpainted carpentry from which, nevertheless, smoke rose through chimneys into a cloudless sky. Pastel mobile homes perched on cinderblock feet in bleak squares of grass. Red-cheeked plastic Santas waved gaily from the bland roofs of ranch-style bungalows. Wrecked automobiles clustered as if in herds, overgrown with ropes of kudzu vine. The images, the courses of the roads, struck him as familiar but oddly changed. Scoured in white light.

For a while he would forget Ford, then glimpse him. The landscape absorbed Dan, and he studied the line of ragged trees, the swoop and rise of the high-tension wire, the slant of an untended road sign; and suddenly, turning his head, he would find Ford driving the car.

Highway 70 gave way to the less-traveled Highway 58 beyond Kinston. The roads forked at a clapboard service station over which soared a sign bearing a blue neon bird, wings flapping at the same electronic interval as when Dan first remembered seeing it, years ago, Dan small and quiet, peering over the backseat of his father's car.

Soon the car crossed into Forrester County, and he read the first road signs for Somersville and Potter's Lake.

Along these roads stretched a chain of houses in which Dan had lived during his childhood. The thought of the houses, and of Ford seeing the houses, filled him with quiet apprehension. The first appeared beyond Potter's Lake, a white, tiled cottage nestled on a low rise, impossibly tiny, porch fallen to ruins. Dan had intended to point out the house to Ford but at the last moment his arm collapsed to his side and no words emerged from anywhere. The house seemed so small and shabby, even he could hardly believe he had once lived there.

The next was worse, a heap of boards sitting neglected in high grass behind a broad fig bush. Empty windows. Barns tumbling to wreckage behind. The yard had dwindled to a small tangle of weeds surrounded by old farm equipment. *I lived here once.* He turned to Ford and imagined the words. Impossible.

Silence soon began to choke him, and he stared fixedly at the road. Ford must have felt the change, because he asked, "Did you live around here?"

Roads, houses, even trees, alive in his memory, passed by him in a dull stream.

"I have something to show you," Dan said, as the car crossed the bridge over the Eleanor River.

Wooden frame buildings formed something called the Harvey Crossroads. Ford eyed Dan cautiously. "Where?"

"Turn right on this road. Not far."

The woods had been larger when he was a boy. But farther down the road little had changed; the same barns stood in the same fields he remembered, the same farm-houses hanging back half-hidden in the shade of sweet-gum trees. Beneath another bridge, the Eleanor River twisted back on herself, clotted water overhung with shadows; downriver from the bridge was the railroad trestle, and beyond opened the broad field of his memory, once littered with cornstalks but planted now with clover. In the center of the bleak field stood the house, sentinel in its plowed ground, guarded by huge old trees. When his family had lived there, the children named the place the Circle House. The yard consumed the house in weeds and grass, and the structure itself sagged, empty.

Ford studied the tiny house in perfect silence. He slowed the car and parked on the shoulder.

Dan stepped into December wind. The smell of the air entranced him, he studied the horizon in amazement. The line of pines encircled the flat plate of earth, ragged and gaunt. Hardly different at all. Beyond the broad ditch and yard, knee-deep in weed, stretched the flatness of the field. Beyond those trees ran the river, drifting within her shadowed banks, flowing silkily, darkly through the pilings of the bridge.

Ford appeared at his side and studied him. "Here?"

Dan nodded. He studied the weathered clapboard of the front, the sagging tin roof, the concrete porch with cracked steps, ivy covering one wall. The front door hung inward on its hinges. Paint flaked from gray wood. White-washed boards covered some of the windows. The house stared blindly forward.

Do you recognize me? Did you think I would ever come back? His body rebelled when he reached the front porch steps. He took a deep breath, watching his feet, which refused to move until he reminded himself the house was empty and a foot lifted. Found the next step. Ford hung at his elbow, as if afraid he might fall.

He climbed to the concrete porch. Stepping with squared shoulders to the open door, he peered inside.

No image of the past remained, not the least flicker. The empty front room echoed with the sound of his breath. Dry leaves clacked on the floor when the wind slid through the crack in the door; Dan pushed the door open as the wind gusted, and the room shook with a rattling like bones.

Ford's expression changed when he saw the shabby interior. Part of the floor had rotted away, in the corner where the long-ago couch had rested. An old tin chimney flue lay collapsed in one corner, fallen from the wreck of an oil furnace, installed after the Crells abandoned the place. The sight of the machine eased Dan, giving evidence of other inhabitants. He had pictured the house as eternally empty, abandoned since the last stick of Crell furniture rolled away in Papa's truck.

Both men crept forward, careful of the weak floor. The kitchen offered hardly enough room for them, narrower than Dan recalled. Ford had to stoop in one place where the ceiling sagged. Yellow grocery flyers littered the empty gap where Mama's stove had nested. The sink tumbled brown with dead spiders and insect wings, a slight

breeze stirring from the partly open window. Dry linoleum curled across the floor, cracking underfoot. The back
door, incongruously locked, yielded to force and swung
inward.

Outside, a porch had run the length of the house, but
now it plunged downward into weeds. Wooden steps
hung at a precarious angle. Behind the house, the old
block shed stood firmly behind the tangle of an overgrown quince. At the center of the yard the headlights of
an old car reflected the swaying grass. Rust ate its metal
skin and its cloth interior hung in rags.

The door that had once led to the children's bedroom
swayed wildly as wind rushed across the field. "That was
our bedroom." Dan pointed.

"You're not going to try to get out there."

"No." Laughing softly. "This place is a mess."

Turning abruptly. Sliding past Ford, who crowded him
against the door. They looked at each other. Ford said,
"This place has been empty for years."

"I know. I think I'm glad." Speaking matter-of-factly.
"I'm almost ready to go. There's just one more room I want
to see."

In the living room he hesitated. Ford waited behind
him. On the far wall, between the high bookshelves (which
had made his mother proud, when she first saw the
house), the closed doorway, perfectly preserved, stilled
him. His parents' bedroom. He reached for the loose enam-
eled doorknob and turned it. The door opened silently.
The room, dappled with midday light, welcomed him.

Cobwebbed windows admitted a landscape of the side yard, the field, the line of trees along the river. Part of this room had survived, but in the place where his parents bed had stood a great split had opened, as if lightning had slashed the wall like an ax. The room lay open to sky, the roof collapsed above it. Dan stared stupidly through the broken floor to the ground under the house. A plastic doll's foot lay half buried in the soft earth.

"That floor's not going to hold you up, Danny."

"I know. I'm not going any further." Searching the room, as if he might have left something here, those many years ago. Glancing at what remained of the bathroom, the steady drip, drip of water now silenced, the sink tumbled onto the floor, staining the floorboards with a stream of rust. Turning, Dan almost began the short walk to Ford, who waited in the doorway.

But for a moment, as if beyond the window another time existed, he glimpsed his mother, young and slim, as real as if she were actually there, stepping across that snow-covered field, wearing the red dress Dan had loved. Arms wrapped in a thin sweater, she moved deliberately across the furrows, at last raising her head to scan the house. . . .

He moved to the window, heedless of the groaning floorboards; Ford said, "Danny, I swear, I'm coming in after you if you don't come out." But Dan had reached the window and lay his hand against the sill. Vision suddenly blurred and he could hardly see the field or the line of trees beyond. "I should have gone to the river," he said.

"The river?"

"Past those trees." He studied the ragged gray line beyond the field. "I used to walk out there."

He forgot when and where he was, he became that
eight-year-old again, staring across the field at the pale
walls of this house, low under the trees, stubby and non-
descript on its cinderblock pilings. He could almost smell
the river through the glass; and suddenly he was there,
stepping along the bank tangled with honeysuckle, with
husks of cattail, with thick beds of fern.

"I would go to the river whenever I could. Unless it
was dark, then I had to stay in the house. When I was at
the river, I couldn't hear Mom and Dad anymore. It was
peaceful." *And I used to lie in the dead honeysuckle and dream
of a cave beneath the river, a man like you in the cave, and one
day a lion in a golden field.* An arm circled Dan from behind.
*One day a lion in a gold field gashed my thigh, and I slept for a
hundred days in your arms,* and the two stood silently
watching the distant line of the river through the trees.

"I used to dream about you at the river," Dan said.
"You lived under the water, and you took care of me."

"Me?"

"I didn't know it was you at the time. But it was."

He turned to where Ford stood behind him. The
shock on Ford's face confirmed for Dan that he himself
was crying, though he could not feel his tears. Head resting against the now familiar roundness of Ford's shoulder,
Dan found he could see the field again. Bare of any habi-
tant. Clean of snow. The present reasserted itself. Today

was Christmas Eve, and Dan had grown far past the eight-year-old who once wandered by that river. Now Mama lived an hour down the road, and she no longer owned the red dress. But as he and Ford traced their way across the weakened floor, he again felt his own ghost in the house, the small boy who still wandered in these rooms, searching for what he had lost.

Early in the afternoon they entered the Gardens of Calvary Perpetual Care Cemetery, and Ford stopped the car inside the gate.

Flabbergasted, he scanned the field of graves, and Dan's heart sank as he studied the unfolding of surprise across his face.

"You weren't kidding," Ford said. "They live in a graveyard."

"They own it. It's how they make a living. I must have told you that a dozen times."

The Gardens of Calvary occupied a low, rolling field, once farmland, surrounded by a sweep of pine for most of its perimeter, save one side, where a ditch and apple orchard separated the dead from the fallow field beyond. At the center of the burial spaces stood a marble Jesus, gleaming white, on a brick pedestal, arms spread downward in a gesture of blessing, face turned heavenward, as if announcing ownership of all these graves. At the base of the brick pedestal, rows of poinsettias lifted verdant and red leaves as a carpet for Jesus' feet.

Surrounding the standing Christ, on all sides, bronze markers lay flat in the dry winter grass. Graves reached to the foot of the apple trees on one side, but elsewhere the population of deceased had only partially filled the field, and grave markers were visible only as depressions in the grass. Here was a cemetery designed for the convenience of the lawn mower, lacking standing tombstones altogether.

"What do you do when you own a graveyard?"

"Sell graves. Dig graves. Keep the grass mowed. Bury people. Mom runs the office. That's it, back there in the trees. It's also their house."

Far at the back of the field, beneath the enormous branches of a pecan tree, a small, neat trailer nested among well-tended shrubs and dark-leaved plum trees. Shadows of interwoven branches dappled the cream walls. An office had been added to the front of the trailer and that door opened now. A trim woman hesitated behind the aluminum storm door, glare obscuring her face. "That's Mom." Dan felt the hand in his stomach again, along with another feeling, the warm rush of her presence. "She's trying to figure out if it's us or if it's somebody who's come to visit a grave."

Ford studied her. "I bet she knows it's us." Ford released the brake and eased the car along the loop road.

She must have suspected, at least, for she continued to wait in the open doorway as the car slipped past rows of flowerpots, neat brass markers nestled in dry grass; past the mausoleum atop which another Christ, also bleached white as bone, knelt in prayer. As the car neared the gravel parking area in front of the cemetery office, she waved and stepped free of the doorway.

Seeing her again, all Dan's fear returned. Mother and son watched each other, exchanging code. Then Mother turned her eyes calmly to Ford, nodding hello.

Even in her mid-fifties Ellen Crell Burley retained the dark curls of her youth, the graceful hands, slim figure, fine skin, and strong facial bones that characterized her and that she had passed to her children. Wrapping a sweater close around her, she inspected Ford's parking. The car stopped, and Dan opened the door.

Detachment flooded him with the winter air. Distant, hovering above himself, he crossed the gravel to embrace her, cheeks touching, her kiss cool and dry. Hearing Ford's footsteps behind him.

She turned to Ford, her face a calm mask. "Well, I guess I know who you are."

"Yes, ma'am, I guess you do," Ford said. "I'm glad to meet you."

Ford and Ellen studied each other. Dan stepped back, making room. Ford leaned over Dan's mother and embraced her gently.

She endured the touch with a slight smile. She had an aversion to hugs; even her children only occasionally strayed close enough for contact, knowing not to linger. Pulling away from him, she said, "Danny told me you were tall, Ford, but I didn't know you were this tall."

"Danny told me you were pretty, but he didn't tell me you were this pretty," Ford's voice edged with the social tone Dan expected. "Thank you for letting me come for Christmas."

"We're glad to have you."

Inside, she said, "You can both put your things in the bedroom. I made some room in the closet."

The low ceiling of the office almost brushed the top of Ford's hair. Mom lifted her glasses to her eyes momentarily. "Well, Ford, you can almost stand up straight in here, can't you? My husband built this room onto the trailer, and he's right short. So he didn't think about how low he got the ceiling."

Ford laughed. "I'm fine."

The office contained a metal desk and side chairs, a typewriter, telephone, and answering machine. Two filing cabinets occupied one corner. Propped against one wall, a display of bronze and stone grave markers offered the customer a sample of the possible sizes and decorative borders of eternity. Over the display, framed behind glass, hung a neat drawing of the cemetery with the grave plots precisely laid out.

Adjoining the office was a small den that Ellen had filled with Norfolk island pine, Chinese evergreen, areca palm, and wandering Jew, along with heavy wooden furniture of no particular type, and thick shag carpeting of many brown shades. This room had also been added and lay one step below the broad doorway to the original living area. The twinned rooms had always impressed Dan as pleasant in the past but with Ford standing at their center, illuminated in afternoon light, the furniture became awkward, the wood carving graceless and clumsy, the carpet garish.

Mom waited on the steps, hands in the pockets of her sweater. "Danny. Bring the bags in here, son. Show Ford where to go." She met his gaze perfectly, with a slight smile. He stepped past Ford, and she received him again, embracing him briefly. "Did you boys have a good trip? I told you I would have picked you up at Raleigh."

"Yes, ma'am, we knew you would have, but I like to drive. I don't get to do a whole lot of it, I'm at the hospital so much."

"You're a pediatrician, is that right?" Mom liked doctors.

"Yes, ma'am."

Dan stood with the hanging bag in the small bedroom that occupied the end of the trailer. This room had been assigned to Dan whenever he came home to the Gardens of Calvary over the last years, and he had grown familiar with its cramped spaces. While Ellen Burley, since her second marriage, had adapted to life in a mobile home, she bore only contempt for what she called trailer furniture. She had stocked each of her small rooms with sturdy stuff from a real furniture store. The bedroom held a large, cherry bed, a matching dresser with a broad mirror and attendant bric-a-brac, and a chest of drawers, equally burly, which projected inches beyond its alcove, past the doors of the closet. The one window, at the end of the trailer, opened onto a view of the silver propane gas tank outside, supported on legs of spider steel.

"Smells good in here," Ford said.

"That's my pies," Mom answered, and Dan inhaled the floodtide of vanilla, the unmistakable odor of coconut cream and warm meringue. "I was so busy cooking I didn't even notice what time it was till you drove up."

"We took our time. We drove down through some towns where you folks used to live. Somersville and Potter's Lake."

Mom turned to Dan in surprise. "Why did you come through Potter's Lake? You know that's not the fastest way."

"I asked him to," Ford said. "I wanted to see what the country was like."

Mom laughed hesitantly, eyeing them both. An edge of fear crossed her face, then smoothed away. "Well, now you know. Do you want to unpack right now, or do you want something to eat?"

"I want to unpack these clothes." Dan found himself shy of meeting her gaze. "We ate at Bob and Jean's."

"You can't get anything fit to eat at that place. Too greasy. And me with a refrigerator full of food. I could have made you a sandwich."

Ford chuckled and lifted white boxes of Dan's blood medicine from the suitcase and Mom said, "I need to put those in the refrigerator, don't I?"

"Yes, ma'am." Ford handed her the boxes. "I'd do it myself but I don't want to be poking around in your kitchen."

"Lord, you better not be." She studied the boxes. Turning to Dan. "I think I'll put this out in Ray's shed. I got an old refrigerator out there. Hang everything in the closet, Danny. I got my stuff shoved out of the way, I made some room."

In the silence, after she vanished, they each took a breath. Ford studied the room. "This is tiny."

"I told you it was."

Beyond the window, Mom slipped into the shed with the boxes of Dan's medicine.

The two men wedged themselves into the space between the bed and the closet. Standing close. Aware of the open bedroom door. Ford said, "I think I like tiny. I've never stayed in a trailer before."

"She still hasn't said where we're going to sleep."

"You look like your mother. Did you know that?"

"Nobody else says so." Dan lowered his eyes, hearing her footsteps.

She stood in the doorway a moment, watching. The two men no longer touched but still stood close. She inspected them both, first Ford, then Dan. Who met her gaze.

She sensed a closeness that made her uncomfortable. At least, Dan thought she did. "You boys take your time. Come in the kitchen when you're unpacked." Vanishing.

Ford said, after a moment, "Why don't you go on out there and let me finish this. I bet she'd like to talk to you."

In the kitchen, Mom peeled cooking apples over

a stainless-steel bowl. When Dan entered, she merely glanced up, focusing on her work. "Ray doesn't like his apple pie with peelings in it. Otherwise I wouldn't even bother with this. I don't mind the peelings myself."

Dan stood next to her, one arm around her shoulders. "It's good to be here." A pause of slight awkwardness. "We have to wrap some presents. I have to, I mean."

She smiled, not looking at him. "I got ribbons all ready for you. And some pretty paper." She continued, all the while, peeling apples, her concentration fixed on the spiral of peel drooping into the pot. From the bedroom came the echo of Ford, whistling. Mother laughed softly, and shook her head.

Dan said, "This is sort of funny, isn't it?"

"It's right unusual, I guess. What did Ford's parents say?"

Dan lowered his voice. "They told us not to come at all. It really hurt his feelings."

"That's what Ray wanted me to tell you. But I told him there wasn't any way I could do that. And he hasn't said anything about it since."

"Where is he now? Is he mad?"

"He's at the mall. I think he's all right. But he's not saying much, these last few days."

Dan said, "He never says that much. I hope he acts okay."

"He's doing his best, son." Handing Dan a slice of apple, patting his arm. "Sit down at the table, you worry me standing there like that."

She poured fresh coffee from the pot, wordlessly. Dan said, "I'm half asleep after the ride."

"I'll be glad to make you something to eat if you're hungry. Ray and me already had a sandwich, and he can't eat again till supper, because of his diet. I try to eat like he does. Your sister wanted to make lasagna, but I told her Ray can't eat it and I don't need it as fat as I'm getting to be. Ray would sit right here and eat a mountain of it and then belch half the night and tell me how his stomach hurts. And I have enough trouble sleeping."

"When is Allen getting here?"

"Sometime tomorrow. Him and Cherise are going to stop by to see you, and then they're driving on to see Cherise's parents. Then they're going to stop back by here the day after Christmas and spend the night."

"Did you tell him about Ford?"

Mom answered, quietly, "I told him you were bringing a friend home with you. And that's all."

Dan accepted the slight admonition in her tone. "When does Cherise have the baby?"

"She's due in March, but she's so big you'd think it was next week. Some women show and some women don't; but Cherise, she shows."

Hesitating, listening to the wind against the sides of the trailer, Dan asked, finally, "Have you heard from Duck?"

"He calls me sometimes. He called a couple of weeks ago." She paused, but Dan knew to wait. "He told me he doesn't want to come home. So I don't fight with him about it."

"At least he's talking to you now. Does he tell you where he is?"

"He says he's in New Mexico. But I don't know whether to believe him."

"Is he all right?"

"He says he is. I think he's still drinking pretty much. I try not to worry about it."

Ford emerged from the bedroom, and Dan's mother turned toward him at the sound. Her expression stiffened slightly. "Come join us in here. I made Danny a cup of coffee. You want one?"

Ford slid into a seat across from Dan. Even seated, his presence dominated the room, his shoulders monumental, his size almost an embarrassment. Mom set the coffee cup in front of him and asked, in a brisker tone, "Do you boys ever cook at your house, or do you eat out all the time?"

"We cook when I'm home," Ford said, "which is not much."

"Danny cooks too? I didn't even think he knew how. He used to eat in restaurants all the time. I couldn't believe it when he told me. Wasting all that money."

"Mama thinks eating out is taking a bologna sandwich to the yard," Dan said, and she laughed, almost relaxed.

They sat together awkwardly; Dan froze and could think of nothing at all to say. Till finally Ford stood. "I need to call the hospital."

Something about his expression touched a chord in

Mom. She warmed toward Ford all in a moment. "You can use the phone in the office if you want to. It's that room where we came in. You can be by yourself in there."

When he was gone, Mom poured the cooked apples into pie crusts. "Is he calling about a patient?"

"Yes, ma'am. A sick little boy."

"He reminds me of one of your doctors when you were in Chapel Hill, that first time. I bet you don't remember him, do you?"

Dan felt a prickle at the base of his skull. "No, ma'am."

"He was one of the interns. I don't remember what his name was. But he was real nice to me. And he always acted like he was so worried about you. Ford reminds me of him. He was tall like that." They heard Ford's voice from the other room, muffled. "I guess he got the call through."

Mom watched him, tangible as a touch. "I'm glad you came."

"So am I."

"Ford seems like a real good person," spoken haltingly, though; and she could not look him in the eye. "He has a lot of money, doesn't he? You can tell."

Not a sound from the other room; they were both listening. "He must be finished."

But the silence went on too long. Dan stood and stuck his head in the office. He found Ford staring out the window with the phone receiver in his lap. "They have the kid back in surgery. Too much bleeding. I couldn't get Russell, he's with the surgeons."

"Who did you talk to?"

"The floor nurse. He's been in the OR about an hour." Shoulders wracked with sudden tension. "I don't think this kid's going to make it. I had a bad feeling when I left."

"Do you think it would be any different if you were there?" Gently pressing his body against the back of Ford's neck.

Mom called, from the den, out of sight of the door, "Everything all right?"

"Yes, ma'am," Ford called. Taking a deep breath, he stood. "Come on, there's no reason to sit out here. I'll call again later."

During the lull in her cooking, Mother took them on a tour of her yard, and they walked among the various flower beds as she pointed out the shrubs and flowers. She named the colors of all the azaleas, even though all were bloomless and green. "Have you always lived on cemeteries?" Ford asked, looking around at the graves, the closest of them being across the paved loop road.

Mom laughed. "No. This is my first one. But I'll tell you one thing. It's quiet. And nobody bothers you."

Her vegetable garden bore witness to her careful frugality; neatly laid out on an otherwise untilled portion of the land, it had continued to bear collards for her table even in deepest autumn. She described, matter-of-factly, what types of vegetables each row had yielded, and how many quarts of peas, beans, and corn she had frozen. "We got a mess of field peas this year. I must have put up sixty quarts. But the butterbeans didn't do anything."

A car pulled into the gate, and its lone occupant opened the driver-side door. A woman with her hair tied up in a dark scarf carried a foil-clad poinsettia carefully into the field of graves. Stopping at last, she knelt to touch the bronze plaque nested in dry grass, setting the poinsettia into the bronze vase. She adjusted the flower to make the picture perfect, then remained kneeling, longer than her knees might have wished, as evidenced by the difficulty with which she stood. Mom said, "Her husband died two years ago. She brings flowers out here almost every month."

"You have people out here all the time, don't you?" Ford asked.

"Except at night. Sometimes people will ride through here at night, but they don't stop."

The woman returned to her car as another vehicle passed through the gate. At the sight of this one, Mom said, "There's Ray with my Christmas present."

Ray Burley parked beside Ford's rented sedan and emerged with his collar upturned. From the backseat he retrieved large gray shopping bags of the department-store type and, arms full, he spied the party approaching from the garden. Neatly dressed in gray slacks, a precise jacket, and well-shined shoes. His expression bland, only the sharpness of his gaze warned of danger in his scrutiny of Ford. His jaw was set in a line indicating discomfort. "I see you boys got here."

"Hey, Ray." Dan moved to help with the bags. He hugged Ray quickly and shyly, feeling the man's resistance.

Ray handed him one of the bags. "Don't let your mother

grab that out of your hands. She's liable to try anything to find out what's in there."

"Ray, this is Ford McKinney. Ford, this is my second dad."

Ray's eyes glittered. After a moment he offered his hand. "Pleased to meet you."

"Pleased to meet you, sir. Thank you for having me."

Ray nodded, somewhat stiffly. "You have a good trip?"

"Yes, sir," Dan said. "We didn't have any trouble at all."

Ray inspected Ford up and down. Nothing could be read in his face. The inspection ended, and Ray ambled toward the house, passing the rented car, which he stopped to inspect. Hesitating a moment, then stopping. Turning to Ford, he asked, "This yours?"

"Till tomorrow night," Ford said.

Ray stooped to look at the interior and patted the side mirror. Deadpan, looking Ford in the eye, "You don't let Danny drive it, do you?"

Ford choked on a laugh and answered, "No, sir, I don't."

"That's good."

Everyone headed inside. Mom said, "Danny drug Ford all through the fields getting here. Took him through Potter's Lake, and you know that adds a good hour to go that way."

"Not much to Potter's Lake, is there?" Ray said. They were all sitting in the kitchen. "You grew up in Savannah. That right?"

"Sure is."

"Pretty town."

"Did you live there?" Ford asked.

Ray, worrying a bottle cap between his fingertips, glanced at Ford, then back at the bottle cap. "I sold spaces at a cemetery right outside of Savannah for a while. Fairway Oaks."

"He keeps telling me he'll take me down there one day," Mom said, "when we get a camper."

Dan had always considered his stepfather handsome, with his strong nose and jaw, clear blue eyes and neatly trimmed hair. Ray stood four or five inches shorter than Dan, stocky-framed and solid, but with a salesman's smooth, tan body. Mom stood briefly beside him, stroking his shoulders as he talked to Ford. "This your first Christmas away from home?" Ray asked.

"Yes, sir, it is. And it feels a little odd."

Ray chuckled. "You ought to talk to my children. They don't come home for Christmas, and they don't even think twice about it. Ellen's children come to see her. But mine don't. Unless they need money."

"Your boys come to see you," Mom said, "almost every year."

"How many children do you have?" Ford asked.

"Six. Three sons and three daughters." Sipping coffee, he gestured to the pictures on the divider of shelves that separated the kitchen from the living room. "Most of my kids live in Louisiana."

Mom added, "The oldest boys are really sweet. They built my shelves for me."

Ray nodded with a touch of pride. "Built that shed out back too."

"Do you do much carpentry?" Ford asked.

"I do a little," Ray said. "That's why we built that shed. I got me a good shop out there."

"I've been trying to set up a woodworking shop at home," Ford said, "if I could ever get time."

"It takes some doing, all right. Took me four, five years to get mine like I wanted it. I still don't have a good lathe like I want."

"He's making me a cabinet for the bathroom," Mom said. "I can't find anything in the stores that will fit the space I got. Ray's good with that stuff."

Ford said, "My dad has a shop. And there's plenty of room in my basement for one, if I knew what to do to get started."

The pause lengthened. Dan could tell Ray was considering the thing, turning it over. After a while he pushed back his chair and stood, saying to Ford, "Come on out and look at my shop."

Nobody said a word as Ray led Ford out the back door. Mom watched as they crossed the yard. "That wasn't too bad."

"No, it wasn't."

"You want to wrap your presents while they're out there? I got all the gift-wrapping stuff back in my bedroom."

He retrieved the gifts he had packed. Mom pulled out her bag of Christmas wrapping paper from the closet. Dan displayed his gifts, and Mom asked the price of each. "Son, you spent too much money."

"No, I didn't. I'm doing fine." Pleased at her admonition, nonetheless. "Wait till you see what I got you."

"Lord help me, I'll feel so guilty about whatever it is I won't be able to use it."

"Now, Mama, it's my money, and I can spend it on Christmas if I want to."

She fretted another moment or so but was obviously pleased. This game repeated itself every Christmas, and Dan found himself relieved at its cycle this year, restoring, in some way, his sense of normalcy. She laid out rolls of paper on her bed, arranging scissors and tape. The game of Dan wrapping his own presents also replayed itself each time he came home, since Mom invariably wrapped the gifts herself. "Your sister bought that power saw like Ray wanted. You can write her a check for your half. Ray will really like that. And I got him that lathe he keeps talking about. I don't even half know what it is, but he wants it. I hid it in the vault behind the shed. He'll be surprised because he doesn't think I could manage something as big as that."

"What did Ray get you?"

Mom laughed. "I don't know, I can't figure it out this year. I guess I'll have to wait. What did you give Ford?"

"I gave him a sweater and some other stuff. A watch." Tense, suddenly, but forcing speech. "I have one more present for him. But I'm scared to give it to him. I don't know what he'll think."

This present openness of conversation disturbed his mother, but she persevered. "What is it?"

She understood his hesitation when she saw the box, and a slight cast of fear overlay her features. Dan opened the blue velvet lid. A gold ring nested in white satin, a plain band inlaid with fine geometric tracings. He handed the box to her. "This is a wedding ring," she said.

"It's not, really." Dan blushed. "I don't even know if he'll wear it."

Disturbed, she touched the ring with her fingertip. He could see her sadness was real. "It worries me. I guess I always hoped you'd change your mind and find you a wife."

"I won't ever have a wife. I'm not looking for one. I told you that a long time ago."

She nodded. "But you were never with anybody before. So I could pretend." The moment lengthened. "Seems like nothing is ever the way it ought to be. And this is one more thing."

Returning to the bed, she took up the Christmas paper again. She rested the box in sight, open, to show the ring. Finally she asked, "Are you happy?"

"Yes, ma'am." A knot of feeling rising in his throat.

"That's good." She touched the ring again. Closing the box, lifting it, she met his eye. "Do you want me to wrap it?"

Ford and Ray spent a peaceful half hour in the shed while the sun sank, and Dan and his mother arranged the new gifts under the tree. Mom switched on the television with its soft background chatter of Christmas greetings from the local stations.

"Do you have any shopping to do?" Mom asked, pulling out her butcher block from the top of the refrigerator. "I need to make one more trip to the mall tonight. To pick up something for Cherise."

"I wouldn't mind going out there, but I don't think I need to buy anything else."

"It's going to be a mess, trying to shop tonight. But all I got her so far is a sconce. You know how she likes that colonial-type stuff. And I think I ought to get her something else."

"Are you getting along with her?"

"Oh, yeah," Mom said, "we're doing fine. I went up to Greensboro to see her and your brother, and her and me had a real nice talk. Allen is doing real good. He's running that whole branch of the bank. And they think he'll go to the district office pretty soon."

"Allen always had the knack for making money, didn't he?"

Mom laughed. "He sure did. And for spending every penny of it." She had begun to cut up a whole, raw chicken. The white, elastic skin stretched and parted. Bone cartilage glistened. "I thought I'd fry this chicken. I'll bake a piece each for me and Ray. How does that sound?"

"You know how that sounds to me. I'll sit here while you fry chicken any day."

Pleased, she added, "And I can cook some vegetables

out of the freezer. They won't be like right out of the garden, like you used to get. But it tastes better than what you buy in the store. To me it does, anyway."

They sat peacefully in the kitchen until Amy arrived. Her small car slid beneath the branches of the pecan tree, and Amy waved, cigarette in hand. Through the windshield Dan glimpsed her pale face beneath dark, short curls, her smile flashing. A slight haunted look to her eyes. Cigarette bobbing, she looked around the yard as if expecting to find someone else. Beside her, strapped into the passenger seat, Jason waved his small white hand.

They stepped free of the car. She wore her hair neat and short and rinsed it with a red-tinged henna. On her face, along with the requisite makeup, eyeliner, and mascara, she had that hard-edged expression Dan remembered from childhood. Only when she watched Jason, standing on tiptoe to embrace his uncle, the hardness vanished.

"Welcome," she said. "Did Mom tell you me and her had a fight about supper?"

"Hush, Amy."

"We did. I'm sorry I was so ugly." She matter-of-factly pecked Mom's cheek. "I bet we're having chicken. Right?"

"I like Nanna's fried chicken," Jason announced, whirling around the yard with a plastic jet.

"Tell Uncle Dan who's coming to see you tonight," Amy said.

Jason screamed, "Santa Claus! And he's bringing me a whole bunch of stuff."

"Well that's good," Dan said. "I bet you can hardly wait, can you?"

Jason shook his head furiously. Amy said, "I won't have any trouble getting him to bed tonight." Looking around the yard. "Did your friend come with you?"

"Him and Ray are in the shed looking at Ray's shop," Mom said. "Get Jason's toys and come on in the house—it's too cold to stand around out here."

Amy opened the hatch of the small car and Dan hefted the laundry basket full of bright plastic toys that traveled with Jason from house to house. The child played inside the trailer adjacent to the kitchen, where Mom and Amy could keep an eye on him while they drank coffee. Dan set down the basket of toys. Jason asked, "Will you play with me, Uncle Dan?"

Through the window Dan could see Ray and Ford leaving the shed. Ray toured the exterior of the shed with Ford briefly, showing off the lumber rack and the shelter under which Ray kept the machinery for tending the cemetery grounds. Amy noted this movement from her kitchen vantage, leaning over to look out the window. "Is that him?" She glanced at Dan, who had knelt to help Jason with the basket of toys. "He's good-looking." Amy tapped the cigarette on the ashtray.

"Who is?" asked Jason.

"Nobody," Mom said. "Play with your toys."

"Ray must like him," Amy said, "because he's sure showing off that shed."

"Am I good-looking, Nanna?" Jason asked.

"Yes, honey," Mom said, "you're a handsome little boy."

Amy looked at Dan and grinned. "I never had a boyfriend who looked like that."

"My daddy's not good-looking," Jason announced. "He's fat."

For a moment. The juxtaposition of Ford's presence with theirs. The faces of his family swelling out of the past. A fist formed in his solar plexus.

Ford entered the kitchen and their eyes met. Dan forced a smile and introduced them. Amy had snuffed out her most recent cigarette and offered her hand. Her smile tensed.

Amy reached for her coffee. "Jason. This is Ford. He's a friend of your Uncle Dan's."

Jason looked up. Ford said, "Hello, Jason."

"Say hello."

Jason opened his mouth but could not speak at first. Ford knelt behind Ray, bringing his face a little closer. "Did I hear you say something about toys?" Ford asked.

Dan wandered into the room where Ray sat, bathed in lamplight and basking in the voice from the television. Jason appeared at the side of Dan's chair and watched his uncle. "Plug in the Christmas tree, Uncle Dan." So he knelt along the paneled wall and fumbled for the end of the extension cord that powered the Christmas lights. He slid the plug neatly into the wall, and the tree glowed.

When Dan was a child, his mother's Christmas tree had always been a spruce, but nowadays Mom preferred the plastic variety, perfectly shaped, simulating the real tree in every way but texture and smell. On plastic branches hung strings of small colored lights, each of the strings blinking in sequence, the lights illuminating wooden and plastic Christmas ornaments. Plastic snow completed the picture, sprinkled over the tree and its ornaments as well as over the packages and fleecy cotton beneath the tree. Jason knelt beneath the tree and pointed to packages, saying, "This one is mine, Uncle Dan. But I'm not supposed to touch it."

The blinking Christmas lights, the wrapped gifts, even the plastic tree, opened Dan to the fullness of the past, the fact of Christmas. Once a year, like clockwork, the holiday revisited him with dread. What he remembered, the image he could never refuse, was himself, was his brothers and sisters on the Christmas Eves of the past, a receding parade of cramped living rooms in small houses, of open-flame gas heaters hissing dryly, heating their ceramic bricks red hot. Each year, on Christmas Eve, breathless, five anxious children facing the shrine of a Christmas tree, strung with large, hot lights, glass ornaments, and strands of silver tinsel.

Jason's voice, lilting, singing the fragments of a Christmas hymn, startled Dan—was it Jason singing or was it Grove, from a long time ago? Dan closed his eyes, and his brother Grove was there, lying on the couch in pajamas during one of the intervals when he couldn't walk. *Grove watched the colored lights of the tree and sang at the top of his lungs, happy at the thought of toys.* The exact image flooded Dan, and he himself stood in that former room over his brother, changing the bag of ice on Grove's swollen knee, watching a television newscaster present the inevitable holiday announcement, *a mysterious unidentified flying object sighted crossing south from the Arctic circle. . . .*

Uneasy, Dan stood. Focusing with effort on the present, the nephew, the Christmas tree, Ray in the recliner. Dan listened for sounds from the kitchen.

He lifted the half-melted, hardly cold ice bag from Grove's swollen knee, gently, as Grove watched him. The newly filled bag of ice awaited, surface stiff and hard, in Dan's other hand. He gave the fresh ice to Grove, to place on the tender, ballooned flesh. New ice caused pain because the ice bag remained stiff until the ice had partly melted, and the stiffness made the swollen joint ache; but partly melted ice wasn't cold enough to numb the nerves. Grove's face was damp with sweat, the lights of the Christmas tree glittering. "Thank you," he said, settling the ice bag gingerly against the blue-veined skin, and lying back with his arm across his eyes.

Jason sat on the arm of Ray's chair, hands on his knees, watching television with a serious expression. Tonight's weather woman, whose mass of auburn hair nearly filled the width of the weather map, announced with wide-eyed wonder at the end of the five-day forecast that a mysterious radar blip had just been sighted in the north and was thought to resemble a sleigh pulled by reindeer. . . .

Sound fading to silence, then a roaring in his head. *Grove's face burst into a smile of pure radiance.* Jason shrieked, and whirled to Ray. "Did you hear that?" Jason asked, and Ray laughed.

Jason turned to Uncle Dan. "They saw Santa Claus in the sky." He slid down from the arm of the recliner and ran to tell his mother.

Dan went to the bedroom, stood there with the door closed and took deep breaths. Dim lamplight brought the walls close; he kept his back to the mirror, facing the window. Bare dirt in the side yard, gray under the arc light. Headlights from a car cruising the loop road gave him a start. *The sound of his father's truck pulling into the yard, light splashing the chaineyball tree. The sound of his footsteps on the stoop, his hand on the door.* The door to the bedroom opened and Ford said, "Where are you?"

Dan turned. Faced with Ford's large body, he felt a need to shut off the memories, to return to the room. As if he were leaning against the strong shoulders and chest. "I'm getting ready for dinner."

"Oh." Ford nodded. Closing the door behind him, closing the door to the bathroom as well, and crossing to Dan. The two stood together watching the car exit through the gate, red lights receding. Wind resounded. "This is peaceful."

"Is it?"

He could feel Ford's nod. "I like everybody. Your sister is fine. And Jason's great."

"He's so solemn. He acts like a little old man."

Ford laughed. "He's like you. Your mom showed me a picture when you were that age."

Muffled, the sound of Ellen's voice from beyond the door. "No, Jason, don't go in there."

Ford leaned momentarily close to Dan, saying, "We probably better quit hiding. Are you all right?"

"Yes," Dan said. "But I wouldn't be, if you weren't here."

As always in Dan's house, the business of eating was conducted quickly, in near silence. The thought of Ford during his family's mealtime had provided Dan one of his chief dreads, but Ford simply joined the general quiet and spoke when addressed. Dan momentarily sank into his fear of his family, into a flash of unreasonable anger at some coarseness in Amy's voice, or at Ray's noisy way of drinking tea or the drone of the television behind the meal, and suddenly Ford moved into his field of vision, serving himself seconds from the plate of chicken, ready with a compliment on Mom's cooking. That face, that voice, at this table.

———❦———

Following supper came the trip to the mall. Dan found Ford in the bedroom, gazing vacantly at the window. Underneath his stillness waited an unspoken ache. Dan could see it in the face, the softness of the gray eyes, the boyish hunger of the mouth. Ford lifted the sweater over his head. "I feel a little lost."

The collapse began at the center of his face, spread outward. He sat on the bed, and Dan quietly pulled Ford's head into his lap, gathering the boy against him. "What is your family doing tonight?"

"Grandmother's party. They'll be arriving right about now."

"Do you think Courtenay and her husband went home?"

"I'm sure they did. And I'm sure she's giving Mom and Dad fits." Pausing. "She really does like you, you know."

Dan laughed, softly. "Yes, I know. Except when she's around me."

"I mean it."

"I mean it, too. She likes me fine. She's just not sure if she likes anybody with you." Hearing the sounds of preparation rising to a peak, he added, "But she's getting used to the idea. Come on. You're the pilot for this expedition."

Ford laughed, said yes, but lingered. "I love you, Danny."

Closing his eyes at the unexpected declaration, Dan took a deep breath. A strong hand pressed his face. "You're calling me Danny a lot these days."

"I like it." Pause. Then, small voiced, "Say you love me, too."

Dan sighed, leaning down to the man's ear, whispering, "I love you, too."

Through the holiday night along darkened roads; through the quiet hamlet of Wickham, where the Main Street telephone poles had been transformed to large candy canes; through the countryside to the four-lane highway and along the highway to Foxbriar Mall they traveled, not quite a family, yet not quite anything else. Ray, Ellen, and Amy squeezed into the back seat, placing Jason between

Ford and Dan, where he chanted the few words he could recall of "We Wish You a Merry Christmas."

In the mall, Ray and Ellen quickly vanished beyond an island of concrete swans swimming through a lake of carefully tended ferns. The others moved more slowly through the broad space, showered from above with holiday music and stunned by the glitter of the shops. Voices washed over them; young women with large hairdos discussed the varieties of aftershave their boyfriends fancied; older women in pantsuits opened their bags to allow snaggletoothed daughters to peep at Daddy's Christmas present. In the toy store Jason dashed from aisle to aisle and pointed out, largely to Ford, all the toys he would be receiving from Santa Claus. Then Amy and Dan took Jason to an empty booth at a hamburger place while Ford quietly vanished.

Amy, watching him go, pulled a cigarette from her purse and lit it. Eyeing Dan. "You won't yell at me as long as I don't smoke around Ford, will you?"

"I wasn't fussing at you because of him," Dan said, though something sank in his gut. "I just wish you wouldn't smoke."

"I figured maybe Ford thinks it's common to smoke, or something." She lit the cigarette and inhaled self-consciously, glancing at the other shoppers and blowing her smoke across a low planter full of plastic snake plant. "Mama had me so worried about him being here, telling me how rich he is and how old his family is and all that stuff."

"She was worried?" Dan asked.

"You know she was. It was all she would talk about. I guess she thought he was going to walk in the house with his nose up in the air, or something." Pausing to wipe Jason's chin. He went on chewing contentedly.

"What do you think now?"

"I think he's nice." Amy spoke with self-conscious brightness. "He doesn't act like he's better than us at all."

"He's not better than us."

"You know what I mean." Amy reached for the ashtray. "He doesn't act like he thinks he is. What is his family like?"

"I've only met his sister. Her name is Courtenay. She's fine. We don't get along all that well when we're together, but I like her."

"She doesn't think you're good enough for him?"

Dan shook his head, "Not so much that. They're close, Ford and her. They looked after each other when they were growing up, sort of like you and me. I think she feels like I'm taking him away from her. And she worries about him." He sipped his sweet, flat Coke. "We get along better than we used to."

Amy snuffed out the cigarette. She was thinking about something else now. "I went to see Papa's grave last week. I took him a poinsettia. I figured nobody else would do it —his brothers and sisters don't pay him any mind."

"Did anybody ever get him a gravestone?"

"No. Allen won't spend any money on it. And I don't have it to spend."

"He was my real granddaddy," Jason announced, following the conversation with great seriousness. "But I like Granddaddy Ray."

"So do I," Dan said.

Amy pulled the child against her side and lay her head atop his. "You went with me to that graveyard, didn't you, sweet boy? And you carried the flower for me so I wouldn't have to."

"It was heavy," Jason said, sighing.

"Do you ever miss him?" Amy asked.

The cold hand closed on Dan's throat. "No."

"I do. I know it's stupid."

"I went to the Circle House today. With Ford. Do you remember which one that was?"

She paled slightly. "Why?"

"We were close to it. I wondered if it was still there."

"Was it?"

He nodded. "It's falling down. Nobody lives there. Our bedroom is off the foundation, and there's a big hole in the floor in Mama and Papa's room."

"I'm glad of it." Unable to look Dan in the eye. She embraced Jason again. "I wish you could forget about that place."

Dan sipped his Coke in silence. Returning to the moment at the window, the image of Mama in the red dress, the fear in Ford's eyes. "I wish I could too."

"What did Ford say? About the house?"

"It scared him. I had told him we were poor, but I don't think he realized what I meant till he saw where we lived."

Amy laughed. "You should've told him that was one of the nice places."

"I did."

She worried the cigarette pack with her fingertip. "Did you tell him what happened there?"

"No."

"Why did we name that one the Circle House?"

"Don't you remember?" Dan asked. "You came up with it. Because the rooms opened into a circle and there weren't any dead ends in the house. So when Papa chased Mama there, she could always get away from him."

With jarring suddenness, Ford loomed over the table and the present reasserted itself. Amy shoved the ashtray to the side, and Ford slid into the booth beside Dan. "Did you find what you wanted?" Amy asked, instantly public.

"Oh, yes. It was right there."

Ford asked Amy to help him pick out a gift for Mrs. Burley.

Jason accompanied Ford this time, the child's hand small within the clasp of the man's. "Mama, now you walk behind me and him. Okay?"

At a shop called Élan, Ford and Jason paused to review various flowing scarves, wool jackets, alligator purses, and other items in the window, Ford requesting Jason's five-year-old opinion on which of the displayed wares would please Jason's nanna. Jason selected a large, wide gold-plated belt and Ford pretended to consider it, rubbing chin with forefinger and kneeling next to Jason for a serious discussion of the belt's merits. "Your Nanna might think it's too heavy," Ford said. "It looks like to me it could be."

Jason considered, tucked in his lower lip and nodded. "Probably," he said, "because it's gold."

Amy knelt on his other side. "She might like a scarf."

Jason shook his head wisely. "No, she wouldn't. Nanna don't like scarfs like that one." He sighed and threw up his hands. "We better go in the store and look at some other stuff."

They wandered from there to another shop, Helene's, moving slowly through the shifting crowd. Overhearing conversations, *Mom won't like that, she looks awful in that color. That's too high, I can't pay that. Can you believe how precious this is, just the most darling little outfit?* Dan's attention strayed somewhat, and when he turned to find Ford already paying for a long-waisted red wool jacket, he eyed the obviously expensive item with some surprise. Stepping toward the cashier, he touched the price label, read it and looked at Ford. Eyebrows raised. "Too much," he said.

Ford's jaw set in a line. "Jason likes it, and I like it."

Jason said, "It's red, Uncle Dan, and Nanna likes red. And it makes her look pretty."

Dan shook his head slowly, backing away. Ford watched the retreat, and Dan felt his hurt. But his jaw was set, and he completed the purchase quickly. The cashier pointed the way to gift wrap and Ford headed there without a backward glance.

"How much does it cost?" Amy asked, and Dan answered. She blew out breath in slight surprise. "That's more than I spent on her."

Dan felt a sinking in his middle. "That's more than you and me both spent on her."

Jason said, "It's from me and Ford. And Nanna will like it a whole lot."

Amy quipped, "I sure hope he buys me a present." Watching Dan's clear disapproval with amusement. "You're mad, aren't you? Can't he afford it?"

"Oh, he can afford it, all right." More than mad. He controlled himself. "I better hush. The one thing we fight about is money."

"That's what me and Hank fought about most of the time," Amy said. "You better be careful. You don't want to end up like I did."

From across the crowded sales floor, Ford glanced at Dan carefully, brows knit together. Prepared, with stubbornness, for argument. Dan met his glance, unable to soften his expression.

—— ❦ ——

At home again, after a mostly silent drive, they parted ways quickly. Ford and Jason arranged Ford's packages under the tree. Ford used the phone to call the hospital, learned his patient had lived through surgery and was recovering, then said good night. Amy and Jason drove home to make a bologna sandwich for Santa Claus. Ray and Mom went to bed.

Dan sat up alone in the living room, staring into the

plastic tree. No clear line of thought carried him. On the floor lay the offending Christmas package, the expensive gift. Watching it, he remembered the moment in the mall, his coldness at the thought of Ford's unnecessary, irritating extravagance. Now, distant from his own sudden harshness, he saw only Ford's fear in its aftermath. *What does it matter how much money he spends on my mother? Why do I fight him about money? What am I defending?*

He flicked off the television and knelt to unplug the Christmas lights. He closed his eyes and imagined the rooms of the house on Clifton Heights opening round him one by one. He set the thermostat for its night duty and returned to the living room, switching off lamps. He stood at the window in the dark and waited till he could identify all the sounds in the house, the ticking of the electric clock, the drone of the refrigerator's compressor, the slow drip of water into the stainless steel sink. The click of the furnace as the thermostat cycled. He stood there waiting for something; he could almost name it. Then the feeling ebbed, and he faced the bedroom. He undressed and slipped between the sheets. Ford was already asleep.

Late in the night he felt Ford leave the bed, head to the other room, make a phone call. He was away only a little while. When he came back, Dan settled against him, and, after a moment, Ford turned and they lay across one another in the dark.

"He's all right."

"Yes. Sorry, I didn't mean for you to wake up."

"It's okay." Tasting salt on Ford's skin. "I'm sorry I was such a jerk. About the present."

Ford never answered, but turned on top of Dan and murmured against his neck. As soon as that, asleep again.

—◦◦◦—

Ellen Burley rose early on the fifty-fifth Christmas morning of her life. She washed her face in the large bathroom at the end of the trailer, removing the two strips of tape which she placed on the side curls of her hairdo before sleep each evening. As always, she was careful to close the door to keep from waking Ray. Once upon a time in their marriage Ray had risen with her, but since his second heart attack he had begun to lay abed longer than she, sometimes an hour or more.

She had a fondness for the peace of early hours, begun in her first marriage when early morning had been her refuge. As long as she rose out of bed in time to wander in the silent house before children or husband awakened, she gained precious minutes of privacy. This was a time she could trust, whatever had happened the day before. The habit of solitary mornings carried itself forward from the storms of her first marriage to the relative peace of her second; she habitually rose close to dawn to make coffee, sit in her kitchen, and sip from the warm cup, in company with herself.

To her surprise, then, this morning she found her kitchen already smelling of coffee. Buttoning her housecoat, she reached for a clean cup from the cabinet. Tasting. She carried the cup to the outer room, where she found Ford standing at the windows beside the Christmas tree. Hearing her, he turned, smiling. "Good morning," he said. "I got up early and helped myself. I hope you don't mind."

"No, I don't mind." Ellen seated herself in her own recliner. "I think I'll leave the heat alone a few minutes. Ray has that blanket turned up like a toaster."

Ford said, "I'm not cold." As an afterthought, adding, "Merry Christmas."

"Merry Christmas."

He sat on the couch. Not a stranger anymore. She examined him as he wrapped his robe more closely around his knees, his dark hair in need of a comb, the strong bones of his face shaded by morning beard. They peacefully sat together watching the Christmas tree, colors dulled in the pale of morning. She sipped her coffee slowly, counting the layers of light in the sky, opening as the sun rose, clouds appearing beyond the windows. "I feel like I ought to know you, Ford, we talk so much on the phone. But I guess now that you're here I'm shy."

"I know it was hard for you when Danny asked you if I could come."

"Danny was right unpleasant about it. He was so sure I was going to say no." Another moment of silence. "How is his health?"

"He's fine." Ford looked her in the eye. "His cell counts are fine."

"That means he's not any worse than before."

"It means his immune system is still functioning really well and that he's not likely to get sick any time soon." He answered calmly. But there was, in his face, so much of heartache, she could not meet his eye without feeling the same wrenching within herself. Rising, she reached for his empty cup. She found when she was near him that she had grown fond of him, and she touched the top of his head when she came back.

He smiled, settling back against the couch. Looking around the comfortable, close room. "I like your house. It feels like you."

She set the coffee on her side table, placed precisely where she liked it, and reclined in the chair. "When I was young I used to dream about owning a house, just about any house, that I could keep clean, like I wanted it. My mama was a bad housekeeper." She felt momentarily uncomfortable, until she looked at Ford again and noted the interest with which he listened. "We did own one for a while, too; my first husband and me, I mean. Danny's father. A little tiny house. But you'd have thought it was a mansion from the way we acted about it." She laughed softly.

"Danny doesn't talk about his daddy much."

"I don't imagine so."

"Why?"

"None of us talk about my first husband very often. I don't know if that's good or not."

Ford appeared to ponder that; then he looked her in the eye again. His face was very clear; she could read every thought in it. "On the way here Danny took me to a house. It was the only place we stopped."

She asked, a hush around her voice, "Where was it, do you know?"

"Near a crossroads," Ford said, "a little white house in a field," and stopped, looking at her.

"Harvey Crossroads."

"That sounds right."

She looked out the window, beyond the little scrap of front yard across the Christmas graves to the mausoleum, framed against apple trees. "I like to go for a walk on Christmas morning. Would you like to come with me? All you need to do is throw on a coat, we're not going that far."

The coats waited on the stand in the office; she tied a scarf around her hair too. When Ford buttoned the dark draping over his pajamas, she saw the presence of a younger boy in him, suddenly afraid to have awakened on Christmas morning in such a strange place. She waited till he was close and opened the door. They were met face-on by a blast of winter. "You might want a hat," she said, opening the storm door and stepping onto the gravel outside.

He produced a cap from the pocket of the coat and put it on. Ellen slipped her hands in her pockets and ambled along the edge of the parking spaces, in the shadow of the sycamore and pecan trees. Biting wind swept across the foil-wrapped pots of poinsettias, ripping leaves from plants, sending them tumbling across the rough grass. Ford looked around, at the curve of road, the mausoleum and statue of Jesus. They headed for the far corner of the cemetery.

She asked, "What did Danny tell you about that house?"

"Not much," Ford said. "We walked around inside."

She could hear his hesitation. From his reticence, his air of vague fear, she gathered he lived with Danny in uneasy truce, and this thought disturbed her. For the first time, on the walk, she studied his anxious expression. "He wouldn't tell me anything about the place, except that his father killed a dog there."

Striding to the edge of the narrow ditch that separated the Gardens of Calvary from the apple orchard, she reached for Ford's hand. He supported her as she took the long step.

They walked in silence across the sparse, brown grass, along the soft mulch of rotting leaves and occasional apple husks, shadows tracing their faces. She felt him waiting for her to go on talking, and chose her words carefully. "Danny was eight years old when we lived in that house. We didn't live there long. But I guess he would remember it pretty strong." Pause. "That was one of the worst times for fighting. My husband, Danny's daddy, hadn't been drinking for a while but he started up again. And around Thanksgiving we had a big fight, him and me." Near the center of the orchard, she pulled the coat close against her. Letting him know, by her hesitation, that she wished to refrain from stating the cause of the fight. "It was a bad fight, and it went on for three or four days, and Bobjay started drinking again. And in the middle of it he chased me out into the woods. He was so drunk he couldn't follow me. This was at night, and all the children had run out after me too. I think it had snowed. Anyway," shoving her arms to the bottom of the coat, "he couldn't get to me but this dog come up to him and he killed the dog. It was a mongrel the children had taken up, I couldn't stand the mutt myself. But he killed it."

She saw by Ford's face that this was enough, that this story explained the house to his satisfaction, and she paused. Powerfully tempted to say no more.

"How did he kill it?"

"He had a butcher knife," she said, matter-of-factly. "He was chasing me with it."

"And your kids were right there."

"Oh, yes."

Shock registered on his face. Again she felt convinced that she could stop the story here if she wished. The rest would be hard to get out. But Ford's earnestness, and the discomfort she had felt, when she wondered whether Ford would stay with Danny, made her pause. She asked, "Are you and Danny having a hard time?"

The question surprised them both, Ellen more than Ford, when she heard its echo and realized how easily it had crossed her lips.

He considered his answer, and they wandered toward the edge of the orchard, a field which had once been farmland but which recently had been sold to a large corporation. Soybean remains rattled. Each moment the sky became a fiercer blue.

"There's some way he's afraid of me that I don't understand. Like in that house, the one he took me to see. When I found him in that bedroom, crying. And he wouldn't say why, and I was scared to ask."

"Which bedroom?" she asked, finally facing the moment, her voice suddenly small.

"The one at the front. The floor's fallen through now."

She gazed across the bare field, almost seeing the house herself, like an island under a canopy of trees within the sea of plowed ground, and the small figure of her son, her oldest boy, at the edge of the trees, vanishing toward the river.

"A bad thing happened to Danny in that room," she began, and then fell silent again. Ford waited. She said, "Maybe he'll tell you about it one of these days."

"What happened?"

She shook her head, and said nothing else. She stepped toward the interior of the orchard as if reaching for the protection of the trees. She heard the sound of his footsteps. She refused to look at his face.

They walked slowly through the orchard, and Ford slid his arm around her shoulders. She found herself curiously glad of the touch; though she was also glad, a few moments later, when he knew to withdraw the embrace.

<hr />

Once across the ditch, they approached the corner of the mausoleum, and she knelt at the lower tier of graves.

The mausoleum itself rose about as high as Ford's shoulders, faced with turquoise-veined marble. Christ knelt in prayer on the top. The structure gave an impression of compactness and starkness, with its backdrop of leafless trees and vases full of Christmas flowers.

On the lowest grave, near which Ellen knelt, a small Christmas tree rested in the bronze flower stand, a perfect miniature fir with tiny decorations. She touched the tree lovingly, glad to see that the wind had spared it any damage.

When she looked up at Ford, he was reading the name on the bronze marker, and she watched as the realization penetrated him slowly. Grover Douglas Crell.

"This was your youngest son."

She answered, without rancor, "He still is."

"I'm sorry. Yes." He met her eye. "I guess I never stopped to think he would be out here."

She kept her voice in a gentle range of tones, though as always, when she knelt near this particular spot, her head was full of screaming. "I couldn't put him in the ground." Standing, she smoothed her coat again. "This is why I go for a walk on Christmas morning," she continued. "I only stay for a minute."

She had kept control of her breathing and now sighed, deeply. Linking arms with Ford, feeling sudden affection, they headed inside.

<hr>

In the house they were greeted by the rush of air through the furnace. Ray stirred in the kitchen. Ellen, untying the scarf, peered at him. "We were out at the mausoleum."

"I saw you," Ray said, in a morning voice, "I got up after you went out."

"I wanted you to stay in bed."

Ray shuffled into the living room in his slippers, passing Ellen, kissing her cheek dryly. "This is good coffee. Merry Christmas."

"Merry Christmas," Ford said. "You should have got up and walked with us."

"It's too cold to be walking around. And Ellen is so stingy she won't turn up the heat in the morning, so I got to spare myself the best I can."

"That's right. I like to keep him with a little bit of a chill on him." Laughing, she moved into her kitchen.

A moment later, the bedroom door opened, and Danny emerged, scratching his head. He said good morning and kissed her cheek in much the same manner as Ray had. She felt his reticence and thought of what Ford had told her, directly and indirectly.

"You guys have been up for a while."

"Ford and me already went for a walk." She set a cup in front of him.

"That's fine, as long as you don't try to drag me out there in this cold, not this time of day."

Ford loomed in the doorway. "Listen to him, like a little bit of cold would shrivel him up. What are you doing out of bed so early, old man?"

Danny reddened slightly. "Have we heard from Amy yet? Is Jason awake?"

They drove to Wickham to see. Amy lived in a small apartment at the back of a large house on the outskirts of town, a neighborhood called Piney. Winter-wrapped children played in brown yards, a tiny girl in a blue parka on a bike with training wheels, a teenage boy with a kite and no wind, a father and son with walkie-talkies, antennae shivering. Amy met them at the door, her own pink, quilted housecoat buttoned to the neck. Cigarette waving she said, "I didn't even call you, I knew you'd be showing up over here pretty soon."

Ellen laughed. "Is he awake?"

"Lord, yes. He's been up about an hour, and he's about to bust. Hey, Ford. Hey, Danny. Merry Christmas."

Jason, still rubbing his eyes, gazed solemnly as they entered. When he saw Ellen, he announced, "Nanna, I got everything."

They headed to the other room, where Jason steered his electric race car on its first lap around the track. Ellen arranged herself comfortably on the couch, sweater riding her shoulders, and she became the grandmother, fondly watching her daughter, her son, her daughter's son. Her son's friend. Out loud, she appreciated Jason's talent as a race car driver; she occasionally received a "Look, Nanna," and dutifully looked. Danny held Jason in his lap, patiently teaching him the ins and outs of steering, as Jason raced his red car against Ford's black one. She found she had sat on one of his toys, a superhero doll, and when she asked him what it was he said, "Kattermarroons," or some word that sounded to her like "Kattermarroons," and so she was allowed to nod in that slightly bewildered way; she was the grandma, she was supposed to ask what it was, she was supposed to be bewildered. And she was, most of all, by her son, who could hardly look his friend in the eye.

At the cemetery, a vapor trail vanished upward from the furnace flue, and in the front yard Ray puttered in fur-lined slippers, wrapped in his winter coat. Poinsettia pots had overturned throughout the memorial garden, and he held two of the damaged pots aloft toward her. "The wind broke the flowers off. It's gusting pretty good out here."

"Which ones were they?"

"Willis Palmer and the little Harvey girl."

"The wind gets pretty bad over there because there's no hedge. You should let me plant some hedge like I want to."

The family opened gifts that ran the gamut of the expected. Danny needed disks for his computer and got two boxes. Amy liked gold chains, and Danny and Ellen had bought her one. Ray could always use another tool for his woodshop and received two this year.

But this year there were Ford's gifts as well, lavish by family standards, though no one said a word. In fact, Ellen found herself only mildly surprised at the cashmere sweater for Amy, the silver pen for Ray, the He-Man castle for Jason; and the lovely wool jacket in the box marked with her name surprised her in a pleasing if uncertain way.

The discomfort of the moment might have passed quickly if she had not noticed Danny's uneasiness. She lay the jacket tenderly across the back of the couch, and Danny rose from his seat, ostensibly for coffee since he carried his cup; but Ford watched him leave.

———⊶⊷———

When the phone rang, as she fried the last of the breakfast ham, the sound of another son's distant voice disarmed her completely. Duck said, "Hey, Mom, I bet you can't guess who this is," and she felt warmth flood her and sat down at once.

"Duck, my God."

"You didn't think I'd call, did you? I must've scared you better than I thought." His deep voice, resembling so much the gravelly tones of his father, raised the hair on the back of her neck.

"You scared me pretty good, all right. I wish you were here."

"Let's don't start about that," he said. "Did everybody else get there?"

"Allen hasn't come yet, but he should be on his way by now. Him and Cherise are driving from Asheville. You know they live in Asheville now."

"No, I didn't know that. How's Jason?"

She laughed and said, "I'm surprised you can't hear him. He's playing in the other room. He's had him a big Christmas so far."

"I ordered him a little Indian poncho out of a catalog,

but I didn't do it till yesterday, so God knows when he'll get it."

She pressed the receiver against her ear so hard it hurt. The hollow sound of distance had begun to swallow his voice. "Are you going to do anything special for Christmas? Do you have someplace to eat?"

"Oh, yeah. I got friends out here. Don't worry about me. I even got me a Christmas card, from my job. I'm having me a big old time."

"I'm glad you won't be by yourself." She felt herself begin to dissolve a little. "Where are you? Are you still in that place in New Mexico?"

"That's right."

"But you won't give me your address."

"Mama, now let's don't start all that. All right?" The line went silent for a moment. "I better go, before I run up this phone bill. It ain't mine. Now look, Merry Christmas and all that stuff. All right? I'll talk to you soon." He sounded suddenly a little sad himself.

"Please call me soon."

"I will."

She knew she would like to cry and refused to allow herself the luxury. The others appeared in the doorway, apparently drawn by the sound of her voice and the silence surrounding the conversation. Ray asked, "Was that Duck?"

"That was him."

"I told you he would call," Amy said.

"I need to sit still for a minute."

"I don't think he's in New Mexico," Danny said, "not calling this early."

Ellen laughed. "That's exactly what I was thinking—you're suspicious like I am." Standing, surveying them all, and neatly flipping the ham in the frying pan. "Now you all go about your business, I'm not going to have a fit or anything."

On Christmas morning, as she had for years in kitchens in many houses, she prepared turkey, dressing, pies, gravies, and the veil to the past thinned. Today she knew she was in the kitchen of the house at the back of the Gardens of Calvary (she never called it anything but a house), but at certain moments she went hazy on the year. Or, with her hand plunged deep into the turkey, she went blurry on which kitchen counter it was; maybe she stood at the steel sink in the house behind the restaurant in Potter's Lake, or maybe in the little yellow house beside the railroad depot and the dock where the lime barges loaded.

A Brunswick stew recipe from her mother-in-law, Mrs. Crell, two pages of close, faded writing on yellowed paper, neat letters not very well practiced, recorded either by the mother-in-law herself or by one of her daughters, and gravely handed to Ellen in the first year of her marriage, almost as a trust. Icebox fruitcake, made of graham cracker softened with egg and sugar, raisins, coconut, candied fruits, and pecans gathered from the yard. A confection like candy, and Ellen always remembered to say, "Danny likes this as much as I do. Allen likes it pretty good too, but Danny really likes it." While she made the cake, shaped it with her hands, to something that would fit the refrigerator, where it would set until Christmas Day.

At some point, she also said, "When I was little, I swore my children would have better Christmases than I did." The audience for this one did not matter as much. But she said it.

After she had been cooking for a while, she sat on the sofa next to Amy and closed her eyes. A feeling of peace rose in her like a tide, the sounds of her children, the gentleness of the day.

"Poor Mama, all she ever does is cook," Amy said.

"I'm all right." Then she drifted again, feeling Amy pass by, her voice added to those in the inner room, hearing something like *Nanna and Grandpa are asleep out there, don't make too much noise,* and the low muttering of the television, the distant calls of birds.

Her inner clock notified her when the rest must end. The kitchen awaited her as she had left it, oven ablaze, cooking utensils laid out on the counters, chopping block carefully cleaned. From the television in the outer room came the music of the holiday. Ellen sang along with the carol in a low tone, occasionally studying the highway to determine whether Allen was on it. The kitchen brightened with the lengthening of day. The angle of light, the image of the cemetery beyond the window, and the vision of her hands, preparing food as she had done all her life;

all was peaceful, as far as she could tell. The boys built their tower of plastic blocks; Amy smoked and day-dreamed; Ray absorbed television. Whatever Danny felt, he kept hidden, as he had always done. Soon Allen and Cherise arrived, and the house felt full and noisy. Allen Crell was the handsomest of her sons, with his father's strong build and square-boned face; his hair was lighter and finer than Danny's, his body thicker, his skin coars-ened by golf-course sun. As a branch manager for a bank, he carried himself with the air of a squire. Cherise was a perfect match for him, fresh and pretty. Once introduc-tions were made, Allen asked, in his booming voice, "Mama, are you cooking? You better be."

Amy and Cherise set the table. The good Lenox china she had bought herself was handed out of the cabinet carefully. The pair had set her table before and did a fair job, using cloth napkins and good stainless flatware, and when she inspected their work she thought the table looked pretty, even though the dinner plates were a trifle large.

"There's plenty of room," Cherise said, using her sweetest voice. "We're all family." Though she said this with a hair of hesitation.

"That's right, we're all family," Amy agreed. "We'll sit on top of each other."

Meanwhile Ellen brewed tea, checked the progress of the dressing, transferred food to serving dishes and, when all was ready, retrieved the last items baking in the oven. At the last moment she scanned the kitchen, which was soon to become a dining room, and with that in mind she covered the stove burners with their metal covers, changed dirty kitchen towels for clean ones, fluffed the curtains at the windows, and, briefly, opened the back door to clear the air.

The arrangement of bodies at the table became, with the addition of Allen and Cherise, even more ludicrous than the night before. Serving would have deteriorated into a total comedy except that Ellen had already anticipated the difficulty and simply served everyone herself.

The men finished their meal first and departed from the table, while the women lingered over smidgens of collards and stuffing with gravy. Danny appeared at a loss as to where he fit, and drifted somewhere between. Finally he came to rest leaning in the doorway beside the refrigerator.

He had the look on his face which she remembered most clearly from his boyhood—a layer of calm over a layer of fear, and the sense that even when motionless he was attempting to recede. She stood beside him and slipped her arm around his waist. He acknowledged her presence, but his attention remained focused on his brother, Allen, beside Ford in the living room.

"Seems odd." He spoke in a tone meant to reach only as far as her hearing. "Doesn't it?"

"It's what you wanted," she said.

"Oh, yes. I know that."

From the couch, Allen said, "What are you two talking about up there?"

"None of your business. I have secrets with Danny just like I have secrets with you."

"Well I guess it's all right then." Allen smoothed hair that had strayed over his forward bald spot. "At least you finally got out of that kitchen."

Ford said, "My mother doesn't cook on Christmas, but that's probably just as well."

Allen laughed. Ellen said, "Ford, you shouldn't talk about your mother like that."

"Oh, it's true. I love her to death, but the only meal she cooks is Christmas breakfast, and that's enough."

"Do you have somebody who cooks for you?" Allen asked, then grimaced and amended, "I mean, does your mama have somebody who cooks for her?"

"Yes, she does, thank God." General laughter.

"Is that true?" Allen asked, turning to Danny, "Does she really cook that bad?"

The question hovered in all innocence through the silence that followed. "I don't know." Danny's air, as he spoke, communicated much more.

Ford said, "They've never met," in a small voice.

The awkward moment passed. Ford and Allen returned to a discussion of golf, and Allen, who always traveled with his clubs, offered to show the set to Ford. They piled on coats and stepped outside and soon could be seen through the front blinds, Ford testing the swing of a club, Allen standing to one side, cigarette behind his ear. Ellen settled the blinds back into place. Cherise appeared in the doorway, asking where Ellen kept her little plastic containers, for what was left of the collards. Then she looked around. "Where's Allen?"

"Showing Ford his golf clubs."

Cherise eyed the doorway suspiciously. "Showing Ford?"

She found the kitchen mostly set to rights. The collards were hardly worth saving so she got a fork and finished them, solving the problem of the plastic container. Amy and Cherise leaned against the countertops.

"It just seems odd," Cherise was saying. "That's all I meant."

"He's a really nice guy." Amy looked vaguely irritated.

"Who, Ford?" Ellen asked.

"Yes, ma'am. I was just telling Amy that it sure seems odd having him here for Christmas. When it's usually just family, I mean."

Amy started to speak but held her tongue. Ellen studied Cherise. "You don't think there's anything wrong with it, do you?"

"Well, it's not in the Bible." She stopped there, abruptly. Amy and Ellen watched and waited, forcing her to continue. "It's Danny's business what he does with his life, I guess."

Ellen lowered her voice slightly. "I don't exactly know what you mean. We all got used to you when you were new."

"Yes, ma'am." Cherise swallowed.

Afterward Ellen rinsed dishes in the sink, stacking

them neatly in the drainer. Suddenly the rooms had the feeling of imminent parting, as Cherise, maybe angry at what Ellen had said, asked about the time and reminded Allen that they would need to be leaving soon, if they were going to get to her parents' house by dark. Amy noted that she should go home soon too, since Jason's dad was coming to pick him up. "I'm glad he's sleeping a little bit, I don't think he got a whole lot of rest last night."

Silence, rest, peace among the family and good will on earth, like a moment of carol. Only the slight irritation of the conversation with Cherise, and soon she would be gone. Ellen was satisfied. The rest was beyond anyone's control, as far as she could see.

Dan stood at the edge of the graves. Wind lifted treetops, leaves, and petals of flowers; wind tossed apple branches beyond the ditch; wind rushed over the length of the trailer. The long day nearly over, sun slanted from the western line of trees. Amy and Jason, Allen and Cherise had driven away, the family gathered in the yard to say good-bye. Mom still waited in the doorway, and Ford stood behind her, watching uneasily, as if Dan might explode. But he went on surveying the graves.

An ache in his shoulder grew fierce as wind poured through his jacket. The pain had begun in the joint early in the afternoon, for no reason Dan could think of. Some force had torn a tiny blood vessel somewhere in his shoulder. At first he had wondered whether the hurt was real or whether it would go away, but by now Dan could be certain he was bleeding. The muscle blew itself up like a balloon one blood cell at a time. The process would not stop until Dan took the medicine that enabled his blood to clot. Dan understood this as a fact.

But all day he had kept the pain secret, had even ignored it himself. Now, near sunset, it increased. But instead of heading into the house and asking for what he needed, he headed away from the trailer and the figures in the doorway.

He was numb inside. Hours at home, in the midst of his family, always wiped him clean of feeling. Today, with Ford, the process had become distorted and terrifying, leaving Dan no retreat except the coldness and distance that were like trademarks.

Kneeling at the edge of the mausoleum with his hand along the marble, spelling his brother's name with his fingertips, G-r-o-v-e-r. His brother inside the mausoleum, embalmed and silent, dressed in the blue suit that seemed somehow pathetic in Dan's memory, the country child in the country suit, broken and gone.

"I am not going to talk to you," Dan said. "You're dead."

His mother had told him the story of the miniature Christmas tree and the sight of it, poised in the bronze vase on the front of the mausoleum, made him heavy and sad. He touched Grove's name again, moving carefully. The cold of the marble raced through his fingertips and flowered in his shoulder, the pain from the hemorrhage cutting sharp and deep. He must return to the trailer, gather up the boxes of his medicine, mix it into the proper form and transfuse it into his veins. He must take care of himself. He had performed the procedure a hundred times but he could not bring himself to picture it today.

You should let somebody help you, Grove said. *That's all you have to do. You already know it but you're a chickenshit, that's why you're putting words in my mouth.*

"I said I'm not going to talk to you."

Silence. Sunset touched the earth with fire on all sides. Dan stood slowly.

Ford had moved to the edge of the yard and stood there. He showed his anxiety in the rigid lines of his arms plunged into the leather pockets. Dan felt the pull of that being, the hunger. *I will take care of myself.*

"Sure you will."

Mom stood in the doorway of the trailer. Her own anxiety was just as plain, though Dan could not have said what were his clues.

Turning to the grave a last moment, he shut off all the voices and sighed. Following the loop road, he returned.

———— ❧ ————

Inside, he could hear the low sound of Ford's voice, a vibration that passed through walls. In the office, Ford huddled over the phone, astonishingly small and fragile. "I'm sorry, Mother," Ford said, "we were busy all morning, and I couldn't get to the phone." Pause. "Well, it's not like that." Rubbing his forehead with fingers. "I told you, I couldn't get to a phone, I'm sorry." Ford closed his eyes and rubbed his forehead as if it hurt. "Mother, I didn't ruin your Christmas. Your Christmas was ruined a long time ago." Pause. "You know exactly what I mean." Pause. "I've had a wonderful holiday. His family is great." Swallowing. "No, it's not very big." Brows furrowing momentarily. "No, just the family. Dan's brother and his sister and his sister-in-law." Pause. "Well, I still don't see why you didn't go to Uncle Reuben's. But that's up to you."

He turned in the chair, and Dan ducked out of sight. His heart was pounding. He was surprised at the strength of his reaction. Ford was listening now, the tinny, distant sound of his mother's voice audible in his silence. Finally, Ford interrupted to say, "This is no use, Mother. Goodbye. I'll talk to you soon."

As he hung up the phone, Dan slipped away. Ford found him in the kitchen. A clock murmured behind him. Other sounds joined in the steady rhythm. Ford was scowling. Dan stood nervously to pour himself water; but when he rose he moved abruptly and pain lit his shoulder.

Ford asked, sharply, "What's wrong?"

The throbbing pain had yet to peak. Dan stood still and Ford faced him. Searching his face.

"My shoulder."

"Bleeding?" Dan nodded, "How long?" Ford slid his hand inside Dan's sweater.

"I don't know. I noticed it a while back."

"And you didn't say anything." Changes played over

Ford's face. Dan read his companion's exhaustion and sudden anger. "I can't believe you still do this as many times as I've yelled at you about it. You cannot let yourself bleed one minute longer than you have to."

"I know that, Ford."

"Then what is the problem? I'm right here. Your medicine is right here. All I have to do is give it to you."

"I know. Look—"

"Never mind," Ford snapped, "where did your mother put the boxes?"

"In the shop. In Ray's refrigerator."

The rest of the medical paraphernalia Dan had stashed in the chest of drawers in the bedroom. Wishing to be elsewhere when Ford returned, he headed there to fetch it. Mom appeared in the doorway. "Son, what's wrong?"

Small-voiced, he answered, "I'm bleeding in my shoulder," opening the chest of drawers, searching for the syringes, tourniquet, and alcohol swabs. "Ford's upset about it."

"Oh my goodness," Mom said. "Why is he mad?"

"He always wants me to tell him the second I start bleeding, and I never do." Feeling suddenly tired, he sagged against the heavy wooden chest, facing a picture of himself at eight, framed on the wall. Dan tried to find a position in which his shoulder would stop hurting. From the kitchen came sounds of Ford returning, large footfalls accompanied by the rustling of paper. Mom, over her shoulder, called, "We're in here."

"Did he tell you what happened?" Ford asked, as Dan applied himself to his search for butterfly needles and alcohol swabs.

"Yes. It's just like him." Her tone was mocking but gentle. "He never could pick a good time to get sick."

This, delivered in Mom's best offhand manner, quieted Ford somewhat. Dan and Ford faced each other across the room. "You didn't forget anything, did you?"

"No, I didn't." Stomach beginning to knot. "I brought three butterflies, I hope that's enough."

"I don't think I'll miss your veins twice."

Knowing no response would meet with friendlier reception, Dan remained silent. Ford sullenly watched him.

In the kitchen, boxes of dried blood protein sat on the table. The process of mixing medication to treat his hemophilia had evolved, for Dan, the character of a ceremony. He opened the boxes, laying out the contents —dehydrated Factor VIII protein in one large vacuum-sealed jar and sterile water for reconstitution in another. Ford joined him at the table and began to prepare the other box. Dan remained silent, puncturing the nipple of the vacuum jar with one end of the double-needle. A thin stream of sterile water jetted into the white latticework of the protein, which instantly collapsed into wet clumps.

Mom asked, "Do you boys have everything you need in here? Because I want to stay out of your way." Not waiting for an answer, she leaned from behind Dan to kiss his forehead. "I know you'll be fine when you get your medicine." She hesitated, then touched Ford affectionately as well. "Looks like you have somebody to take care of you, anyway. Your very own doctor."

In the quiet that followed, Ford's anger began to soften. Dan waited, the bottle of diluted medicine warming in his hand. Finally, Ford said, "This mess with my family is getting out of hand. I think my parents' solution to this is going to be to make me choose between them and you."

Edges of fear prickled Dan. The butterfly needle on the table caught his eye. "I think that's exactly what they're trying to do."

During the transfusion they hardly said a word. Ford slowly squeezed the syringe and the yellowish fluid vanished through the butterfly needle and into Dan's body. Dan always imagined he could feel the medicine as it circulated through him, awakening his bloodstream, filling him with well-being. Adding to him the one tiny ingredient he lacked. Ford removed the needle, careful of the drop of blood at the tip. He slid the plastic sheath over the needle and packed all the jars and wrappers neatly into the medicine box. His careful movements gave Dan a slight feeling of discomfiture, though he said nothing. Ford cleared the table, and Dan slid a Band-Aid over the needle puncture, pressing down to stop the oozing blood. They were done. His shoulder ached, but soon the ache would be less.

They moved to the outer room to sit with Mom and Ray. A slight coolness between them still. After a few minutes Ray announced he was going to bed, but Mom said, "I think I'll sit up with the boys a few more minutes." Ray vanished toward the bedroom, slippers making soft brushing sounds along the kitchen linoleum. Mom took the remote control from the arm of his chair and turned off the television. She tucked her robe under her knees. "How's your shoulder, son?"

"Better."

"Is there enough for another dose before we leave tomorrow?" Ford asked. "I didn't check when I was out there, I was so mad."

"There's enough."

"You were mad, weren't you?" Mom asked, chuckling. "I used to get mad like that when Danny or Grove would tell me they were bleeding. I would fuss and fuss and rush around, until finally I realized it didn't do a bit of good."

"I'm a doctor, you'd think I would know that."

He spoke in an almost surly way, and Dan realized he had forgotten the need for charm. Mom must have realized it too, because she smiled. Some troublesome thought came to her as she watched Ford, and Dan was afraid she was sorry Ford had come. But when she spoke, he understood he had guessed wrong.

"Ford, did Dan give you that present he showed me?"

"We traded presents before we came," Ford answered.

"I'm talking about the present he showed me yesterday."

Ford looked at Dan suspiciously, and Dan's heart began to pound.

"Good night, boys. Ford, make sure he gives it to you."

"What was that all about?" Ford asked, when she was gone.

Fear engulfed Dan and he stood. "I do have another present for you. I showed it to her yesterday."

He headed for the bedroom. Ford followed him there, though they left the door open. Blood rising through his cheeks, Dan reached for his bag from the shelf of the closet, then froze. Unable to turn. Ford said, "You're really scared. This must be something."

At first he could not find it, the wrapped box in the dark bag; then his fingertips brushed the paper surface. He had an impulse to shove the whole bag at Ford and let him fish it out for himself. But he saw Ford waiting. So he lifted the box out of the bag, sat down on the bed, and cradled it in his palms.

The marriage summit, as Ford came to think of it, took place the January after Ford's first night with Dan. Dr. and Mrs. McKinney drove from Savannah for a long weekend and stayed in Ford's guest room, a room Ford's mother appreciated very much since she had decorated it herself. Ford watched her unpack on the sunny Friday afternoon. His father roamed another part of the house, audible only by the murmuring of ice in his cocktail glass. They planned to stay in Atlanta overnight, then drive to Nashville for the wedding anniversary of a friend.

Mother and Father were at their most cordial, but something in their manner indicated to Ford that their enthusiasm for this discussion had waned somewhat. Ford himself had felt willing enough to listen to his parents when they suggested the talk, but now, faced with them in the flesh, he found himself sullen and unwilling. The fact of Dan had changed things in ways that Ford had only begun to understand. Watching his mother unpack, he resented the assurance with which she laid her clothing into the drawers of the empty dresser. She unfolded her sky blue nightgown and hung it in the closet. Surveying the Queen Anne bed, the Empire wardrobe, she smiled brightly, pleased with herself. "This is such a nice room," she said, "it's a shame you don't get more use out of it."

"I could get a roommate, I guess."

"You know that's not what I mean."

"I suppose I could open a bed-and-breakfast."

"Oh, Ford, stop. You think you're being clever, but you're not."

Father joined them, and the talk passed to more mundane topics, including hospital gossip and family news. Grandmother Strachn had fallen in the bathroom and fractured her wrist; her bones were slow to heal. "I hold Rose accountable," Mother declared, "and I've told her so. Imagine, letting a woman of Mother's age bathe unattended." Courtenay had indeed moved into an apartment of her own, and Mother found it lacking, though she had only heard it described. "Some little rat's nest of a place, you mark my words. Courtenay enjoys tormenting me with this low-class behavior of hers." She had finished unpacking, and the conversation had moved, by then, to the sun porch, where she admired the blooming of the camellias beyond the glass walls. "I've sent her some nice magazines with decorating ideas, but she hasn't said a word of thanks or asked for a bit of advice."

"Courtenay's got her own mind, Mother," Father said. "Both our children do." With a sharp glance at Ford.

They all understood the reference he was making, just as they understood the moment had come to have the promised discussion. But now that Father had come to the point of it, his reluctance became ever plainer. They lingered on the sun porch discussing Ford's suggestions for a dinner restaurant. Mother gossiped more about Rose, who had begun to date a man who worked for the Social Security Administration— "I can't imagine anyone more tedious," she sniffed. "He might as well be a grocer."

But finally, in the restaurant, with their dinner orders placed and wine in their glasses, Father took a deep breath and began. "Well, son, are you dating anybody these days? Your mother says you haven't mentioned a name."

The name was on the tip of his tongue and stayed there. "I don't have a girlfriend, if that's what you mean."

"What else would I mean?"

"I go out with friends. Russell Cohen, the guy I told you about—"

"The Jew," Mother reminded Father.

"Oh, yes."

"I have a few Christian friends, too," Ford added.

"Don't be a bore, Ford. I was only reminding your father who he was."

"We have Jewish friends too, you know," Father said.

Ford apologized, and an awkward lull ensued. A busboy filled their water glasses. Father became increasingly discomfited in the silence, and finally asked, "Are you still seeing your therapist?"

"No, sir. I stopped a while back."

This was news to his parents, and his mother stepped in. "You didn't mention this at Christmas when we talked. And I know I mentioned her."

"We didn't actually talk at Christmas."

"We most certainly did. I told you that I thought she was responsible for this whole attitude of yours, that you can drift toward the future without any plans or prospects."

"I stopped seeing her before Christmas."

"I thought she was helping you."

"She was. She did." He watched his father fidget with his silverware, straightening the knife and fork. "So now I'm cured, and I don't see her anymore."

"You should answer your mother's question and stop being a smart aleck," Father said, his tone darkening. "Was it all that therapy that got you so confused on the subject of marriage?"

"I'm not confused."

He laughed in a fairly sinister way. "Oh, yes, you are."

"Dad, I really don't see the point in discussing marriage when there's not anybody I'm interested in marrying, not right now."

It seemed to Ford, watching his father, that there was another part to the question, that the words were almost formed on his father's lips, a specific question with nouns and verbs, but that his father pushed it back. So Ford continued, noncommittally, "I don't know what I'm interested in that way, Dad. I'm sorry but that's the best answer I can give you. I don't know any women I'm interested in marrying or even dating, at the moment. Maybe that will change. Who knows?"

"How can you be so casual?" Father flung down his napkin and would have gone on but for Mother's touch on his arm.

Mother spoke more gently. "It's very hard for us to understand, Ford. We thought you were quite happy with Haviland Barrows, we thought you two were perfect for each other. Then suddenly you broke her heart and the story was all over Savannah. And you've never given the least explanation."

"I never loved Haviland, Mother."

"You said you did."

"Well, I was wrong."

"How do you know you were wrong?" she asked, but a shrill note entered her voice, and the question immediately embarrassed her.

"Mother, please."

They sat in uncomfortable silence. Except for Father's scowling, the dinner table became almost serene. When Mother spoke again, it was to relate a bit of gossip about the hard times that had befallen the Barrowses. Father allowed himself to be drawn into speculation on exactly where all the money had gone, and his manner gradually softened to geniality. The difficulty ended. But Ford understood from glances his parents traded that their questions about him had become more urgent than before. Only their fear kept them from asking questions to which he would have to give more specific answers. Sooner or later they would figure it out, he was sure of that.

Telling Dan about the conversation, Ford had found himself more confused and upset than he had realized, both from the memory of his parents' visit and from Dan's reaction. Ford told the story on his first overnight visit to Dan's apartment; they had seen each other only a couple of times and were still uncertain of each other. Dan thought the story of the conversation amusing. "Are you really that much of a coward?" he asked.

Ford felt himself flushing. "I'm not a coward. What do you mean?"

"Tell your parents the truth."

A knot of fear settled in Ford's stomach. "Tell them about you, you mean."

"That's one way to do it."

"But what if things don't work out for you and me?"

Dan blew out breath impatiently. "So? You're still going to be gay, aren't you?"

"I'm not gay. I never said that."

"Well, you may not be, but you sure fooled me a couple of times."

The fear persisted, and Ford fought off a feeling of

panic. "Telling my parents about all this stuff is not as simple as you make it sound."

"Yes, it is."

That he would insist in this way made Ford furious, and he spoke sharply, unable to contain the anger. "Well, I said it isn't, and you're just going to have to believe me."

Dan's eyes narrowed in anger as well, but he let the moment pass.

They avoided the topic of Ford's parents for a long time after that.

———⊶⊷———

In those early days, through the first winter, they were together two or three times a week, dating, as Dan called it, using the word deliberately, since it clearly disturbed Ford.

Ford's reluctance on that subject—the reality of his feelings for Dan—struck Dan as amusing. Standing together in line for a movie, or waiting for a table at a restaurant, Ford's stiff posture and glances at the rest of the crowd made it clear he was terrified of what people might think. Once, while they were waiting to be seated at a jazz club near Buckhead, Dan touched Ford on the forearm, a brief gesture but clearly an intimate one. Ford nearly jumped out of his skin, then blushed, and said nothing. He pouted for the rest of the evening, then, in the car, asked, "Do you have to put your hands all over me in public like that?"

"Like what? Like when I touched your arm?"

"I was so embarrassed."

"You reacted like I'd stuck my hand down your pants or something."

"What did you expect me to do?"

Dan chuckled, though the conversation had begun to sting a little. "Were you embarrassed when Haviland Barrows touched you in public? Or one of those other women you told me about?"

"You don't have to make a big deal out of this. I just think it's stupid when a couple is all over each other in front of other people."

"I wasn't all over you, I laid my hand on your arm for a couple of seconds. Maybe you should call that therapist of yours again. It sounds like to me you need a booster shot."

"What the hell is that supposed to mean?"

"Maybe you need some help getting through all this."

"Getting through what?"

Dan allowed a silence to pool and spread. "People are going to know about us, Ford. And I don't see anything wrong with that."

"I don't see why. It's nobody's business what we do in private."

"Oh, please."

"No, I mean it. We don't have to be a couple like that. We don't have to walk down the street holding hands and that kind of crap."

"Why is that crap?"

"Men don't do that stuff. Kissing good-bye in airports and all that mess."

"Why not? What's wrong with it?"

"It's silly. It's not necessary."

"You're just afraid people are going to know something about you that you don't want them to know. And you think I'm going to help you keep your secret."

Ford exploded, gripping the steering wheel. "Look, stop pushing me. Now I've told you I don't want you touching me when we're out together and I mean it. And I don't want to talk about it anymore."

Dan, furious, faced the passenger window and said nothing at all. They were silent the rest of the way home, and Dan slept in his apartment that night, alone for the first time in days. He could no more endure it than Ford could, and the next time they were together, it was as if the conversation had never taken place at all. Rather than provoke the fight again, Dan accepted the slight bitter aftertaste, and trusted time to make or break the rules.

It was in planning a trip to New Orleans that they discovered the argument about money.

"Buying first-class tickets is ridiculous." Dan waved airline ticket portfolios over Ford's kitchen counter. "Look at these prices! I've never paid this much money for an airline ticket in my life."

"I always fly first class," Ford said.

"Well, I don't."

"There's no room for my legs in those seats at the back."

"Well, you're crazy if you think I'm spending this much to go to New Orleans."

"I'll pay for the ticket. I told you that."

"No way."

Ford gaped at him, red-faced. "You're being ridiculous. I have plenty of money, I can afford it."

"I can afford it, too, if we buy tickets that don't cost my whole month's salary."

"Well, I'm not changing these tickets."

"Fine. I'll buy myself a ticket."

"In coach?"

"Yes."

"But then we can't sit together."

Dan shrugged again.

"But I've already bought you this ticket."

"I'm sure you can get your money back. And this way you won't get embarrassed that people might think we're actually traveling together."

Gorges rising, they glared at each other. Ford, stunned speechless, slammed the ticket on the counter and stalked away.

So they flew to New Orleans in separate cabins on the same plane, Ford sipping his first-class cocktail while Dan drank a free soda from the drink cart. The separation brought a coolness between them that lasted through their first night in the hotel.

Waking beside each other in the strange room, however, they thawed somewhat. By the time they ordered breakfast, the argument was forgotten, or at least sub-

merged by the fact that they were, after all, together in
a new place. From the hotel they walked down Bourbon
Street, past T-shirt shops, oyster bars, strip joints closed
for the morning; past yellow carts shaped like hot dogs
and Takee-Outee stands where the egg rolls dripped with
southern grease. In the lower Quarter they found several
gay bars, all of which Ford refused to enter, and one gay
disco frequented by hustlers and transvestites, some of
whom appeared to have been hanging around the dance
floor since the night before. Dan persuaded Ford to enter
by going inside himself, and they ordered morning drinks,
and watched the flashing lights of the mostly empty dance
floor. They spent an uncomfortable few minutes at the bar,
Ford laughing outright when Dan asked whether he
wanted to dance. "No way," Ford said, "you'll never get me
out there in front of all these people."

"Why not?"

"Are you crazy? I can't dance."

"Not even drunk?"

"No way."

Dan eyed him sullenly, unconvinced; then he let the
subject drop. They left soon after, when the bartender sidled up to Ford across the bar and started to flirt with
him so openly that a visible blush rose up from Ford's
collar like a tide. Dan hardly knew whether to be jealous
of the bartender or amused at Ford's discomfiture.

For the rest of the trip they spent their time in the
places where heterosexuals drank and ate, leaving Dan
with the feeling that he had crashed a fraternity mixer or

a Shriners' meeting. They watched an early Mardi Gras parade, and begged for beads and doubloons with the rest of the crowd. They ate beignets in the Café du Monde and wandered along the river walk, where the Mississippi River flowed muddily past, and they took a ride on a riverboat, listening to what was billed as New Orleans jazz. Now and then on the street they passed a pair of men standing too close to each other or holding hands right out in the open; Ford could hardly keep from gaping.

"There's a lot of gay people here," Ford said.

"No shit," Dan answered, but later, reflected that, for the first time, Ford had spoken the word himself.

Checking out of the hotel at the end of their vacation, they quarreled again about splitting the bill; in the end Dan paid his share and Ford accepted the money, mouth set in a stubborn line.

Times of awkwardness alternated with times of harmony, when it seemed to both of them that they had always been together and always would be. Their sex was like a signpost for all the rest: sometimes their bodies blended as easily as on the first night; at other times they met like blunt objects, colliding with graceless thuds and thumps. At such times, Dan's questions about Ford came to the fore.

"You never kiss me," Dan said, one day in late spring. "Why is that?"

"I do so kiss you sometimes."

"No, you don't."

They were lying on Ford's bed, the windows open, listening to warblers in the yard. Dan's question drifted outward and dissipated to the point that he wondered whether he had asked it at all. "Are you going to answer me?"

Anger settled as a stillness over Ford's features. "This is stupid, I don't want to talk about it."

"Do you think it's not safe or something?"

"Dan, please." Rolling over to face the window, throwing an arm over his eyes. Soon, as happened so often, his breathing deepened, and he was gone.

He fell asleep; he was tired. He worked long hours at the hospital, sometimes two days without stopping, or even more. At home, he slept. In the middle of a conversation, he lay his head on a pillow, and, as long as Dan was close by, he drifted away. Without a thought or a care, complacent, he slept hours and hours, and Dan sat there, maddened by the regular rhythm of Ford's breathing, wishing he understood why Ford wanted him there at all.

"Are you comfortable having sex with me?" Dan asked. "I was pretty sure you were, at first. But are you now?"

Groggy, irritable, Ford shook his head, not as if in answer but as if the question should not have been asked at all. He lumbered to the bedroom and lay down again.

"I need to know," Dan said, but his voice echoed and no one answered.

They talked about spending more time alone, each of them. Dan said, "What difference would it make? You're never awake when I'm here. Why do you want me with you if you're going to sleep all the time?" And he would go home for the evening instead of sitting in Ford's house, with Ford exhausted, snoring on the couch or on the bed. Dan would sit with his cats and a book and stare at the wall above the book and hold the thought of Ford in his mind, the sweetness of Ford without any verbs, any action; and late in the night there would come a knock on the door, the turning of a key, and Ford would slide beside him in his narrower bed and say, "I couldn't rest."

On Dan's couch, with the cats curled above him on the back, Ford lay his head on his arms and dreamed. The dreams became a kind of conversation; he dreamed Dan had died and his parents would not let him go to the funeral; he dreamed Dan had another boyfriend whom he liked better, who lived in a room in Ford's house that Ford had never seen before; he dreamed of a younger Danny bleeding in a hospital bed, and Courtenay stayed with him day and night but she would never let Ford in the room at all. He dreamed of Danny dead or dying in a hundred ways, and from this he might have understood something of his own fears; but instead he slept, and when he woke he worked to forget the dreams, to ignore them, to bury them out of sight.

"Do you think if you finish your residency you'll ever get enough sleep that we can talk again?" Dan asked.

Ford laughed and answered, "No, I don't think it's possible. I think I'll have to sleep for a hundred years or so, if I want to catch up."

"That's what I figured."

"Is it really that bad?"

"Well, you've been home for ten minutes and you're already nodding. I expect you'll be asleep in my lap in another ten minutes or so."

Ford stretched and tried to sit up in a more alert posture. "Is there something you want to talk about?"

"There's lots of things. The future. You and me. Whether or not you're happy. What to do about your parents. What to do about my parents."

"None of that sounds very interesting." Ford yawned and settled his head against Dan's shoulder. "Except maybe the future. When I won't be so sleepy anymore."

And settled his head into Dan's lap, a weight that increased as Ford's breathing deepened. And slept. While Dan waited and watched, loving the shape of his head, the curl of his hair. Loving the close weight, the near warmth.

Loving Ford became simple in the quiet, when Ford breathed in and out like regular tides, when his eyelids fluttered over his eyes, when his brow smoothed out like a child's. Lying beside him, or holding him in his lap or against his shoulders, or even watching him across a room, Dan could love him easily and without effort, as long as he was resting. In the stillness of Ford's house, in the closeness of Dan's, the feeling that was so precious to them both unfolded like a flower blooming, and the simplicity of their togetherness rose from the feeling like sweet scent. At moments, if he could have remembered it, Dan understood that their best place was this silence. Ford could love him more easily without words, merely with his presence. Words created the future, exacerbated problems, raised barriers between them. But in the silence of Ford's sleep, Ford could love Dan easily; in the stillness of Ford's rest, Dan could adore him without question or fear.

"I wish you would get tested," Dan said, in June as their first summer was approaching. "For the virus, I mean."

Their nights together had increased by then, till they were nearly always sleeping side by side. Their sex had increased as well, and some of the harmony Dan felt, in order to make the request, came from that.

Ford roused himself and blinked in a drowsy way. "Why? Do you think you've given it to me?"

Dan blushed. "No, I don't think I've given it to you. But it would be nice to know."

"You hardly ever let yourself ejaculate within ten miles of me, Danny. Where do you think I'm going to get the virus from? From kissing you? All you ever do is complain I don't kiss you enough."

"I would just like to know for sure."

"I think you should forget about it."

"Oh, sure." Pause. "It's just a blood test."

"Drop it."

"But why? What's wrong with my asking?"

"It's none of your business, that's what's wrong."

"Don't be silly—"

Ford gave him a warning look, and a clear note of belligerence crept into his voice. "I said, drop it. I don't want to talk about it." Then added, "For all you know I've been tested every month. If I get the test, and I think I need to tell you something about it, I'll let you know."

And turned his face toward Dan's stomach. And he slept, his warm breath filling Dan's T-shirt.

Ford could stay awake for sex, even after the longest hospital shift. He might fall asleep immediately afterward, but during, he had great stamina and attention to detail. They came to agreements. For oral sex, Ford never wore a condom; for anal sex he always carefully sheathed himself. Dan wore a condom whenever Ford touched his cock, unless Ford worked him by hand, in which circumstance Dan relished the touch of skin on skin. Ford, who hated the taste of rubbers, gave Dan fewer and fewer blow jobs as time went by, and Dan never asked why, since it was easy enough to guess. Dan was never the active partner in anal sex for the same reason: the risk was too great, in his mind. If they did not have sex before Ford fell asleep, they had it after. Sometimes Ford woke after a few hours of sleep, in the early morning or near dawn, and simply pressed himself against Dan till Dan felt the warmth and woke up. In spite of the danger, their bodies learned and remembered. Dan became adept at taking Ford's cock inside him, at moving his hips in a rhythm that could bring Ford close to orgasm or delay it in a maddening, electrifying way. Ford grew expert in touching Dan at certain points, drawing his nails along the sides of Dan's thighs or rubbing fingertips along Dan's exposed glans, and his reward was the shivering intake of Dan's breath, the sudden thrusting of his hips and a helpless collapse of orgasm that Ford was allowed to witness. In spite of the poisonous fluid, in spite of Dan's reticence and fear.

It was safe sex because they agreed that it was so. Yet it never quite felt safe. So they closed their eyes to any danger, and never, or rarely, spoke about it.

"I don't see what the problem is." Exasperated, Dan pulled away from Ford's bare shoulder, then felt the absence and hovered. "You're hardly ever here anyway. What's wrong with me going to some rehearsals?"

"We'll never see each other if you get yourself in another play."

"Sure we will."

"When? You'll be gone every night for weeks, you'll start hanging around with the actors, you'll be drunk when you do come home."

"I beg your pardon."

"Danny, you know I'm telling the truth."

"No, I'm talking about the coming home part. This is not my home."

Ford sighed. "Don't change the subject." He spoke using his tenderest tones, repeating what he had said before. "If you do this, I'll never see you. I don't like that."

"I can't sit in this house forever waiting for you to show up. You just fall asleep as soon as you get here."

"That's not true."

"It's true more than half the time."

But the idea had agitated Ford. "Please don't do this. Not this time."

Dan waited long enough to let Ford know he had

heard and that he was considering. "Why is this so important right now?"

"I'm getting used to having you around. I don't want to get used to anything else."

It seemed to Dan there was a threat implied in this, or a fear that was larger than the subject at hand. "I don't want to stop being in shows forever."

"Just now," Ford repeated. "Just for right now."

—— ∞∞∞ ——

At the hospital they had developed the habit of keeping their paths separate when Ford was scheduled to do his Grady rotations; so Dan was surprised one day when, after he had found a quiet corner of the cafeteria, Ford crossed the room with his lunch tray and sat at his table. He eyed Dan in a tentative way, with little boy eyes, wide and round. "I saw you and missed you," he said, his tone hushed.

A dozen sarcastic replies formed and died on Dan's lips. He found he could say nothing at all. They looked at each other and then away. "You look sleepy," Dan said, after a silence. "You were restless last night."

"Bad dreams," Ford answered.

"What?"

He shook his head, and they ate without speaking. But he had dreamed that he woke up and their bed was empty, and then he had gone looking for Dan but Dan was nowhere to be found: not in Ford's house, not in his apartment, not anywhere; and then Ford roamed the halls of the hospital looking for Dan, and all Ford's friends, Russell and Dorothy and everyone else, were trying to help; and soon he was close enough to see Dan disappearing ahead of him down long corridors, around corners, into stairwells. He remained certain he would find Dan, but he never did. When he woke, realizing with relief that the absence was only a dream, he nevertheless felt as if something had been taken from him. He found himself more tired than before he slept.

Finally Ford said, "I had one good dream, though. I dreamed you got rid of your cats and moved into my house."

This was a lie; he remembered no such dream. But the thought had come to him recently and had persisted.

"There's nobody in the world who would want my cats," Dan answered, and that was the end of the conversation. Though later, alone at his desk, Dan realized what Ford had suggested, that it was momentous, really; and all the more momentous for his having made the suggestion at the hospital.

"I like Dorothy fine," Dan said, "and Eva is fun. We're going to a movie next week."

"I know. I heard you ask her."

"Well, I need something to do all that time you're at the hospital."

Ford leaned back onto Dan's couch, satisfied with

himself. In Dan's apartment he always felt vaguely uncomfortable, the small rooms squeezing against his ribs so that it was hard to breathe. Dan eased against him, and Ford was struck again by the fact that he felt so easy with Dan today. Some days even the sound of Dan's voice came at him like a pressure, so that when Dan spoke Ford wanted him to stop speaking, and when Dan looked at him Ford wanted him to stop looking.

"Dinner was Dorothy's idea," Ford explained. "She's been talking to me at the hospital a lot."

"I was pretty amazed." His smile was warm and satisfied and made Ford ache, a little. "It's nice to be out with other people."

"Dorothy told me everybody at the hospital knows what's going on with you and me."

"I told you they would."

The thought still gave Ford a cold spot of fear in his stomach. But he closed his mouth on it. "She says we should live together," Ford added, carefully. "She thinks everybody should be like she is with Eva."

"She's like a little husband with Eva, isn't she?"

"It's pretty funny."

The conversation eased into silence. Soon they packed a bag with fresh clothes for Dan and headed to Ford's house again. But they were both aware that Ford had made the suggestion for the second time. Dan should move into Ford's house and they should live together.

<hr />

Dan thought about leaving Ford. Not going anywhere, but leaving. Saying, I don't want to see you anymore. We've taken this as far as we can, but I think it's time to stop.

Ford thought about leaving Dan. Going somewhere to get away from Dan, someplace like San Francisco or Sheridan, Wyoming. Saying, I don't think we can work this out. I don't think I'm sexual, really, I don't think I know how to be.

Dan became cold to Ford. Not in behavior but in his mind, in his way of thinking about Ford. He said, in his thoughts: You're a self-centered rich prick, and I don't need any more of you in my life. I don't need your glances of disapproval at my language, your contempt for my cheap clothes, your bad attitude about my apartment. What I need is a man who isn't afraid to love me, and you're afraid of me nearly all the time, in nearly every way that one man can fear another. He said, in his thoughts: You really aren't as bright as I am and that's a problem, and it isn't going away; it's a problem that will get bigger as time goes by, as you age and become uninteresting to me, except in the physical way, and I could possibly even tire of that. Tire of watching you take off your shirt, tire of the swell of your arms as you curl dumbbells in the bedroom. Tire even of that.

Ford became honest with Dan. In his mind, without words, he told Dan the brutal truth. He said: You're a killer and you're killing me. You have a poison in you that is eating me, too, and you know it and you don't care, you smile at me and ask me, why don't I kiss you? Why don't

I want you? And I have to close my mouth when we kiss. And I have to wonder whether you will want to make love tonight, or whether there will be a poison in your ass when I stick my cock inside, or whether the condom will be all right this time, or whether I will squeeze you too hard and you will start to bleed, and then I will have to feel bad because you are so delicate. You really aren't as bright as I am and that's a problem; you don't see the world as clearly as I do, and sometimes your breath smells good to me and sometimes the exact same smell repulses me. And I could possibly get tired of that. Of your fine-boned shoulders and your collarbone like two wings.

And they would wonder, without words, without sound: Why do men stay together? It is easy to understand why they fuck, but why do they stay together, what is the answer? Why do they live in the same house, share meals together, argue about money and parents, why do they have pets, plant begonias, bring home birthday cakes? Where are the children, where is the sense of permanence, what is the tie that binds?

Yet they slept peacefully, side by side, and the body of one became adjusted to the rhythm of the other, and the breathing of one slowed the breathing of the other, and they dreamed in tandem and shared fragments of each other's dreams, and they grew more like each other day by day, not in personality but in the fissures of the brain, because, seeing the same things every day, day after day, they laid down crevices in themselves that were the same shape, that were the same events written into memory, and this was enough, without words, to keep them silent about the fact of their hates and their fears, their deep concerns about each other, and the certainty that one of them would die first and neither of them knew which one it would be. The certainty that one of them would leave first, and that only by waiting could they learn which of the two.

⸻ ∞ ⸻

In September they planned a trip to the beach but, days before the trip, Dan struck his elbow against the corner of a metal filing cabinet. The impact caused him to bleed in the joint, the first time he had a bleeding episode in which Ford became involved. The effusion of blood was more severe than Dan at first judged, and the joint swelled badly and its range of motion diminished. Fearing the needed wait in the emergency clinic, Dan hurried home to his own supply of medicine, which he stored in his apartment's refrigerator.

It happened that Ford stopped by the Blue Ridge Avenue apartment building and knocked on the door in the somewhat dilapidated hallway, just as Dan removed the butterfly needle from his arm. Dan answered the door still holding a cotton swab over the venous puncture, and Ford noted the unusual pose. "What happened?"

"I have a bleed in my elbow," Dan answered. "I just gave myself medicine."

Ford stepped to the center of the apartment's living room, late sun dappling his arms. He had come straight from the hospital, as he usually did these days, and seemed to Dan once again grumpy and in need of sleep. "I can't believe you did this yourself and didn't call me."

"I always do this myself."

Ford watched him, shaking his head. "I'm sorry. I'm tired, I didn't mean to snap." Looking around the rooms, stretching his shoulders. "Could we go to my house? I need room to move. Maybe I won't be so grouchy then."

A moment's tension. *We never stay here.*

At home, Ford led Dan into the kitchen where the light was strong, sat him on a stool and carefully removed his shirt. Ford touched the bruised joint carefully and looked at Dan, the edge of anger returning, along with a glimpse of another feeling, a kind of anguish. "This has been bleeding a lot longer than an hour or two," he said harshly. "Look at this. It must hurt like hell."

"It hurts some," Dan said.

Ford headed to his bedroom still muttering aloud, "I can't believe you let this happen when all you had to do was make one telephone call," returning with a medicine bottle that he was in the act of uncapping as he walked. "Take two of these. You're going to bed when they hit. Do you want your arm wrapped?"

The careful tending was new for Dan and eased something deep in him, beyond the reach of pain or painkiller. He found himself suddenly allowing rest. Leaning against Ford, letting the arm relax. The narcotics soon took effect. The painkiller tinged the pleasant moments with a lace of surreality; the ache in Dan's arm dulled and became unmomentous. After a while, Ford said, "All right, bedtime boy, let's go."

"Where?" voice fuzzy with the drug.

Ford laughed softly. "Where else? My room." After a moment, "When do you need to take another shot?"

"Tomorrow."

"You have the stuff at your apartment?"

Dan nodded against his chest, drowsy and vaguely rising. Ford led him to the bedroom, pulled down the bedcovers. "Get in, before you fall down."

Warmth settled round him, a hand resting on his brow, and then the weight of Ford on the bed. Watching. "This is better than being sick by yourself, right?"

"Yes." Dan turned his face into the feather pillow. "I'm sorry."

"Don't be," hand along the edge of the blankets. "You'll get used to letting me help you one of these days."

Toward morning, the bleeding started again. Dan awoke to the certainty, a telltale ache burning along his arm. In the moment before waking, he could not tell where he was, whether he was in his own bed in his apartment, *whether he was in the Circle House, walking in the field with the sound of his father's voice behind him, and his shoulder was aching and he kept it a secret from everyone. He had awakened in the dark and his shoulder was aching and he was afraid to call out—his father would wake up and be angry and nothing would happen anyway, Dan would go on hurting, and if he moved too much, Allen would mutter in his sleep,* but it was Ford who slept, deeply, beside him, lost in accumulated exhaustion, legs tossed over Dan's, making Dan afraid to stir and, because of that, even more uncomfortable.

When the pain no longer allowed him to lie still, he sat up in bed with the blankets around his waist, holding his arm against his side, searching out the clock, which let him know dawn was close.

Ford stirred and Dan tried to settle back into bed, but his arm coursed with pain from the motion and he failed to restore himself beneath the blankets. Ford murmured and rose partly out of bed himself. Eyes opening, seeing Dan, suddenly his face flooded with consciousness. "What's the matter?" he asked, with effort to make words so soon out of sleep. He pulled himself closer to Dan. "Has it started bleeding again?"

He nodded. Ford moved toward him, kissing his forehead softly. The press of the body eased Dan's panic. From Ford he felt no anger. "I'm sorry to wake you up," he whispered, and Ford pulled him close, in a caress.

Ford headed to the bathroom. Light flooded the doorway and spilled across polished hardwood. Returning in jeans, he proffered a cup of water and more painkiller, sitting on the bed, light along bare shoulders and arms. "Tell me what I need to get when I go to your apartment."

Taking the pills, Dan asked, "Do you want me to go with you?"

"I wouldn't be giving you narcotics if I wanted you to

go with me." Listening to Dan's descriptions, most of which Ford already knew. "I'll feed the cats. I'm keeping you here today."

"I thought you were on call."

"No, I'm off the whole day."

He rose, dressed, found Dan's keys in Dan's pants. "Lie down and rest. Don't get up and try walking around, you'll fall flat on your face. I'll be back in a few minutes."

When Dan was alone in the dark house, he could feel the current of the painkiller rising. Dullness returned to the bursting in his elbow, the edge of pain vanishing; and dread returned, too, that he would drift into sleep and dream about his father again. He lay still and breathed deeply.

"Dan, I hate to wake you up, but I can't give you this shot in here."

Sitting up suddenly, blinking, he noted vague daylight smeared on the windows as Ford steadied his shoulder. Dizzy, the painkiller rushing in his head. Ford slid a loose robe over his shoulders, and they headed to the kitchen.

When he saw the large syringe and its familiar murky contents, he felt the slight panic again. Ford touched Dan's bare arm, seeking a vein. "Do you trust me to do this? I'm pretty good at it."

"I'll try."

The sight of the syringe in Ford's hands made him want to jump out of the chair.

"Calm down. It's all right."

"I know it is. I don't know why I'm being like this."

"There's two of you sometimes," Ford said, evenly. Through the painkiller, Dan felt distant surprise to hear his own thoughts echoed. "That's why." He chuckled briefly. "What would you do if you were by yourself? You can't give yourself a shot, not with your arm like it is."

"I probably wouldn't give myself one."

Ford nodded. "That's what I thought." This time there was no anger in his voice. The transfusion lasted till light seeped up the panes of the kitchen windows, the sounds of morning birdcalls reaching them from the yard.

"You're not using your arm till I say you're using your arm. I'm going to make you a bed in the den and you're staying there. You're going to let me take care of you. We can fight about it if you want to. But I've thought about it, and I know how you are, and I might as well start this fight sooner as later. Okay?"

"Okay."

"Do you want some coffee when I make it?"

"Yes."

By the end of the day he understood, again, how much his life had changed. All day he lay in peace, tended by the careful hands of the doctor, surrounded by the spacious, comfortable rooms. Dan bore it without protest. In the evening, Ford prepared another infusion of anti-hemophilic factor and administered the injection again, without objection from Dan. With, in fact, relief. "Residents aren't supposed to be any good at that. How come you are?"

"I'm good at a lot of things I'm not supposed to be good at."

———— ⚬⚭⚬ ————

A week later, with the arm healed or at least mostly healed, they headed to Grayton Beach.

Lunar Cove stood just behind the dune line. When they approached the house from behind, Dan thought there must have been some mistake. The size made him certain this must be an apartment building, not a house. They stopped at a garage large enough for three cars. No entrance was apparent from outside. Ford idled the car, "The realtor said you have to go in through the garages. It's for security."

"This is it? That's all one house?"

"Sure," Ford said. "It's not that big."

Ford, at the garage door, fumbled with a series of locks. He gave a heave and rolled the heavy door upward. "Remind me not to let you do that. You did pack medicine. Right?"

"Yes. I did." Stepping into the huge garage.

Ford tossed him the key and he caught it. Stairs led to the back door of the house. The lock turned smoothly, and the house opened with a small intake of air.

Afternoon light flooded a neat anteroom leading immediately to a broad kitchen, windows facing the dunes on one side and the parking lot on the other. The room outclassed any kitchen Dan had ever seen, even in houses where people resided year round.

Hearing Ford on the stairs, he went into the next room.

Broad windows opened onto the sea. Past the dunes azure waves were breaking, the white sand gleamed. Blue sky burned fiercely beyond the broad-beamed posts of a porch, beyond the carpet, the fireplace, the carved wooden doors, the staircase sweeping upward to more rooms.

From the kitchen came sounds of Ford's cautious entry. "Dan," he called, his deep voice echoing in the kitchen.

"In here." Dan touched the cool stone mantle.

Ford carried their luggage to the bedroom. The suite proved as spacious as anything on the lower floor. The same broad glass windows and hefty wooden beams. French doors opened onto a balcony, where they faced the ocean wind.

"How is your arm? No pain?"

"None. I think it's okay."

After a moment, Ford asked, "Do you like the house?"

"It's really something."

Watching Dan earnestly. "I wanted us to have something nice."

Inside, Dan opened his suitcase to begin unpacking. On impulse, and without stopping to consider his actions, he opened Ford's as well.

"What are you doing?"

"Unpacking you."

There was something touching about his surprise. "Why?"

"I wanted to do it."

When he was done, they walked beyond the dune line, where heat rose from the sand in waves. Blue-green water glittered all the way to the horizon.

"This is great." Dan turned from side to side, noting the bare expanse. "There's nobody here."

Ford gave him a playful slap on the shoulder and trotted toward the water. Wind tugged at Dan's loose shirt and tossed his curls to tangles. Feeling the sharpness of it in his face and the heat on his arms and neck, he closed his eyes and sighed. The surf penetrated his consciousness, soft-rolling and repeated waves surging one over another and whispering across sand. Shore and sea curving toward the horizon. He rolled up his jeans and slipped off his sneakers and socks. Nearly October, but the sun was still warm. Nesting his shoes in the sand well clear of the waves, he headed toward Ford, who was splashing in the water.

On the horizon along the beach, half-obscured by haze or low clouds, a city lay before them. Its glass towers gleamed in the color along the horizon, the flame of pink where the sun had begun to settle and refract. They waded past an abandoned sailboat, block clanging dully against the mast. Deeply tangled happiness and something else mixed strangely inside. "This was a good thing to do. I'm glad we could manage it."

"It was touch and go there for a while. Russell wanted

me to take his next couple of shifts. He's got a bad cold. But I told him he'd have to be a lot sicker to keep me from taking my week off."

"You're both back at Grady when? Four weeks?"

Ford sighed. "Almost six." Kicking at the water.

After dinner, they sipped armagnac in the broad porch swing. Spread before them were the glittering tops of waves, the carpet of luminous sand, the speckled backs of dunes, under stars and moon. He glimpsed a large, dark bird, escaped from the marshes, flying low over the water. Headlights swept past them as a jeep drove toward the beach and parked along the water's edge. Dan, in spite of himself, felt proud to display himself beside Ford on the porch of the biggest house on the beach. The liquor bit his throat with smoke and dusk. Each beat of wave onto shore released that urban tension. In the silence their bodies continued to speak. Wind blew out from land to gulf.

Helicopters patrolled the lower reaches of clouds along the shoreline, repeatedly, and Dan wondered whether some invading navy were poised beyond the horizon. "Must be looking for drugs," Ford murmured after the sky patroller passed ominously overhead. He moved his head against Dan's shoulder for just a moment and sighed. "We're the squires of the beach, you and me."

"What is Dorothy going to say when she sees this place? She always acts like she's in some kind of contest with you anyway."

Ford laughed, spreading his arm along the swing back

and pushing gently with his foot to make the contraption sway. "She'll go down to the realtor and see if there's something bigger she can rent."

"We should all go to dinner tomorrow night. Someplace up the coast." Adding, slightly sardonic, "Of course we'll have to take two cars. Dorothy's going to bring her little sports car too, I bet."

"Sure she will. What else? There's nothing wrong with taking two cars."

"Waste of gas."

"You sure are on my case today."

"I just think it's funny for you and Dorothy to drive your little sports cars, both of you, every time we want to go somewhere. She'll be trying to race you. Mark my words."

Ford chuckled. Setting his glass on the side rail, he scanned the beach as if to check for spies, then sprawled in the swing with his head in Dan's lap. Satisfied with himself, Ford said, "I'm not as scared as you think I am."

Their bodies became conscious of being bodies, of being together and of warmth kindling. Dan suppressed the thrill of fear that always accompanied this moment, the slight shrinking at the thought of desire; he traced the line of Ford's jaw with eye and fingertip.

A struggle played itself out on Ford's face, acute, hungry. But then he looked away, and the link between their bodies dissolved as suddenly as it had formed.

Abruptly he said, "Let's go for a walk."

Dan forced himself to stand at once, refusing hesitation. He told himself it was only his fear that let him hear anything ominous in Ford's tone. Ford's white shirt glimmered in moonlight. Dan trotted toward him through the sand. Ford had struck out for the darker edge of gulf, the opposite direction from their afternoon walk, and Dan caught him near the water. He settled his hand firmly onto Ford's shoulder and they walked side by side through the darkness, brushing against each other, aware of their solitude along the darkened strand. There was something Ford wanted to say. Presently he extended his arm around Dan, almost shyly. "There's no getting away from you, is there?"

The tentative question left Dan speechless. Ford continued. "I halfway thought I was bringing you here to break up with you. Either that or to make you move in with me, once and for all. I thought I knew what I wanted to say."

Chilling, even on the summer night. Dan forced himself to speak before ice took hold inside him. "You want to break up? Is that what you said?"

Ford shook his head. "No, that's not what I said. I mean, I can't help thinking about it sometimes." A dreadful pause ensued. "Do you ever think about it?"

"No." Closing his eyes, he suddenly hated the warmth of the arm around his waist. At the point of pushing it away, he felt Ford's arm tighten.

"Don't run away, okay?"

What surprised him was not the urge. What surprised him was the need to stay.

They stood in the dark, Ford's fear overcome by his wish to keep Dan close to his body at that moment. Dan's heart was thudding. "So is that what you brought me out here to do? Is that what you're doing? Breaking up?"

"No." Drowned in wind.

"Then why did you say that?"

Gripped by the arm, Dan wondered how they had both arrived at this moment, so suddenly. "I'm scared," Ford repeated. "That's why."

The simplicity of the statement disarmed them. Dan faced the waves, the shimmering undersides of clouds overhead, and he counted patches of stars in tatters among the cumulus. He felt himself more and more amazed, because he was not afraid. Even now. Even with all this reason. He could only go on being happy, that in the concealment of blue-black night they could share loose embraces on the beach, in the open. Ford allowed the intimacy to go on, and that was all that mattered.

"What are you afraid of?"

"You," Ford answered.

"Why?"

Ford laughed softly. For the first time, the sound lacked gentleness. But his voice, after he composed himself, was gentle. "You really don't know, do you?"

Draping an arm across Dan's shoulder, then glancing around. Too much light, he withdrew the touch. Then realized what he had done and put his hands in his pockets.

"Let's go back."

His suggestion completed the failure. During the long

walk home they kept more distance, as if each had grown more tender since leaving the porch.

Lamps threw trapezoids of light along the bedroom walls. Dan opened the curtains and sliding doors, wind flowing in curves through the fabric. He stepped onto the balcony. Out of range of Ford for the moment, he wanted to collapse, and the panic continued to spread inside. Ford unbuttoned his shirt and let it drop from his shoulders.

When they met eye to eye across that distance, Dan no longer lay out of Ford's reach. Ford stepped onto the balcony and stood near. The warm light poured over the curves of his bare back and arms. His presence indicated invitation, clearer than words but more dangerous. The wish to give in, to lay his hand on that shoulder's lush curve, coursed through Dan with an ache that made him tired. A hint of resentment seized him, since he understood the limits of the offer, that sometimes it offered more than it gave.

Now Ford watched him. Now Dan lay his hand on the curve of forearm, pulsing beneath his palms, and the contact evoked in him desire that was real enough. The bare body moved. Ford played out what he comprehended of the gestures of seduction, and Dan lay his hands on the large body of the boy and worshiped him until they were both aroused. No condom separated them that night; Ford would not stop to find it. But beyond, through Ford's heavy first sleep, lay the long stretch of empty hours, marked by the breaking of waves beyond the dunes.

Dan wakened after a dream he never remembered

afterward, but it had frightened him while he was in it. When he emerged into consciousness, light spilled into the room from the adjacent dressing room, and there he saw Ford's bare thigh through the doorway. An ache radiated from the room, along with the light. Dan sat up, sheets rolled around his waist. Slipping across the room, silent, he appeared in the doorway before Ford even heard him.

The familiar face, the tender gray eyes, locked onto Dan without surprise; within Dan the unstoppable softening commenced and he knelt. Ford lay a hand in his hair. "I couldn't sleep."

"I had a bad dream and it woke me up. I guess I couldn't sleep either."

"We're a mess." Dan could have predicted the next sentences. "I'm sorry, I didn't mean to scare you tonight. You know I couldn't break up—" trembling, "—I can't even say it now."

"Hush."

Shaking his head. "No. I can't do that either." Rubbing his eyes dry.

Clearly, he had been panicked; clearly the panic faded now that he was no longer alone. Dan felt the same ease in himself, the loss of terror from the dream, the certainty of Ford's protection. They rested near each other in the small dressing room. Ford asked, "If you were a woman, would you marry me?"

"What if you were a woman?"

"Answer me."

Dan lay his lips along the edge of Ford's knee, the light feathering of leg hair on the tip of his tongue. What a wrongheaded question, really. But he answered. "Yes. But I think it would still be hard to do."

"But you would want to."

"Yes. It's what I want now."

"Is it?" Ford shook his head. The motion suffused his body with sadness, genuine and bone deep; Dan pressed himself against the younger man. "I mean it."

"Then why won't you move into my house with me? That's what I want. Now." The words rushed out all at once. In their wake, silence.

Dan might have laughed; *but only a few hours ago you said you wanted something else.* "You know I can't move in with you and leave my cats."

"That's an excuse. I'm tired of hearing it."

"What would you do if I moved in with you? You're already so scared of what the neighbors think you won't even walk in the front yard with me. What do you think would happen if I lived there?"

As if each word were painful pressure, Ford shrank, as if he would like to disappear into the wall. They had reached this point of discussion before, hitting the same wall. *If we live together everybody will know. Your parents will know. Your sister will know.*

"How do we get past this?" And suddenly Ford felt tears coming out of himself, running along his face. "Danny, this won't last if we don't do something. If we don't try to live together we won't stay together. We have to do something."

So that was why they had come here, why the big house, why the public contact on the porch. After a moment, Dan stood. "Let's go for another walk. Okay? I can't stay here anymore. And I don't want to sleep."

On the beach, feet in the cool sand, they walked without hurry, unmindful of the hour. The topic which they had suspended in the dressing room of the beach house returned to them along the strand. "If I move in with you, my cats come too."

"Fine," Ford said.

They pushed forward into solitary darkness, a sense of peace spreading across their shores like an entering tide. They sat in the sand watching the water, Ford's head in Dan's lap. He let himself get lost, and this time, the weight of Ford seemed sweet. Water lapped around them near the end of its journey, sand streaming beneath them, drawing them downward, then streaming in to lift them again.

On the following Saturday, Ford drove a moderate-sized orange truck to Dan's apartment building. No more cracked plaster, no more little rooms, no more shabby furniture. What Dan had not packed, he had given away. Ford had asked Russell Cohen to come help with the heavier stuff, and by the time he joined them, the windows and walls were vacant. Dan cleaned the apartment while Russell and Ford hefted boxes and carried them to the back of the truck. Russell, settling a carton of paperback novels against the truck wall, said, "This won't take more than one load. He doesn't have much stuff."

"That's what I think, too," Ford said.

Russell stepped down the metal ramp leading to the truck, eyeing the October street, brown-green. Hemlocks flanked the corners of the yard. Looking Ford in the eye, Russell remarked, with the air of an older brother, "Be a pretty big change, won't it? Having somebody in the house?"

"It'll be a change all right."

"You ready for it?"

Ford shrugged. Later, he returned from the truck to find Russ and Dan talking, Russ saying something about having a yard. How much work it was. Russell had become an expert on yards since he bought his first house, in Dunwoody. Dan said, "I bet that's what this is about. I'm supposed to move over there and become the gardener."

Ford said, "That's right. Your new room is right off the garage. Didn't I show it to you?"

"That's what I thought." Russell hefted another box of books and headed down the stairs. "Suddenly this whole thing makes more sense."

The apartment became more barren by the moment. Boxes and small items of furniture, lamps and paintings, slipped down the stairs and into the truck. Most of the large furniture items, including the bed and sofa, remained in the apartment, Dan having arranged to leave them with the landlady—Ford's house was already full of much better stuff, as they both agreed. Dishes and other implements of kitchen life had been sold or discarded or would remain as well—Dan could hardly add to Ford's pantry. In the end, loading the van occupied only an hour or so, and soon every sign of Dan's occupancy vanished from the aging plaster walls.

Dan boxed the cats, and their frantic crying and scraping of claws filled the rooms. Ford stood next to Dan, studying the dappling of morning light through bedroom windows. "I feel like I already moved out of this room weeks ago," Dan said. Something forlorn in his tone.

"This is pretty scary, huh?"

"A little."

"You want to back out?"

"No way. Do you?"

"No." They stood carefully, neither moving apart nor together. Listening.

At the house on Clifton Heights, the unloading of boxes and furniture passed quickly, and when the last boxes rested in the floor of the storage room, Ford stood in the center of the bedroom and felt the change in his house. Autumn sunlight filled the rooms fronting the street. Had he never noticed this resonance before, the way the light shimmered over the polished furniture and fabric-covered walls? Russell opened the first beer, and Dan and Ford soon followed. On the side porch, in a neat wicker swing, Russell kicked off his shoes, indulging in the pool of sun that heated that part of the house in the morning. Dan sat in an adjacent chair, folding his legs into the cushions. Ford took a place next to him, not daring to look at Russell.

"You'll get lost in all this room, Dan, after that little place you were in." Even one beer made Russell jovial. "I always wondered what McKinney needed with a house this big."

Ford eyed Dan, a careful assessment. "I bought it to please my accountant."

"It's a beautiful place."

"I was right about the yard, though." Russell said. "There's a lot of it."

"I've mostly let it sit there," Ford admitted. "My dad and mom make fun of me. They can tell you exactly what's planted out there and what to do with it, but it all looks like leaves to me."

"I thought your mom had a gardener," Russell said.

"She has a Vietnamese man with a talent for azaleas. We have—they have—the whole front yard done in azaleas and oleander. You should see it."

Russell said, to Dan, laughing softly, "You believe this guy?" and to Ford, "You know we all talk about you at the hospital. Old Savannah. Right?"

"I know you give me a lot of crap. But I expect that from New Jersey types."

Russell gestured to Ford with his beer. "You had a pretty good rotation at Grady last time, my man. Dr. Milliken really likes you, talks about you a lot."

"Does he?" Finding Dan watching him coolly. "I had a good time at Grady. I'll be glad when I get back there."

Russell said, "I bet you will. If my girlfriend worked at Grady, I might get to see her now and then."

He delivered this casually, without any forethought, as if the parallels, in his mind, were exact. Ford felt, for a moment, as if he were sitting naked on the porch and Russell were laughing at him. But when he checked, he found only a sarcastic grin. One beer became two, and the day mellowed. Russell appeared in no hurry to go, and Dan encouraged him to stay with an ease that made Ford oddly happy. Something unsettling about it, yes. But he was glad.

Then Dorothy Ballard's maroon Jaguar motored up the driveway without prelude. Dan leaned forward, and for a moment reminded Ford of the mother in Savannah who surveyed her own territory from the porch with similar assurance. "That's Dorothy's car," Dan said.

"I invited her. We're going to have a party to welcome you. Eva should be here too."

"You didn't tell me anything about a party," Russell complained. "I could have invited Kathleen."

Dan was watching Ford. Trying to figure something out. Ford's heart pounded a little harder. He understood he had done a good thing, that Dan was touched. Dan turned to Russell. "Call her. Tell her to come on over."

They met Dorothy and Eva in the driveway, Eva embracing Dan, stroking his shoulder. Dorothy laughed and clapped Ford on the back, a gesture associated with locker rooms and fine fellows. He had a brief glimpse of how his mother might view the present situation, as if her son were moving among freaks and monsters. Dorothy read his thoughts. "You'll get used to it. I was nervous the whole first year Eva and I lived together."

"I know. I'm not worried about that." Ford gave Dan a guilty glance. "The house already feels different, like there's finally something in it besides furniture and me. I know that's the right thing."

"You tell your folks yet?" Dorothy asked, moving toward the back entrance to the house.

Ford drifted with her, answering, "No."

"Well, you'd better."

Opening the door, and remembering at the last moment that Dorothy did not like to have the door held for her. "I don't want to face my parents right this minute."

"Is Dan on your back about it?"

"No. I think he's scared, too."

"Dan?"

Ford laughed. "Yeah, I know. But he is."

Ford took charge of the November cookout, more like a day in summer he thought, lighting the built-in grill and cleaning the grate. Hovering, at various moments, near Dan. Eva and Dan were methodically laying out steaks and wrapping potatoes. The kitchen had taken on the kind of feeling Ford remembered from preparations for parties given by his parents. He was thinking this was now Dan's kitchen too, this was now a home they shared. In the closet in the bedroom hung Dan's clothes. Boxes of Dan's belongings were scattered through the house. The thought reached Dan. Ford kissed him without warning, on the mouth, in front of Eva.

"You two should do that more often," Eva said, and Ford, embarrassed, hurried out of the room.

Hearing Dan. "Leave him alone, Eva."

The mix of people, odd as it was, worked effortlessly, with Kathleen, Eva, and Dan singing old hymns as they cooked in the kitchen, and Russell listening to the Christian music with only slight skepticism. Dan's tenor and Eva's contralto made eerie harmony, hair-raising. Meanwhile Ford and Dorothy talked over the barbecue. The afternoon blossomed into something Ford could hardly have foreseen.

They ate in the sunroom, beholding afternoon across the backyard. The cooks were praised, and then Russell offered the final toast himself, lifting a beer to Ford and Dan. "Congratulations, to both of you," his face only slightly flushed.

Russell smiled and Ford shook his head in amazement. "Thanks," Ford said, and raised his glass. He turned to Dan. They were together in a room full of other people. The idea hardly seemed credible.

The moment passed in the general melee of cleaning. Near the end of the work the phone rang, and Dan reached for it and said hello.

The change in his face was palpable. He fixed his eyes on Ford. Dan said, "This is Dan Crell, Mrs. McKinney. I'm Ford's friend, we've talked before. He's here. Let me get him." Covering the phone with his hand and saying, with a warning look, "Here she is, my dear."

Ford heard the sound of the words but something in him refused to comprehend. He told himself he ought to take the call on the phone in the den but by that time he held the receiver in his hand already, and his mother's voice spoke in his ear, "Well goodness, Ford, it sounds like you're having a party."

Feeling eyes on him. "I have some friends over."

"That's wonderful. You never talk about entertaining, I wondered if you ever did."

"Well I don't, very often, but this is a special occasion." From somewhere, further words emerged. "We're celebrating because Dan moved in today. With me."

"Who?" she asked, and he could already hear the brittle veneer form around her tone.

"Dan. The man you just talked to."

"He's moved into the house with you?"

Take a deep breath. "Yes."

Frost formed along the telephone line all the way to Savannah. "I guess I'm surprised," she began, more smoothly. "I didn't know you were thinking about having a roommate."

The words seemed innocent enough, but he knew his mother. By now Dan had managed to start conversation, and Ford had moved away from the others. The hollow feeling swelled. "I haven't been thinking about having a roommate."

"Well what do you mean? If you haven't been thinking about it, why do you have one?"

"This doesn't have anything to do with roommates. I wanted to live with Dan. I've been asking him to move in for six months now."

She laughed uncomfortably, with a tone that warned him a sudden change of subject was imminent. "Well, son, I guess I don't see the difference. Now I called to find out when you're getting home for Thanksgiving."

"I'm not coming to Savannah for Thanksgiving, Mother. I'm staying here."

"Are you on call? I thought you told me you weren't."

"No, I'm not on call. Listen, Mother, this is a bad time to talk."

"You're telling me you're staying in Atlanta for the holiday."

"Why don't you let me call you tomorrow, when I don't have so much company?"

Silence. She could hardly object to that. "All right. Try to call after church. But Ford, I'm going to be so upset if you don't have a good reason. Thanksgiving is such an important time for the family."

"I understand that, Mother. But my home is in Atlanta. All right? I'll talk to you tomorrow."

Her good-bye chilled him, and dread of tomorrow's conversation began as soon as he collapsed the phone antenna and rested the receiver in its cradle.

Dan had led the others into the den; Ford could hear their voices as he entered.

Russell offered help immediately. Giving Ford a wry look. "For a minute there, I could have sworn you were talking to my mom."

"Really?" Ford tasted dryness in his mouth.

"Sure. My parents hate Kathleen. Whenever I say her name, my mother goes deaf." Embracing Kathleen loosely around the waist. "You can't let it get to you."

But the phone call had shattered the tranquil afternoon. Russell and Kathleen left after the kitchen was cleaned. Dorothy and Eva stayed longer, playing games of pinochle with Dan and Ford. The conventions of the card game eased them into conversation, and Ford found himself unaccountably more comfortable in the presence of the women and Dan. Eva, while declaring her meld for the coming hand, asked Dan, "Do your parents know you're gay?"

"My father is dead. But my mother knows. I told her when I was still in college." Across his face passed the look that always accompanied moments when Dan spoke of his family, a slatelike blankness. "She was fine about it. We don't talk about it very much. I told her about Ford, and she claims she wants to meet him, but I don't know."

Eva laughed with a soft throaty sound. "My parents had a fit when I told them about Dorothy. I had girlfriends before, but she's the first one I ever told them about. It was really stupid, the way I did it. It was on my dad's birthday. They threw me out of the house. So later I took Dorothy home with me. I didn't tell them I was doing it, I just did. And because they didn't have any time to get ready for it, everything went fine."

"More or less," Dorothy corrected, "the first couple of hours were pretty rotten."

"They were surprised. Then Dorothy started drinking Scotch with my dad. He was so impressed when he found out she was in medical school, he started to like her. He was in the military, but he always wanted to be a doctor."

"My mom was impressed when she found out Ford is a doctor," Dan said. "I guess she thought I would end up hanging around in bathrooms waiting for truck drivers."

Dorothy said, "My folks still don't like it that much when I bring Eva home. They don't know how to act."

Eva added, "Dorothy's family has these huge fights, especially when they try to eat a meal together—"

"I have one sister who's a fundamentalist choir director and one sister who's a schizophrenic with six children and a husband who can't find a job. The choir director hates me because I'm gay, and the schizophrenic hates me because my parents are proud of me. And I have a brother who's probably gay, too, but he's only fourteen and doesn't say a whole lot. So we all get together at mealtimes and scream and have scenes. Eva loves it."

"Truly," Eva said.

Ford felt himself conspicuous by his silence. "I guess my parents are beginning to get the idea."

"You think so?" Eva watched him. "Maybe you should spell it out."

Ford wondered, considering Dan's silence, whether he had put her up to this. As if in response to this unspoken thought, Dan said, "He's doing that already, Eva."

"Well it doesn't sound like he's making it all that clear to me."

"Everything doesn't get said in words." Dan looked out the windows at the lengthening shadows on the lawn. "Mrs. McKinney knows why I'm here."

This statement became, in some way, final, and Eva eased back into her seat. "I still think you have to talk about it directly sooner or later."

The card game continued past sunset but ended soon after, with the veil of streetlight casting pale shadows against the windows. The long day ended. Parting involved many embraces alongside Dorothy's sports car. As Eva prepared to slide down into her seat, she said, "Well, so now there's one more married couple in the world. Good work."

Ford found himself pleased and warm at the words. But Dan said, "We're not married yet."

"No?" Eva asked.

"No," firmly. "We're living together. In Ford's house."

As the car pulled down the driveway, Ford asked, without meeting Dan's eye, "What was all that about?"

"All what? The business about being married?"

"Eva was trying to say something friendly. You didn't have to contradict her."

Dan shrugged. "It's nonsense. You and I aren't married."

The words hurt Ford, but he shrugged and turned

away. "I guess I thought otherwise." He headed into the house again.

"My parents were married. Your parents are married. Is that how you want us to end up?"

Something in the words, in the callous tone, made Ford afraid. He tried to clear his head of the afternoon's Scotch and turned to Dan. "And why is this my house?"

The catch in his voice must have warned Dan that this was, in fact, the more important question. "You're paying for it."

"It's our house. We live in it."

Dan shook his head. "Your name is on the deed. I'm living with you. I'm paying you rent."

"I never said a word about rent—"

"I know you didn't. But I'm going to pay. I'm not going to live here for nothing. That isn't fair to you, and I wouldn't know how to deal with it."

"What do you mean, fair to me? When you want to know what's fair to me, why don't you ask me? I have plenty of money, there's no reason for you to pay me anything for living here."

"Of course there is. I can't let you support me like I'm some kind of wife."

"Why can't you?"

Dan looked at Ford as if he must be mad. "Because that's not what I am."

"Why do you have to keep saying that? Do you have to talk about this place like I'm a landlord?"

Dan turned, after a moment, and spoke with forced

calm, riding his own wave of fear. "I don't mean to sound like that. You're not my landlord. I'm living with you because I've never wanted to do anything more in my life. So I have to find some way to stay here, in this house. With you and all your money."

"Stop talking about my money!" The echo of his shout astonished him. He watched the color drain from Dan's face. Without another word, Dan turned and walked away.

Ford found him in the door of the library. The language of the man's body spoke of fear and refusal. "I didn't mean to yell."

"It's okay."

"But I can't stand it when you throw my money in my face. It shouldn't make any difference how much money I have."

Silence greeted this statement. Moving in the shadows, Dan switched on a porcelain lamp that flooded the immaculate room with light. Polished furnishings, deep-pile oriental carpet, ebony carvings, an old tapestry, all filled the room with their presence and dignity. Dan's gesture made itself plain. "It does makes a difference. I'm sorry. But it does."

"Why? I mean it, I want to know. Why should it make a difference that I have money and you don't?"

"Why don't you ask your parents? They can give you the answer."

Ford sank into the nearest chair, closing his eyes. Sickness filled him suddenly. "Why are you doing this? Do you want to ruin everything before we even get started?"

"I've tried to talk about this before. But you act like it's all a joke when I talk about paying rent and paying for my part of the bills." Suddenly the voice of melody became like steel. "I need to pay my share. Don't you understand that? Or else I won't know how to live here."

The ache swelled inside Ford. As suddenly as he had seated himself in the chair he hurled himself out of it and out of the room. Without intending any particular direction, he headed outdoors. Into the trees in the backyard he walked, beneath the mottled shadows of leaves illuminated by lamplight. He listened. Wondering whether he had come here to test Dan, to determine whether Dan might follow him. He heard no sound and proceeded deeper into the yard.

Even that late in the year, the singing of crickets surrounded him. Under the oak tree he cloaked himself in gloom. Balmy night air calmed him gradually. He watched Dan emerge from the house, wander to the parked car, step to the edge of the house, look down the driveway. Ford, breathless now, stood hidden among the deep trees and plantings.

The terror returned to him in waves. He pictured himself storming back into the house and throwing Dan's boxes, Dan's cats, Dan's clothes, into the yard. Words tangled in his head from an argument that had flown by so fast, Ford had hardly understood it. *I need to pay my share. Or I won't know how to act. My share.*

Then his mother's voice on the phone, *I didn't know you were thinking about having a roommate.* "I don't," he whispered, as if he were answering a question spoken only moments ago. "I don't want a roommate."

What do you want? the sound so real he nearly turned to find its source, be it Shaun Gould or Dan or Eva or his own conscience. *What do you want?*

Dan rounded the corner, heading for the back door. Standing in the doorway, nearly obscured by shadow, Dan called, once, softly, "Ford?"

He found Dan in the bedroom lying facedown on the bed. When he lay his hand on Dan's shoulder Dan murmured but kept his face turned away; Ford explained, "I went for a walk. To calm down."

More murmuring toward the wall. Ford touched the back of the neck, the tender softness. "I'm sorry we had a fight."

"So am I." Ford knew from the voice that Dan had been crying, that he was ashamed for Ford to see. Ford pulled Dan against him slowly. Dan said, "I don't know how to explain to you why this is important to me. I don't want you to resent me for living here, I don't want you to think I'm here because of money—"

"Hush. We'll talk about that stuff later. We'll do a budget and you can pay your share and that's that." Dan's grip on him tightened till it seemed he wanted to squeeze Ford inside his own body. After a while, Ford said, "I just want to make sure you're not my roommate. I want you to be something else." Which was as much as he could manage without faltering.

Maybe the evening would have ended on that note,

with their deep feelings once again exposed, with the link between them resonant and full. But touch and closeness led to more, and soon they were trying to make love on the bed, undressing one another carefully, with tenderness. Desire wakened in Ford slowly, and he felt a strange resistance in himself that he ignored, touching Dan as he had done many times, by now. Wanting and not wanting became tangled as their limbs. Ford reached for the condom, the constant companion of their sex. Tearing open the antiseptic pouch, he opened the slim plastic sheath. He looked at the flimsy latex with sudden weariness.

The feeling might have been as much alcohol and the length of the day as reluctance to clothe himself in rubber. But he held the slim plastic with loathing. Dan saw his expression and moved away from him. His face crumpled and he slid to the mattress, curled in a ball.

Ford hovered over him, numb and taken aback. The condom slid from his fingertips. Dan was hardly breathing. Slowly, tenderly, he eased himself behind Dan and engulfed the man with his body; and when Dan allowed the touch, Ford was flooded with gratitude. They said nothing. The limp condom lay among the sheets till Ford nudged it over the edge of the mattress.

The next day, in conversation with his mother, Ford held fast to his earlier assertion that Dan was simply someone he wanted in the house. But no further confession would come. The words *Dan is my lover* refused to emerge. Conversation turned to holidays and Ford explained he wanted to stay in Atlanta for Thanksgiving to catch up on his sleep. But he would be home for Christmas.

———◈◈◈———

Over this treacherous ground he and Dan marched through Thanksgiving into the Christmas holidays. The flu season hit Atlanta at about this time, and Ford's nights were spent tending the sick children of poor people, who had no choice but to come to the public emergency room at night or in the wee hours of the morning. When he managed even a few hours at home, he slept or grumbled about his need to sleep. How Dan felt during those days, Ford could hardly tell. His silence was fearful at times. At other times, it seemed Dan hated the season itself, and every Christmas carol, every Christmas tree in every window.

Neither man mentioned the incident with the condom. The subject remained too dangerous for conversation. Furthermore, for the weeks that followed, nearly everything managed to conspire to separate them physically, and a kind of grayness settled over the house. When Ford was at home, he found no evidence that Dan wanted him at all.

Two weeks before Christmas, Dan walked into an open drawer of his desk at work, bashing his kneecap, spouting an effusion of blood that guaranteed him several days in bed. Ford tended Dan as best he could, given the little time he had. Dan simmered, full of some anger Ford could hardly understand. Outwardly he professed guilt at the burden he had become to Ford, and inwardly he seemed angry at Ford's nurselike goodness.

Matters came to a head when, with Dan nearly able to stand, the knee bleed started again, with the joint still weak and painful. Dan tried to walk too early, lost his balance and fell. Knowing nothing of this, Ford returned to the house after midnight and found Dan surrounded by the paraphernalia of his medication: a tourniquet, syringes, jars of sterile water, and butterfly needles. Dan, pale as a ghost and near tears, refused even to look at him when he entered.

"What's going on?"

"I fell."

Fear and anger boiled in Ford, but he held his tongue. He counted five needles on the newspaper spread on the low table, each oozing blood. The tourniquet loosely encircled Dan's upper arm. But the syringes were still full of medication, and Dan's arm was a map of needle punctures.

"You couldn't find a vein, could you?"

"No." Weariness. "I'll try again in a minute."

"Don't be stupid. I'm here now, I'll do it."

Dan closed his eyes and tears drained along his cheeks. "I can do it. I just need to rest for a minute." A sound of desperation in his voice.

"Let me help you. Please."

Dan shook his head. "You shouldn't take the chance. You know how filthy my blood is."

Said in that frozen tone, the statement cut far deeper

than any accusation. The wounded arm oozed beads of blood. Scalded, Ford felt the fury inside him mount to the point that he could no longer control it; he rose up from the couch and stumbled into the kitchen. He hardly knew what he was doing or which room he was in, but a sound rose out of him, an anger that made no words. Slamming his fists against cabinet doors, sweeping dishes off the counter with arcs of his arms, smashing glass and shouting, loud and uncivilized as he had never dreamed he could be, a shaking rage that left him crumpled against the sink.

Silence. He leaned against the wooden surface, the handle of the cabinet door pressing his cheek.

Then a sound, a stifled breath. Ford opened his eyes. Dan, trembling, clutched the doorway for support. Standing with effort but helpless to advance across the field of shattered glass. They watched each other.

"Go back to the couch."

"No."

"Get off your leg," feeling his voice rise, a note of hysteria.

"Help me," Dan said. "Then I'll go."

"I can't."

"If you don't come over here, I'll come over there to you."

As if to prove his seriousness, Dan took a small step forward. The effort seemed unimaginable. Bare feet landed near shards of china. Ford jumped up at once. Dan waited, holding the edge of the counter to steady himself. The swollen knee, bent so the joint could accommodate its wealth of free blood, shook, and each quiver registered as pain on Dan's face. Ford crossed the room, glass crunching beneath his shoes. He stood in front of Dan.

He could not recall so much tension between their bodies, not since the first day when he visited Dan in his office, after writing the note. He drew Dan toward him to support him; Dan looped an arm around his neck and across his shoulders. Together they returned to the couch in the den. Ford lowered Dan gently into the cushions, catching sight of the wounded knee again, and the arm marked with needle wounds, purpling and swollen. Dan winced when the knee moved wrongly, and pain brought sweat rolling from his brow.

Ford shook his head. "I knew I should have tried to get home today." The sight of the now-worthless needles with their oozing plastic tubes filled him with nausea. "Your poor arm. How many times did you try?"

"Count," Dan said, eyes still closed. "One more and I think I would have put a gun to my head."

Waiting a moment. "Can I try?"

"Yes," almost as a sigh.

Ford applied the tourniquet to Dan's right arm. He took no chance on the smaller veins of Dan's hand but inserted the needle deftly into the antecubital veins that crossed the inner elbow. Dan lay with his eyes closed, heartbeat subsiding. Ford mopped his brow with a cloth. The medicine eased into Dan's veins. Near the end of the transfusion, Dan asked, "What's happened to us?"

The question echoed. "I don't know," Ford answered. "I'm scared of you."

Dan laughed. "Tell me some news."

"At least we're talking about it now." Ford touched the tender flesh where the needle entered the vein. "What are we going to do?"

"Give up. Quit. I'll find an apartment."

The words had a finality that sank into Ford. "Is that what you want?"

The laughter pulsed out again, deep and dark. "No. It's not what I want."

Silence. The syringe had nearly emptied into Dan's veins. Last shreds of fluid eased down the plastic tubing, vanishing. Ford removed the needle and applied pressure to the vein. Tension coursed through Dan's arm, the whole body wracked with it. Ford found painkillers and gave him a dose calculated to break the cycle. Too exhausted to speak, they watched each other.

Finally the Demerol took effect and Dan drowsed. Ford covered the injection needles, one by one, and wiped the blood from the glass tabletop, carefully shielding his fingers. He capped the plastic tubes from which seeped blood and reconstituted protein, making the room less morbid. He swept the kitchen free of glass. Careful to make as little noise as possible, he mopped as well, afterward throwing away the mop head. The work took a long time. When it was done and he had gotten up as much glass as he could, he stood over Dan, who finally slept. No question, tonight, of moving Dan to a bed. Nor could

Ford face the bedroom alone. He brought a mattress from the roll-away cot and made himself comfortable at the foot of the couch. They slept side by side through the night.

———∽∾∽———

Dan's leg healed in time for him to limp home for Christmas, and Ford drove him to the airport. He himself had duty at Grady through Christmas Day but planned to fly to Savannah after that. Dan, still favoring the leg, packed clothing and gifts into a suitcase too large for him to manage with the weak knee, and Ford carried the luggage to the car. Only when he walked out of the house, suitcase heavy at the end of his arm, did the realization came to him that Dan would be leaving within minutes. He stowed the suitcase in the trunk of his car as Dan stepped carefully out of the house.

A pale wash of winter sky hovered over lanes of asphalt. They **rode** in silence across sweeps of freeway bridge as jets mounted upward into clouds.

"Are you okay?" Ford asked awkwardly.

"I'm all right." But the distance between them persisted, or so Ford thought. He steered into Short-Term Parking, found nothing, and decided to improvise; he left the slim car in an illegal space near a crosswalk. Dan would be able to walk that far.

When he switched off the engine, the sounds of the airport permeated the car. Dan was looking out the other window, jaw working. "Is something wrong?" Ford asked.

Dan looked him in the eye and lay his hand along the

back of Ford's neck, into Ford's hair. The sudden tenderness was more terrifying than any amount of anger could have been. "I don't want to go. It's Christmas and I want to stay here."

Christmas. Music drifted through the car, played from the radio of someone passing by outside the car. They sat until the sound faded. "I don't want you to go either. Why didn't we think about this?"

"I don't know. Sometimes I think we like to pretend we're not really together and stuff like holidays doesn't matter."

Cars passed in a steady stream. Dan's hand soothed his neck, tucked beneath the collar of his shirt. "I guess it's too late to do anything about it now."

"I guess so."

But they lingered anyway, until Dan said, "We better get inside. I've got a ways to go."

Even in that tenderness, Ford hesitated to kiss. They joined the crowds heading into the glass doors. Ford handled the luggage, led Dan to the gate.

"I'll call you on Christmas."

"After midnight? I won't be home till then."

Dan shrugged. "It's not like I'll have anything else to do."

"Things will be slow at the hospital. I may be able to get to a phone during the day. Did you write down your mom's number?"

"On the bulletin board in the kitchen," Dan said.

Ford sighed. Again afraid, in that public space, to do

more than embrace Dan in a brotherly way. Dan vanished into the jetway.

At home, Ford wandered the rooms like a bachelor. It's Christmas Eve, he thought, poured himself a drink, and sat in the den by himself. He was glad when Dan called from the Charlotte airport to say he was lonely. Glad again when Dan called from home to say he had arrived. After that, properly narcotized, Ford went to bed, the bedroom feeling hollow, the bed suddenly enormous. Ford wakened often to the shadows of branches silhouetted by streetlight, swaying in bursts of winter wind against the frame of the window. The quiet house unnerved him and he was relieved when the alarm clock rang, before dawn.

On Christmas Day, from a telephone in the doctor's room on the ninth floor of Grady, Ford dialed the number for Dan's home in North Carolina.

A rich, languid voice answered. Ford said, "You must be Dan's mom. You sure sound like him."

Her laughter had the same warmth, and the same edge. "This is Ford, isn't it? Danny said you might call."

"Yes, ma'am. I finally got to a phone." Ford suddenly felt awkwardness, wondering what she knew. He proceeded uneasily. "Sounds like you folks are having a good Christmas."

"Oh, we're doing all right," she replied. "Danny's nephew is crawling all over him with a truck and a robot.

He got a new robot for Christmas." She spoke easily, as if she had been talking to Ford on Christmas afternoons for decades. With a slight change of tone. "Danny acts like you're really a good friend to him."

"I'm glad to hear that."

"I guess you wish I would go on and get him, don't you?" She laughed and called to someone at that end of the line.

Warmth shot through Ford as he waited. Dan asked, "Were you talking to my mother? I think she's curious about you."

"Is she?" Ford paused, adding weight to the question that followed. "You told her everything?"

"Yes."

Danny acts like you're a really good friend. They talked a while, about Christmas, about the hospital. Relief underlay the whole talk; whatever had happened, they were together, anyway. Finally a nurse came to the door looking for Ford and the hospital returned to his foreground. "I can't stay on the phone."

"I miss you," Dan said. Almost a whisper.

"I miss you too."

"You're the one who said you have to go. I'm not hanging up."

Ford laughed, eyeing the clock over the doorway. "All right. I'll see you in a couple of days." He rested the phone in the cradle. Suddenly exhausted, as if he had run for miles. And promptly forgot to call his family. He phoned from his car, headed home.

This evening, he dreaded the empty house. Rounding the oak tree, he sat in the swing and let his heels drift above the grass. Tangled in the memory of his mother's voice, he let the familiar tones play in his head. *We certainly have a right to an opinion about someone your sister wants to marry.*

He waited in the living room for the phone to ring. Hoping Dan would call. But they had already talked. The phone was silent all night. Heading to bed, he curled into the bedclothes on Dan's side, as if he could find him there.

———— ∞ ————

The visit to Savannah became a decathlon of wills from the moment Ford's father and mother met him at the airport. That they both found time to greet the plane set him on his guard. In the car, the parents exchanged pleasantries with the son. "You need a haircut." Mother ran manicured nails over the nape of Ford's neck. "I always have to remind you. You need somebody to take care of you, Ford."

"A man needs something like that," Father agreed, "otherwise who'd put up with being married?"

Mother hit at Father's shoulder playfully, and scolded, "You would. You'd put up with almost anything for me."

Sheepishly Father admitted that this was so. They still loved each other, after all this time. Ford let the thought sink in. He said, "I take care of myself pretty well." Heart thudding, he added, "Dan helps out too."

Father asked, "Dan? Your roommate?"

Mother said, "A roommate can't take care of you the

way I'm talking about." Then, brightly and pleasantly, she changed the subject. "You need to visit your Uncle Paul while you're here, Ford. He's awfully sick, and your father says he could die at any time."

"Well, that's not exactly what I said, Jeanine." Glancing at Ford in the rearview mirror, Father spoke doctor to doctor. "He's got liver cancer. On top of everything else. You should see him if you can."

"Uncle Reuben is really upset about it," Mother added. "Uncle Paul couldn't get to the Christmas party last night, and Uncle Reuben didn't have anybody to fight with."

"Uncle Reuben sat in the corner all night and wouldn't talk to anybody," Father's well-tended face showed hints of its age in the corners of his eyes, the whitening of his hair. Father continued, "Reuben's healthy, not a thing wrong with him except he's old. He could last another twenty years."

Early morning over Savannah reminded Ford of other mornings, the road on the way to Country Day School, or the look of the backyard from his bedroom when he first leaned out of bed. The familiarity of the streets echoed with his past, the expectations of it, and all that he was supposed to have been: a part of this city, heir to its upper tiers, guardian of a way of being. The thought had power over him even when he refused it.

Courtenay and her husband, Mike, arrived at the house soon after Ford stored his overnight bag in his old bedroom. Mike set about making breakfast in the kitchen, with Courtenay's help; coffee brewed, drinks poured, the family began its second day of holiday. For distraction Ford studied Mike, the carpenter Courtenay had lived with and then suddenly married. Ford had met him only briefly, but he liked the burly, brown-haired man by instinct. Mike had managed, from his first contact with the McKinneys, to maintain a wall of oblivion to the little insults with which Mother greeted him. He adapted to the family by action: this morning he chopped onions and potatoes, mixing egg and cheese, his strong carpenter's arms moving sinuously as he worked. Ford found himself oddly attracted to the wire-muscled arms, a feeling that frightened him a little.

Mother said, "Mike cooks better than most women I know, Ford. It's amazing. He's almost as good as your grandmother's Millie, at least at breakfast."

"Mother's always amazed when Mike can do anything besides grunt," Courtenay said, and Mike laughed.

"Please, Courtenay, you say the most awful things."

Mike spoke with a slight New England accent. "Courtenay's got no manners." Courtenay stood close to him as he diced ham into fine pieces. "She believes she's entitled to tell her friends exactly what she thinks, whenever she wants to."

Mother purred, "Well, she had every chance to learn manners. We tried to teach her how to behave around civilized people." Speaking brightly, hardly conscious of the edge to her voice, Mother drifted through the kitchen.

Courtenay winked at Ford over the edge of Father's day-after-Christmas newspaper. "Mom's going to start talking about my debut again, any second now. Or my wedding. You watch."

Father chuckled and whispered, "I bet you're right."

From the breakfast room, Mother uttered in her most silken cocktail-party voice, "Of course, I knew we had failed somewhere when she refused to debut with her class. Keith says we stayed a year too long in Atlanta when she was a child. But Ford was even older, and he turned out fine."

"So far, anyway." Courtenay eyed Ford with lowered head.

Mother returned to the kitchen with her glass. "Exactly what is that supposed to mean?"

"Be careful," warned Mike from the stove, "Courtenay's trying to get something started."

"I'm not trying to do anything," Courtenay said. "I simply wanted to point out that Ford might turn out to be as uncouth as I am. One of these days."

"He'd have to work at it." Father swatted Courtenay with folded newsprint. "Even if he did, he'd need years to catch up with you."

Her skirting so close to revelation unnerved Ford, and he gave her a warning look. He said, for the benefit of the others present, "Courtenay knows all my secrets."

The remark created a great deal more discomfort in Ford's parents than he had anticipated. Mother said, "She certainly guards them well," and gave Courtenay a significant glance. Father changed the subject, asking Ford details concerning his second year in the residency program. Ford followed with the expected combination of complaints, enthusiasm, and anecdotes; he emphasized the difficulty of the residency schedule in order to set up his father's usual comparisons to his own residency, back in the days when conditions were even more arduous. This conversation, which provided familiar terrain for all the McKinneys, relaxed them.

Breakfast passed in that easy manner and following it, the family held another gift-exchanging ceremony for Ford's benefit. Mother gave him a new silk suit that was certain to fit since it had been tailored by Mr. Charles, who kept Ford's measurements in his book. The suit, chosen with her usual exquisite sense of what would set off her son's good looks, proved to be the catalyst for further conversation.

"You'll look handsome in that," Courtenay said. "That's your color."

"I knew that fabric was what I wanted the minute I saw it," purred Mother, touching Ford's collar affectionately. "My son certainly does look attractive, doesn't he?"

"I like it. But I don't have time to wear a suit anywhere these days. Not with my schedule."

"Well, surely you could at least find the time to take some nice girl to dinner," Mother continued. "Even one of those women doctors. I think that would be good for you."

"There are a lot of good-looking women going into

medicine, nowadays," Father remarked, "judging from what I saw last time I was in Atlanta. Jeanine, I need another drink. I hardly had a thing to drink yesterday. I need to do better than that today."

The family nested in the back of the house, the casual rooms, as Mother called them, to spend the morning watching movies on Father's new stereo four-head VCR, which had the ability to inset a picture from live television into the same screen as the movie. "I can watch a movie and a football game at the same time," Father said. "This is a terrific machine. I'm even going to learn how to program this one. Listen to that sound. I can tape concerts off Channel 8 and the orchestra will sound just like that."

Mike had read the instructions. "It should be pretty easy to program. Do you want me to set the clock?"

"Sure. Let me watch so I can learn how." They headed for the video box, where Mike demonstrated the various buttons.

Courtenay, briefly intimate with Ford, asked, "How's Dan?"

"Fine. I talked to him yesterday. He's coming back home to Atlanta today. He said he had a good Christmas."

"He lives with you now." Courtenay seemed at odds with that thought.

Ford was aware of his father's increased attention. Feeling more uncomfortable as each second passed, he nevertheless found himself unable to steer conversation in any other direction. "We're still getting used to each other."

"Getting used to what?" Father asked, turning from the VCR lesson.

"My roommate," Ford said.

"What about your roommate?" Mother entered with Father's fresh drink.

Father said, "Ford was complaining about his roommate."

"He wasn't complaining," Courtenay said. "I asked him how they were getting along now that they live together."

The phrasing struck Ford as a dead giveaway. "I wasn't saying anything bad about Dan. I said we're still getting used to each other."

"Well, what's there to get used to?" Mother asked, pitch rising slightly.

For a moment he had an impulse to answer the question. Really answer it. But he swallowed the notion and reached for a little lie. "Nothing, really." As Courtenay watched.

Mike, on the excuse that he had left his drink in the other room, escaped through the doorway. Mother handed Father his drink, and they posed together in the usual arrangement, Mother sheltered near Father's shoulder. Mother gave Ford her raised eyebrow as preface to admonition. "Ford's too old to be having roommates anyway."

"He's frugal," Father offered. "He wants to keep that house payment down."

Courtenay watched Ford. He remembered the suddenness with which he had confessed to Courtenay a year before and felt the sense of waiting from his parents. The moment had arrived, or so it seemed. He might have deflected the remark, easily. Any of a dozen answers might have defused the obvious question; and Ford was mightily tempted to do just that. But he said, finally, with the first flush of morning alcohol pulsing through him, "When are you going to figure this out?"

Father's glance sharpened instantly. "Who? Us? Figure what out?"

"Dan doesn't live at my house because I want to have a roommate. I've told you that before. At least I've told Mom that."

She sipped her own drink and refused to respond. Father glanced at her, and asked, "Ford, what on earth are you trying to say?"

He shook his head, his throat closed with fear.

Courtenay snapped, "How many more clues does he need to give you, Dad?"

"Courtenay, now you stay out of this," Mother began, but Father silenced Mother by wrapping his hand over hers.

"Maybe this is one of those secrets Courtenay was talking about," Father said.

Courtenay said, "It wouldn't have to be a secret if we weren't afraid the two of you would freak out—"

Ford paled. "Be quiet, Courtenay, please." Taking a deep breath. Turning to his parents again. "Dan is not my roommate. He's something else completely." Hardly recognizing his own voice. "He sleeps in my room. With me. His clothes are in my closet. I care about him. Do you get it yet?"

"Ford," Mother began, stricken.

"Don't say anything to him," Father ordered. Looking around the room as if all the objects in it had become foreign to him within the last few seconds. "I can't believe this." Directed to Ford again, vicious, "Do you mean what you're telling me? This man is a homosexual, and you have him in your house?"

"Yes, sir. That's what I mean."

To Courtenay, Father's voice was no less cold. "And you knew about this? And you didn't tell me?"

"Of course I didn't tell you." Courtenay matched his tone.

"Be quiet!" Shaking with rage. Father looked from son to daughter. "You are no children of mine."

Following this pronouncement, he stalked to the door and vanished.

Mother, stunned, drifted after his awesome departure. Face breaking, losing the coldness Ford had expected, she asked, in a tone reeking of pain, "Ford, how could you? How could you tell your father this?"

Wordless, he stood without defense in front of her. Moments later she followed her husband. Courtenay embraced Ford, saying something in his ear, saying, *Don't worry, don't worry, it's going to be all right now,* as he stood there, in the house and yard where he had ranged as the perfect boy in boyhood. Hearing his mother's distant voice calling, down the stairs, "Keith? Keith, are you down there?"

———— ✹ ————

Courtenay and Mike rescued Ford for a few hours, taking him for a drive to calm down and then for a visit to Grandmother Strachn.

Through the nearly empty streets they drove, Courtenay pointing out landmarks to Mike as she steered the van in which they had traveled from New England. This left Ford to himself in the part of the van in which Mike ordinarily hauled lumber and building materials. Seated on a crate, elbows on knees, Ford stared blankly at the familiar contours of houses, churches, and squares. He noted small changes in the landscape, filing them away in the part of his brain that maintained Savannah geography. Otherwise he simply sat there, dull-witted in the aftermath of the conversation.

Relief slowly came to him over the course of the drive. This storm had been so long coming, he hardly knew how to behave now that it had broken. One thought was that Dan would finally be proud of him, that he should tell Dan as soon as he could. But no thought enabled him to forget the image of Father leaving the room in a shaking rage, nor could relief alter the fact that he must face his father again. *You are no children of mine.*

He had feared his mother's reaction as well, but she surprised him. Clearly she had understood the conditions under which Ford and Dan had been living; she had figured it out some time ago. But she had shared none of her insights, and Father's confusion appeared as total as his wall of fury.

Late in the day, Grandmother turned to Courtenay and asked, "Well, how is your mother this morning? I notice the day has passed and she didn't so much as do me the courtesy of a phone call. Yesterday or today." Grandmother lifted her nose deliberately. "Well, I suppose it's the best I can expect from her. She's too busy worrying about whether I'm leaving the house to Rose when I die to bother with something as simple as a phone call." As if reading her grandson's mind, she fastened on him clearly. "Or worrying about whether Ford is getting married. She has to worry a lot about that."

"So she's been talking to you?" Ford asked. "I thought she was keeping pretty quiet."

"Oh, she talks about it, all right." The subject had obviously been on Grandmother's mind as well. "Why don't you just go ahead and tell your parents you're never getting married, Ford?"

The question resounded through the large room, a second parlor, in which a fire burned. Mike ducked his head instinctively, and Courtenay opened her mouth. Ford answered, "I've told them a dozen times, Grandmother. They don't listen."

"For heaven's sake." Sitting back, she contemplated the fire. Impossible, at that moment, to think of her age or weakness. She embodied sharp savagery instead, a bird of prey. "Then they deserve what they get. If I'm not upset about it, why are they? You're my grandson. If you don't want to get married, you shouldn't do it. If I had it to do

over again, I wouldn't get married. Not to your grandfather."

"Grandmother," Courtenay reproved, but found herself cut short.

"I wouldn't. I didn't need his money, my family had
plenty." Grandmother looked at Ford keenly. "Your mother
is afraid I won't leave you this house if you're single when
I die. You tell her I said that's nonsense. She wants to pretend I don't know how conniving she is, but I know my
children. You tell Jeanine I'm leaving you the house whether
you're married or not. Whether you want it or not. And
you're going to let Rose live in it till she dies."

Ford said, "Grandmother, you don't have to think
about things like that."

"You mean I wouldn't have to think about them if I
didn't have a daughter like Jeanine."

They lingered in Grandmother's second parlor through
lunch. Toward the middle of the afternoon, Ford excused
himself to the alcove in the library where Grandmother
kept her telephone. Dialing the familiar number, he
warned himself he was probably too early, Dan might not
be home yet. But the receiver lifted and the voice blossomed across space into Ford's ear.

"Hello," Ford said, "guess what?"

"I already know. Your mother called."

Now Ford heard the weariness in the voice. "What
did she want?"

"She wanted to know if it's true that I am homosexual,

and she asked me what I've done to you to make you think you are. That's about the gist of it. And your father got on the line and threatened to call some folks at Emory and have me fired from my job."

"Oh, Jesus," Ford said, "I'm sorry."

"Don't be." A calm filled the phone. "I'm proud of you. I wish there was something I could do."

"Don't answer the phone anymore. All right?"

"All right. Where are you? You sound better than I thought you would."

"At my grandmother's. Courtenay and Mike are taking care of me right now. But you may get a call from the airport if I decide to come home early."

Ford asked about Dan's knee, his trip, even about the cats. The ease between them surprised Ford a little. Was it as simple as the fact that Ford had finally said something? That he had made a decision?

He told Courtenay about Mother's phone call on the way to van, after kissing Grandmother Strachn good-bye on her tissue-thin cheek. After Courtenay absorbed the surprise, she said, "Well, I don't know if that's a good sign or a bad sign. Was Dan all right?"

"Yes. He was surprised, I guess. But so was I."

At home, they found the house deserted, though the family cars both sat complacently in the parking area behind the house. Mike spotted the parents, who were sitting in the garden, buttoned up in winter coats, sipping some liquid contained in coffee mugs. Between them was a bottle of Scotch and a thermos. They stayed there till after dark, unmoving, with a look as if they dared anyone to approach.

Finally, Mother came inside the house and Father drove away in his car.

Ford met her in the kitchen. She managed a glance at him but she could not meet his eye. "Where's Dad gone?" Ford asked.

"To his office. He had some things he wanted to do."

Ford put his hands in his pockets. "He doesn't want to be around me, does he?"

"Your father had things to do at his office." She repeated the phrase mechanically. "You can't very well blame him if he doesn't feel comfortable around you right now."

"He could try. He has to try sometime."

"Why?" She turned to face him, lit by lightning. "Why does your father have to try anything? Why can't you try something for a change?"

A comforting numbness wrapped him. "Like what?"

"Like behaving the way we raised you to behave. Like coming to your senses. What has this person done to control you this way?"

"Who, Dan? Dan doesn't control me."

"Then I don't know what you call it. He has warped your mind, he has perverted you. He has twisted you up till you think you're the same kind of creature that he is." She stepped to him, took his shoulders in her hands and peered at him earnestly. "But I know you're not. I'm your mother, and I know you're a man. You're not like he is, you're not some kind of homosexual. You're my son and you're a handsome man and you want to do the natural thing. I know you do, or at least I know you will when you come to your senses."

"Mother, I'm in my senses, I'm not crazy."

"Don't tell me that!" Flashing again, backing away from him. "You're sick, you're still sick from whatever happened to you, and that therapist friend of yours did not help you. I don't know who she was, but I mean to find out and I mean to give her a piece of my mind, because if this is the kind of mess she was encouraging you to do, to live with a man and call it natural, well, I tell you what—" Stopping for breath, she sagged against the counter. "Ford, you have to get that man out of your house, or I don't know what I'm going to do."

"I can't do that, Mother."

"Yes, you can."

"Mother, you've talked to him. You know he's not a monster."

She covered her ears. "I haven't talked to him, I don't know what you're talking about."

"You called him today. He told me so."

"I have never talked to that creature. Never." Then, in a low, dangerous voice, "Did you call him from here? Did you call that man from my telephone?"

"No. I called when I was visiting Grandmother."

Nearly shrieking in his face, she hissed, "How dare you! How dare you call that man from my mother's house, how dare you!"

She came so close to hysterical screams that Courtenay

appeared and hovered in the door. Ford turned to her and said, "Take me to the airport. All right?"

"Where are you going?" Mother asked. "Ford, where are you going?"

"I'm going home, Mother." He refused to face her. Afraid his own face would melt. His tie to her felt ruptured, irreparable. "Home," he repeated.

"You can't leave." Half-hearted, like a reflex.

"Yes, I can."

In the end, when there proved to be no seats on any flights, Courtenay and Mike drove him to Atlanta, borrowing Grandmother's Lincoln. Mike steered along the mundane Jim Ellis Freeway through miles of swamp. Ford sprawled in the backseat as if in a wasteland. Holding on to the thought that he would be at home tonight, that he would sleep in his own bed, next to Dan.

Near Clifton Heights, he realized he had never called Dan to say he was coming. No lights shone in the front of the house, except the front porch lamp. Mike steered to the backyard, and Ford guided him to the parking spot under the trees.

The back door opened, light flooded the side yard. Dan appeared. Ford slid from the car eagerly, and Dan called his name, descending the brick steps.

He hesitated a few feet from Ford. He stepped into the orbit of Ford's shoulders and took them in his hands. For a moment, along with sympathy and concern, desire hovered as well. Between them both.

Courtenay and Mike got out of the car, and Ford

thought he ought to move. But Dan's hands held him firmly pinioned, with hardly any pressure at all. Ford stood there and breathed the air of his home, the comforting scent of Dan.

"Was it that bad?"

"Worse." His voice surprised him with its calm.

A moment later, he introduced Courtenay and Mike. Dan had talked to Courtenay a couple of times on the phone and they embraced as near-family members were expected to do, though stiffly. Mike shook Dan's hand with a mildly bemused expression. They sat in the den for a while. Ford and Courtenay told the story of the day. Dan kept his eye on Ford throughout.

Oddly, it was Courtenay who seemed uncomfortable. She spoke to Dan politely, and kept her end of the conversation freely moving; she told the story of Ford's coming out deftly and with enough passion that Ford believed she wanted to accept him as the kind of man he had described. But in Dan's presence, the relationship between Dan and Ford was no longer theoretical. In front of her now was the man with whom Ford slept. Courtenay disguised the feeling easily and with McKinney skill. Ford noticed it all the same, and apparently Mike did as well. He joined the conversation at points, describing the various encounters he had endured with the McKinney parents.

Ford settled Courtenay and Mike into the guest room and said good night. Courtenay kissed Dan's cheek dutifully before going to bed, and they watched each other for a moment with careful scrutiny; Dan vanished soon after. Mike said, in the doorway, "I like him. He's a good guy."

"Yeah." Ford yawned and scratched the back of his head. "I like him too."

"It shows," Courtenay waved good night, adding, almost convincingly, "I'm happy we finally met him."

"You sure?"

"Yes."

He found Dan standing in the doorway to the sunroom. Again, Ford sensed the desire that underlay Dan's tenderness. Sliding his hands up the broad planes of Ford's back, Dan said, "I'm sorry it went so badly."

"At least it's done. I'm home."

"I know. I can't believe it. What time do you go to the hospital tomorrow?"

"Noon. Then I'm on call for three days straight."

Dan blew out breath and shook his head. Ford kept Dan against him. Dan asked, "You're on call New Year's Eve, too, aren't you?"

"Yes." Remembering this house a year ago, this body coming within reach for the first time. Ford waited for his own body to unfold. After a time, with a touch of gruffness, he asked, "How's your leg?"

"Fine," Dan answered, "want to see?"

They headed to the bedroom. Ford found the necessary condom in the table by the side of the bed and laid it in plain sight, as a declaration.

———— ∞ ————

Silence settled over the link between Ford and his father. When Ford telephoned, his mother invariably answered. After her single outburst on the day after Christmas, she continued to talk to Ford as reasonably as ever, with her usual awesome cool. When Ford asked, Will Dad speak to me today? she answered, Why no, son, he's not here right now. He'll be back in a little bit. When Ford said, Tell Dad to call me, she answered, Well, son, you know he probably won't do that right now. When Ford asked, How much longer can this go on? she answered, Now Ford, you've disappointed your father, you know you have. You've disappointed both of us. And you have to live with that.

She would proceed to discuss the family, its concerns, the news from Savannah, the health of his elder uncles, aunts, and grandparents. She spoke without any hint of mocking, and she betrayed no bitterness. Except, if he dared mention Dan, she would say, in her chilliest tones, *I had as soon not discuss your roommate.*

From his father, never a word, neither protest, threat, nor anger. No phone calls to Emory to get Dan fired, no ultimatums. Silence. Stretching over months. Till one day when Ford dialed the familiar number, his father answered.

"Hello, Dad," Ford said.

Silence at the other end of the line, then, "Hello, Ford. How nice that you're calling."

"It's good to talk to you, I'm glad you answered. How have you been?"

"Fine. How have you been?"

"Fine." Ford's voice shook a little, and he fought to

control himself. "Seems like you're never there when I call, these days. Does Mom give you my messages?"

"Well, of course she does, Ford. But I stay pretty busy."

"I know you do." A knot in his throat, intense. "How's the practice?"

"Doing pretty well. Would you like me to get your mother?"

"No, sir, I'd like to talk to you." Putting every ounce of feeling he had into the request.

"Well, son, I don't really feel like talking right now. Let me get your mother for you." Setting down the receiver softly. Ford felt himself nearly strangled. After a few sentences of talk with his mother, he excused himself from the conversation and hung up.

———⦿———

Time passed. Every day, Ford heard the echo of the conversation with his parents, like a song playing over and over in his head. Every day, he saw the change wrought in Dan by the fact of it.

One day, Ford answered the phone and a gentle voice said, "Hello, is Danny there? This is his mother."

"Hello, Mrs. Crell, this is Ford. Danny's not here right now."

In the moment's pause he heard her confusion, and then heard it pass. "Hello Ford. Now listen. I'm Mrs. Burley, not Mrs. Crell, thank God. My first husband's been dead a long time, and I say a little prayer of thanks about it every day."

They laughed in a perfect blend. "Danny's at some weekend meeting the hospital sent him to. He gets back tomorrow."

"How is he doing?"

"Fine, as far as I can tell."

She hesitated a moment, then made her question plain. "I mean, how is his health? Those T-cell things and all. Do you know?"

"He's fine," Ford said, "he really is. He went to the doctor a couple of weeks ago."

"Do you know his doctor? Is he a good one?"

"Yes, ma'am. You can bet I'm not going to let him go to some quack. Dr. Barnes is the best."

She sighed. "You're a doctor, too, right? So I guess you would know."

"Yes, ma'am, I do."

"I worry sometimes." The hesitation in her voice grew less. "Danny used to get sick and not tell me. I don't want him to be like that now."

The ache of tenderness that rose up in Ford made it hard for him to speak. "Don't even think about it," he managed. "If there's something you need to know, I'll call you myself. Okay? But he's as healthy as he can be, right now. His leg has healed up from that bleed he had, and he's been back at work since Christmas."

"That's good to hear."

They talked a while longer, pleasantly, and when he hung up the phone Ford savored the warmth. When Dan came back, Ford told him about the conversation, and the story brought pleasure to them both. It was a pleasure that deepened with time, as, from then on, whenever Dan called his mother or she called him, she spent a few moments talking to Ford. He found himself wishing his own mother had ever been so warm and easy on the phone.

Summer brought the beginning of the last year of Ford's residency, a promotion for Dan, a new car. They fought about money, the house, Courtenay; they went to gay bars, and Ford got all the attention; Dan came home jealous and threw plates. They had a dinner party for Ford's friends and then one for Dan's. At the hospital, their relationship became common knowledge, to the point that one day Dr. Milliken asked Ford to use his influence with Dan to get a new ventilator for the neonatal intensive care unit. As if the request should seem perfectly ordinary.

But with Christmas approaching, the anxiety of what to do for the holidays haunted their thinking. They wakened early one Sunday morning in late autumn and made breakfast. Ford liked to see Dan in their kitchen, moving through the familiar routine in his house robe and soft slippers. His pale handsomeness shone. Ford, seated on a stool, yawned. "This is peaceful. I could get used to waking up with you at home."

"I could get used to having you around in the morning, too. Rough night?"

"Oh, yes." Sighing. "We had a kid come in with bruises all over his skull. His dad claims he fell off a toilet. But we all knew better. The nurses were really upset about it. They wanted to drop the dad on his head a few times."

"The kid all right? Are they going to send him home?"

"We don't know. The social workers were trying to figure it out when I was leaving."

Dan stared fixedly out the window. "Was the mother there?"

"Not while I was on duty."

The fragrance of coffee filled the room. From the back door came the scratching of cats asking to be let in. Ford opened the door, and they rushed to their food. "Did I tell you my mother called yesterday?"

"No. She actually dialed the phone herself? Did she say what she wanted?"

"Oh, yes. She wants to know when I'm coming home for Christmas. I guess Thanksgiving, too. As if nothing had happened." He let the silence lengthen for a moment, then said, "I'm not going home for Thanksgiving. I'm on call."

"What about Christmas?"

"I don't know. What do you think?"

Dan shook his head. "I need to make plane reservations myself, but I don't know when to do it." He busied himself slicing fruit, washing grapes and cherries. "To tell you the truth, I don't want to go home. I want to stay here with you."

The clear, simple statement cut right to the bone. Ford stepped to Dan's side and stood close. "You think we should do that?"

"I think it will hurt my mother's feelings pretty bad if I don't come home." Dan hesitated, putting the knife down. "But I don't see why we should be separated. Do you remember taking me to the airport last year?"

"I didn't want to let you go, I remember that."

Dan lowered his voice to a whisper, a sure sign of uncertainty. "I think my mother would let me bring you. If you could come."

The thought startled Ford. "Have you talked to her about it?"

"No. I wanted to talk to you first." Dan, perhaps to conceal his own nervousness, returned to his labors with fruit and yogurt.

"What about my parents? What do I tell them?"

He expected hesitation, but Dan answered at once. "Tell them what I'm going to tell my mom. I don't come home unless you come with me."

Ford sighed, touching fingertips to wispy curls at the back of Dan's neck. "And I don't go home unless you come with me. Ask me for something easy."

"I wish I could."

Ford pictured his mother's face, replayed her silken voice, smooth and false. "You know what my parents' reaction will be."

"Yes."

"But you think I should say it anyway. Then what?"

Their tenuous peace wavered. "You tell me."

"All right. I say to my mother, Mom, I won't come home unless Dan comes with me. Mom says, Fine, don't come home. And then I have to decide what to do."

Within Dan, palpable to Ford, more tension rose. They were learning to endure such moments; Dan refused to pull away from Ford, and Ford refused to let him. Ford suggested, "Maybe we should both stay here. Have Christmas together here. We can put up a tree and do all that holiday stuff for ourselves. And forget our families."

"I don't think either of us will feel better then. If I could forget my family, I would have done it a long time ago."

Ford had often joked about meeting Dan's mother, getting her blessing. But he still resisted. "We're a family, Dan. You and me. Aren't we?"

Dan thought for a moment. "We could put it off if you want to. I can't stay here for Christmas. It would break my mother's heart. But I can go home by myself one more year. If you want to put it off."

After hesitation of his own, Ford shook his head. "I don't want to be by myself in this house on Christmas Eve, not again."

Dan slipped his arms around Ford's waist, and they stood together in the quiet morning. Ford chuckled. "So I call Mom and tell her. And she tells me to stay home. This is going to be fun."

Half-joking, Dan said, "Maybe we should go, anyway. Show up on their doorstep and make them deal with us."

"I can just see the look on their faces." Ford laughed; and that suggestion was quickly forgotten.

———— ∞∞∞ ————

So events had unfolded, and Ford had come home with Dan, to the Gardens of Calvary, where he sat with the telltale box in his hands. He lifted it from the wrapping in which it had been hidden. He already knew what it was, his heart was pounding. "I don't have one for you."

Dan shrugged. "It's not like I warned you." He was starting to smile. "I was afraid to give this to you. I was afraid you wouldn't want it. But I showed it to my mom, and she wrapped it for me."

He opened the box at last. A gold band rested in satin bedding. "It's your size, or it's supposed to be. I had it matched to your class ring."

Ford studied the gleaming surface. "I like it." Struggling. "I never thought you would do anything like this."

"It's no good if you don't put it on your finger."

Ford studied the edge of the circle as if it were the brink of a precipice. He wanted words but all he could say was, "All right."

"Does it fit?" Dan asked, his voice trembling.

"Oh, yes. It fits fine." A dense weight on his finger, a bright fire. They sat side by side, in silence, deep into the quiet night.

Dan drifted toward day under the weight of Ford's arm. Gray light crept into the trailer bedroom, and Dan remembered where he was. The day after Christmas, at home in the graveyard.

Ford's breath heated his shoulder. The small bed crushed them together pleasantly. Soon they would have to get up, since they needed to leave early for their flight back to Atlanta. But for a few more moments Dan relished the comfort of the bed in the lap of his family, and the sheltering heat of Ford. The gold ring rested comfortably where Dan had dreamed of placing it, more out of instinct than out of any faith in the gesture. But he found he liked seeing it on Ford's hand.

From beyond the closed bedroom door floated soft morning sounds, Mom starting a pot of coffee before waking them. Maybe the sounds penetrated Ford's sleep as well; he murmured, reflexively drawing Dan against him as he came to consciousness.

Ford pulled Dan's face beside his own, their rough cheeks brushing. "Your mom's awake."

"I hear."

Ford's hands pressed along Dan's lower back. "She'll hear us, won't she?"

"These walls are pretty thin."

"How's your shoulder?" Lips so close to Dan's ear, he could feel them move when Ford spoke.

"Aches a little. I guess I better get a shot before we leave."

Still, for whole minutes, they lay together, their hearts pounding, until finally they slid naked out of the knotted sheets. Ford held his hand aloft, displaying the unfamiliar ring. Shaking his head with a laugh.

Dan's mother called from beyond the doorway. Dan showered, favoring his shoulder but hardly noticing the pain, and emerged, freshly shaven and immaculate, from the tiny bathroom. He kissed his mother's cheek and accepted the cup of coffee as Ford prepared the medicine.

"Good morning," Mom said. "How's your shoulder?"

"Better," Dan answered.

Ford added, in a doctor's tone, "And now I want to make sure it stays that way."

"That's a good idea."

She studied the ring on his hand. Her expression wavered from one uncertain emotion to another.

Dan prepared the medicine himself while Ford showered. He rocked the bottle in his hands as his mother watched him. Finally Dan said, "Well, I guess you're satisfied."

"I saw." Mom was trying to smile. "Seeing it makes me feel a little funny."

An edge of his joy escaped him. "It's just a ring."

She lay her hand on his shoulder. "You know that's not true." Unable to say more. But she leaned to kiss his cheek. "I know what it is. I want him to stay with you, too."

Ford returned then, seating himself beside Dan and beginning the injection. Dan hid the catch of happiness inside himself. The subject could submerge into silence now.

The silent transfusion and Ellen's fragrant breakfast made odd partners in the small kitchen. Ford cleaned the table when the injection was done, and, in the midst of the traditional country ham, eggs, and potatoes, they heard stirrings in the distant bedroom. "That's my husband shuffling around in there." Ellen sipped her coffee. "He'll be out here in a minute with that television going." Something in her manner warned Dan that this was a preamble. She took this opportunity as her last to speak to them alone. "I'm glad you two boys spent the holiday with us."

"I am, too," Ford said. "I really appreciate your having me here."

"And I hope you get things all straightened out with your parents," Ellen continued. Her gaze fell on the ring again, and this time she met Ford's eye just afterward. She simply smiled as Ford blushed, worrying the gold band with his fingertips.

Ray appeared moments later, mumbling good mornings as he shuffled to his throne. Soon the sound of the *Early Bird News* pervaded the small rooms, a background that relieved them of the need to speak.

Soon enough, Ford rose from his seat. "Well, we need to get on the road if we're going to make it to Raleigh in time."

"We're all packed," Dan said. "All we have to do is load the car."

"You mean, all I have to do is load the car."

"That's what I mean." Smiling into his cup. Meeting his mother's eyes.

Ray said his good-byes from the television. He stood and shook Ford's hand; if he noted the ring at all he gave no indication. He allowed Dan the usual perfunctory hug with which they greeted and parted; he thanked the boys for coming to Christmas and wished them a safe trip. Ellen walked with them to the parked car. They stood awkwardly in the open space before the trailer as morning birdcalls rose round them. The field of graves with its ornaments of flowers and alabaster Jesuses grew more distinct as day broke fully over the countryside.

After a moment Ellen said, "Well, some people take it the wrong way when I tell them this, because we live in a cemetery. But I sure hope you boys come back and stay longer." The moment of parting, as always, made her sad. Dan felt the cutting himself; they were both bright-eyed. "We sure are a funny bunch of people, aren't we?" she said, running her hand tenderly through his hair.

"We sure are. But I guess it's way too late to do anything about it."

They kissed good-bye, she gave Ford a hug, and they got into the car.

She waited in the yard as the car cruised along the loop road to the gate. Dan felt himself a child again as he lifted his hand to wave good-bye to the dwindling figure framed against the mobile home. The sense of parting seemed endless, as if he had been saying good-bye to her for years.

They drove through the plains of eastern North Carolina. Ford, the precise doctor behind the wheel, was weighed down with some hard thought. For once patient, Dan allowed the miles to pass and silence to linger, till Ford was ready.

Near Smithfield, Ford said, "This was a good thing to do. Your mom really likes me. Did you think so?"

"She said she does."

"Your stepfather was a little uncomfortable, but he was all right about it. About us being there together, I mean."

"If Ray had any acting up to do, he would wait till he was alone with Mom anyway. But I think he was all right."

"The whole holiday would be perfect if we could go to Savannah now."

The ensuing pause seemed calculated. Dan took the bait. "Well, nothing's really stopping us."

Silence grew, and Dan wondered if he had read Ford's signals incorrectly. "Are you serious?"

"Well, it sounds to me like that's what you want to do. Is it?"

Ford admitted, "I've been thinking about it."

"What could they do, throw us out of the house?"

"Yes. For starters."

Dan shrugged. "They're probably going to do that at least once, anyway. So we might as well get it over with." Something deep inside him began to sing. "Maybe if we let them act real ugly, they'll get it out of their system."

"Maybe." For the first time, during a conversation on this subject, Ford smiled. "My dad has a gun—he might shoot you."

"I always thought I'd die young."

"If they throw us out, we'll go down to the beach house. I still have a key."

"You have a beach house?"

"Sure. On Tybee Island." Glancing at Dan, uncertain.

"Well, naturally. I should have known." Sighing. "I

guess I could force myself to spend a couple of nights at the beach."

A light began to break in Ford's face. "Are you sure? Do you think this is a good idea?"

"I'm ready for your parents whenever you are. I know it's not going to be pleasant when I meet them, and I don't expect any miracles. But I don't see any reason to put it off."

Ford nodded, calculating. "So when we get to the airport I buy two plane tickets to Savannah?"

"If there's a flight this time of year."

"There'll be something." Then another thought occurred to him. "Now, I'm paying for this, all right?"

"Fine."

Ford glanced at him as if to confirm that the concession had really been so easy. Raleigh drew nearer. Ford gripped the steering wheel grimly, and the gold ring gleamed.

"Well, what about you?" Dan asked. "Do you think it's a good idea?"

He expected hesitation, but Ford answered at once, and his relief was clear. "I think it's high time."

———— ∞∞ ————

At the airport Ford haggled with a ticket agent for long enough that Dan began to wonder if the trip would prove feasible; but soon they found themselves rushing to a commuter flight on a small concourse that would lead them, following a stop in Myrtle Beach, to their rendezvous with Ford's past.

"I hope we can get a car when we're there," Ford fretted, "you never know, this time of year."

"You can always buy one," Dan said, deadpan.

Ford gave him a warning look as they headed down the concourse. Dan handed boarding passes to the flight attendant and they crossed the open tarmac and ducked into the cabin, finding their seats.

Dan, by the window, surveyed the busy tarmac surrounding the aircraft. Large silver propellers began to turn as the steward sealed the cabin. Leaning against Ford's shoulder, Dan said, "I don't know about this. I don't like flying with these propeller things."

"You'll be fine." Ford returned the pressure.

The cabin attendant, perfectly cosmetologized, leaned over them to say, "If those seats are too narrow, we have a lot of empty space. You're welcome to spread out."

"We're all right," Ford said, "we like tight spaces."

Ford steered the rented car into Savannah before the cocktail hour. Traffic hardly burdened the old streets and squares, even so, and they made good time. When he parked the car on a street off a tree-filled square, he sat with his hands on the wheel as if in disbelief.

Dan's fear surged, and he studied the adjacent houses, all large and prosperous, trying to guess the right one through telepathy or sympathetic connection. The only fact he knew about the house was that the front yard contained azaleas, and all the front yards in sight met that criterion.

"Which one is it?" he asked, and Ford, returning from whatever distance claimed him, gestured to a large white structure, prosperous but rather ordinary to Dan's eyes. A façade of tall windows and an elegant porch overlooked a neatly manicured lawn, the azaleas and oleander interspersed with plantings of other types. The house, surrounded by a wrought iron fence and tall brick corner- and gateposts, spoke with some eloquence of the prosperity of its inhabitants. But its lines of subdued opulence offered little evidence of warmth or imagination. The color was merely white. The windows, seen from outside, were merely richly draped. Like Ford's Atlanta house, every part of it was perfectly accomplished, but somehow forbidding.

"It's big."

White-knuckled, Ford gazed at the structure as if he could see through the walls.

"Are they at home?"

"The cars are out back." He worried the ring on his finger, studied it.

"You can take that off if you want," Dan offered. "If you think it will make this easier."

Ford shook his head quickly. Searching Dan's face. "Are you ready? There's still time to change your mind."

Opening the door, Dan stepped into the cold, damp air.

Ford followed, more slowly. Dan took a moment to gather his coat together. Recognizing Ford's growing paralysis, Dan took a deep breath.

It was as if the house had eyes, as if it were watching

every footfall, judging every breath. The size of it became more evident as they approached, endless windows, steps leading to a high porch. The imposing front door with its brass handle awaited them. Ford said, "I never had to knock before," ashen-faced, and did it.

The door swung open. An elegant woman answered the door, gray-black hair pulled neatly into a bun. Ford's gray eyes were duplicated in her face; she had the sculpted cheekbones, Dan thought, of a fashion model or a glamour queen. Flawless skin, showing the slightest signs of age. She wore light lipstick and hardly any other makeup, her long-lashed eyes blinking in dull surprise. Raising a manicured hand to touch the bun of hair at the nape of her neck, she apparently comprehended the whole situation in a glance. "Ford."

"Hello, Mother," Ford said, near loss of voice. "We came to see you folks."

"What a surprise." When she turned to Dan, coldness crept over her. "You must be Dan."

He offered his hand, and she offered her own. "Yes," he answered, surprised that his voice remained firm. His heart no longer beat so fast, and he controlled his breathing. "I'm certainly pleased to meet you."

She stepped back without a word and allowed them to enter, though she managed never actually to invite them. Dan stepped through the broad doorway, and the house surrounded him instantly with its cool breath of marble, overhead the glittering of a chandelier. Portraits of old men hung on the walls, some oils, some sepia photographs. She gestured gracefully into the parlor, and Dan moved as directed into a sunny, spacious room. On a grand sideboard and an elegant library table stood dozens of framed family photographs. Additional old men judged the room from their vantages on the walls. He faced the woman who had admitted him, even against her better judgment, into this house.

She stood in its center of gravity, allowing the light to frame her dramatically. Making a point of standing, of leaving the men in their coats.

"Did you drive in from Atlanta?" she asked smoothly.

"No," Ford answered, "we flew from North Carolina."

"I wish you had called," she said.

"Why?"

The simple question rendered her suddenly uncertain, and she failed to meet her son's gaze eye to eye. "We've had a very hard holiday. With you not here for the first time. And now you appear at the front door with a guest."

"Dan's not a guest. Is Dad here?"

"No, he's at his office."

"I thought I saw his car," Ford said. "I wanted him to meet Dan."

Again she seemed uncertain, at such depth that Dan felt sorry for her. Nothing in her life could have prepared her for this moment. "You know that's not a good idea."

Ford paled further. Lips set in a line of anger. Before Ford could speak, Dan said, "I'd like very much to meet Dr. McKinney. In fact, I'd consider it an honor."

The mask slipped a little. Her smile wore thin under the effort. "I am very sorry."

Ford, better under control, said, "I'll call him," and headed out of the room.

Mrs. McKinney called sharply, "Ford, don't you dare!" Her face blazed. Dan swallowed. Ford froze in the doorway.

From the back of the house came another voice, "Mother, who is it? Why are you shouting?" Courtenay entered through the butler's pantry. Seeing Dan first, she stopped in her tracks. A wave of realization swept across her face. "Mother, why didn't you say they were here?" Rushing across the room, she embraced Ford at once; he drew her gently to him. "I'm so glad you came. I was thinking I wouldn't see you at all." At the same time, waving to Dan and saying, "Hi. Welcome."

In her presence, Ford found his voice again. "We decided to make the trip this morning. And now Dad's not here."

Courtenay gave him a puzzled look. "Sure he is. He's right down in the shop."

They looked at each other and then at their mother.

Mrs. McKinney kept her cool. "Wherever your father is, he certainly doesn't want to be disturbed."

"I think we should let Dad decide that," Courtenay said. Turning to Dan again, she smiled. "Take off your coat, let me hang it up. You, too, Ford."

She touched his hand tenderly and vanished, and he heard her call downstairs. Ford sank into a nearby chair without a sound. Dan kept his back to the exhibition of family photographs.

Mrs. McKinney remained standing as well. Her expression seemed very much like Ford's, her composure slightly cracked. She drew a deep, audible breath. "I cannot believe you want to put your father through this." Focusing on her son. "You know perfectly well how we feel. Your father is nearly out of his mind."

When Dr. McKinney appeared, she halted.

He, rounding the corner and standing visible in the center of the marble floor, fastened his gaze eye to eye with Dan. They watched each other, almost like children who dare each other to blink. For a moment there was human curiosity, then suddenly Dr. McKinney turned to his son and spoke to his wife. "So Ford's here. And he's brought company."

Ford stood as soon as his father entered and faced him. "I brought Dan. My friend Dan. I want you to meet him. Dan, this is my father."

"I'm pleased to meet you, sir. I think we've spoken on the phone once."

"Have we?" Dr. McKinney addressed him with careful control. "I don't remember."

"Last Christmas."

They were too distant for a handshake. Wiping his hands on a dark shop apron, Dr. McKinney studied the carpet. To Ford he said, "Well, you're here now. What do you want?"

Ford swallowed. "I wanted you to meet him. That's all."

"Well," crisply, "we've met him. And now you can take him away."

"Dad," Courtenay's voice rose in pitch, "don't do this."

Dr. McKinney spoke coolly. "Do what? What business is this of yours, Courtenay?"

"Please, Dad," Courtenay began again.

"Be quiet." Chilling. "You're a guest here, too. I'll thank you to remember that."

Mrs. McKinney, speaking nearly in a hush, faced Dan with her composure partially restored. "I think it might be best that you leave."

A hand of calm passed over him. He had expected more fear, but there was none. They thought to make this a simple moment, almost placid. But Ford said, "He's not leaving by himself."

The words dropped into absolute silence. Ford looked at Dan, then crossed the room to stand beside him. He lay a hand on Dan's shoulder, close, against the tender flesh of the neck. Unmistakably intimate. His father paled.

"Get out," he hissed. "Get out of my house this minute."

"We'll go," Ford said, "but you'd better take a good look at the two of us before we leave. This is me and this is Dan. If you want anything to do with me, you'd better learn to live with him. Because if you want me to choose between him and you, I'm choosing right now. I'm leaving with Dan."

Mrs. McKinney, crumpling at the center, leaned against

her husband, her eyes filling with tears. Dr. McKinney stiffened, his eyes glazed, as if the room had vanished. "I don't have to listen to this nonsense," he snorted. "I'll call the police, and they'll throw you out."

"Do whatever you want, Dad. You won't need the police, but you can call them if you want to." Ford's voice began to tremble, and his grip on Dan tightened. "His family didn't seem to mind when I was with them for Christmas. They gave me a chance. I don't see why you can't give him one."

"I don't, either." Courtenay's small voice hardly carried.

Dead silence followed, through many heartbeats. Finally, voice breaking with genuine pain, Dr. McKinney asked, "Why are you doing this to us?"

Dan closed his eyes. He felt the finality of the moment. When he opened them again, Ford stood in front of him. Face full of sorrow. "Come on, Danny, let's go."

They stepped past the frozen couple. Courtenay rushed to get their coats. Dan headed for the open air, taking a deep breath. Silhouetted against the front door, Ford turned to his parents again. Speaking to their backs. "You don't have to make it like this."

Mrs. McKinney had begun to cry, silent sobs buried against her husband's shoulder. Dr. McKinney whispered, barely audible, "Get out of here. Please."

"We will." Ford pausing, near tears. "We'll be at the beach house tonight. If you change your minds, call us."

They closed the door. Ford hovered aimlessly on the porch, arms drooping. Courtenay embraced him, and Ford held her as if, when he released her, all his ties to her and to the house would vanish. "It's all right, it's all right," Courtenay whispered. "It's over now."

She walked them to the car and waited. Ford kept Dan close to his side, arm looped across Dan's shoulders. Courtenay noted the gold ring, touched it and said, "Look at this."

"Yeah," Ford said. "What do you think about that?"

She searched his face and then turned to Dan. He expected uncertainty in her face, like in his mother's, but found none. "You guys have come a long way."

On Tybee Island, in harsh wind and blazing sunset, they walked along the strand. The drive had calmed them some. As if he had reached safe harbor, Ford faced the choppy Atlantic. Dan waited. In sight of all the houses along the beachfront, Dan folded his arms around Ford's waist.

They stood close, clothed in the slight self-consciousness that they could never escape. Sometimes they walked arm in arm, and sometimes, when people approached, they were merely side by side. The bond between them seemed so clearly visible that acting it out hardly mattered anymore. Anyone who saw them would know. The certainty of that made them feel almost naked.

They reached the breakwater at the south end of the island, where the sea collided with reinforced concrete, exploding in high bursts of foam against a jetty of rocks. Night fell. Stars rose above the eastern horizon. When the beach hung black and deserted on either side and the bite of the wind sharpened, they headed toward the lighthouse again. Ambling. Having no need to speak, they took shelter in each other. *To find a hiding place.*

Close to the beach house now, they faced the darkened Tybee lighthouse. Distant but visible, a ship sailed toward the mouth of the river, headed for Savannah. Farther down the beach walked another couple, maybe even two women or two men, arm in arm along the shore.

"That was hard. Today."

"It could have been worse. And it's over now. Like Courtenay said."

"Do you think it did any good?"

Ford never answered. The ship's horn boomed across the waves. They waited, poised in the wind, under the wheeling of stars. At this moment there seemed so little need to move, when the world remained so full of motion. From somewhere drifted a thread of music, a vestige of Christmas. Dan sang softly with the tune, almost inaudible beneath the wind; but he could feel Ford listening. *To save us all from Satan's power, when we have gone astray.* The song drifted away, but the wind continued. They stood there a long time, water crashing like white fire onto the sand. At last, when the cold grew too much, they headed to the beach house. The song still ran through Dan's head; he sang quietly as they found shelter. He found himself already hoping the phone would ring and a happy ending come, as Ford opened the door and they entered the quiet darkness, together.